SLAY BELLS RING

The Rise of the Banner Elk Slayer

Also by S. David Acuff

Fiction novels

Historian's Proper
High School Masquerade
Slay Bells Ring
The Wrestling Girl

Nonfiction books

Semi-Centurion:
What Doesn't Kill You Makes You Funnier

Screenplays

Masquerade
Moved
Psychedelic Foreclosure
Restoration
The Christian Zombie Movie

S. David Acuff's

SLAY BELLS RING

The Rise of the Banner Elk Slayer

SLAY BELLS RING
2.0 Edition

© Copyright 2023 | S. David Acuff
All rights reserved.

BRAVO BAY BOOKS
Los Angeles, California
bravobaybooks@gmail.com

ISBN: 9798-9888-2930-0 (General)
9798-3927-0965-6 (Amazon)
IMPRINT: Bravo Bay Books

DEDICATION

To all the weirdos like me who need an
extra spicy Christmas adventure from time to time.
Counterprogramming to the sappy sweet Santa songs and
Manger movies. A little cayenne pepper with their eggnog.
And a dash of bourbon from Grandma's secret stash. This
brand-new Christmas horror comedy is for you.

Will we tell people that this novel is destined to
be one of the most influential holiday literary masterpieces
since Dickens' "A Christmas Carol"?

No…but *you* can.

And to Ryan Reynolds/Blake Lively or Emily Blunt/
John Krasinski or Justin Timberlake/Jessica Biel… the first
power couple to option the movie rights
wins Christmas!

Finally, in the words of that famous philosopher
from that one Christmas film in the 80s:
"Yippikiyay…"

How the hell did sh*t get sideways so fast? My original plan had been good, bordering on genius, some might say. Until it wasn't. What do I mean by that? Okay, well, imagine my plan was one of those fluffy soufflés that just needed a skosh more time in the oven to set up. And now, instead of a red-faced Gordon Ramsey yelling how I've "lost the plot" because I'm an "idiot sandwich," imagine it's a frothy, level-4, demon-hound with anger issues pounding down the other side of this dungeon door. The point is, f*ck soufflés. And f*ck meringues, too. And f*ck vampires.

Oh, don't worry, Sister Marguerite assures me I get three f-bombs a year. And those were totally worth it. Who am I? Thank you for asking, I am Daniel Archibald Helsing. Despite the one-star *Yelp!* reviews from my students, I am a decent guy. Trim-ish. Very single, if you don't count a deeply emotional relationship with donuts or my bipolar cat, Sméagol. And, yeah, I've got pop culture references out the ying-yang because growing up my dad was a workaholic bank loan officer and my mom was a 20-inch Zenith television set. I was stuck with that smurfy cocktail of a childhood, so you are, too. You're welcome.

Anyway, I teach math to sixth graders at Cranberry Middle School and a statistics course at Lees-McRae College on Mondays and Wednesdays. And somehow I was appointed the Vice-Chair of the College Herpetology club which is weird because I despise lizards and snakes and herpes.

I do like math, though. No, that's not true. I *love* math. In fact, I'm gonna marry math and have a dozen little integer babies. You could say we go together like Taco Bell and a spastic colon. I get math and it gets me. Despite what Washington tells us, two plus two always equals four. Math is absolute. And I absolutely adore all of my students and have never ever thought of smothering any of them with a throw pillow. Children are a gift from the Lord. Like sunbeams or smallpox. But we've all got bills to pay.

Yes, I am currently single and, yes, I am open to exploring the whole Russian mail-order bride thing because my friend Gator tried it and, hang on, why am I yammering on and on like I'm posting up for FarmersOnly.com? There was something important I was gonna tell you. Oh yeah, one of my students was bleeding out in the next room.

Dammit, Charlie, you better not be dead. You hear me? I roared at her but from a safe place between my own ears. What were we even doing here? I mean this was a helluva way to die. And for the record, I didn't deserve it no matter what the Banner Elk slayer alleged. But, if I'm being completely honest, I didn't *not* deserve it either.

Man. It's been a week. There's all this pressure with the Helsing family business—such that it is—and I've only this instant realized that it's on me if we get eaten alive, guys. But, just in case we do make it out of this basement alive, *I was right, Charlie!* You got that? She was wrong and I was right!

I wiped a trickle of blood and a rogue tear from my flushed, panicky cheeks. WHAM! The growly, ferocious Hell hound was throwing itself bodily against the other side of the oaken chamber door—WHAM! WHAM! —and I didn't know which would buckle first, the door or my scrawny little chicken legs. Chicken legs? Really? Wow, I had a lot of talking points for my therapist, Chrissinde, if I lived to taste another sunrise. Anyway, far be it from me to hyperbolatize with made up words but this, *this* had to be the worse Christmas vacation in the whole history of Christmas vacations.

Some arm-chair horror historians might assume this sordid fluster cluck began 200+ years ago in Transylvania, Romania. But, for one, they've watched way too many Hugh Jackman and Kate Beckinsale latex vamp-fu movies. They're both hot. I get it. But that's Hollywood, not real life. I don't believe in all of that monster mash hooey gooey. It's ridiculous. And I'm a Helsing, born and bred. I would know. Charlie claims this whole thing began three months ago on the night of the Hunter's moon.

And my 40th birthday. But, allow me—the *adult*—to set the record straight.

Things went off the rails last Thursday night at Orphan Fight Club. And our cozy little mountain town of Banner Elk, North Carolina, would never be the same.

CHAPTER 1

"Honey, I hear a lot of negativity about your whole teacher situation," Chrissinde admonished me in our last counseling session. She looked down at me over her black-rimmed Psychiatry nerd glasses. And the mountain twang wasn't softening the blow any. It was still coming across reeeeal judge-y.

"Come on, Sinde, I wouldn't say *negative*," I scrunched up my face at her absurd accusation. "It's just raw honesty."

She narrowed her eyes at me, "Ya called your students 'snotty little terd-muffins' and 'emotional leeches'."

"Emotional leeches of *joy*," I corrected her. "And they are, you have no idea, Sinde, they are little velociraptors probing our mind fences every day for weaknesses and then BAM! Straight for the jugular," I took a much-needed sip of the top shelf whiskey burning a hole in my glass.

"The mind jugular…?" she wasn't buying it.

"Exactly," I drew a thumb across my neck with the accompanying "gkkkkkk!" sound. "Four foot tall joy murderers. All of 'em. Except little Phoebe. She's a sweetheart."

"Ya need a vacation," she threw a dish rag over her shoulder and then placed the Johnny Walker Blue on the shelf behind her. "Or therapy."

I gasped with a hand to my imaginary chest pearls. "Uh, *you're* my therapy," I said matter-of-factly. "See this?" I held up the glass tumbler, "For the bargain price of two ounces of mountain hooch, I not only get all the local gossip…but a bunch of warm fuzzies in my tum-tum." Another sip. "Ah, thanks, Doc, so much healing and closure."

And with a derisive snort she was gone. Sinde hoofed it down to the other end of the bar and yanked a tap handle forward to fill a frothy, bubbly howler of Guinness. She slid it across to some Duck Dynasty dude who thanked her silently with a nod and a grunt. Seriously, was he a prospector from a Bugs Bunny cartoon? In crocs?

Chrissinde Bailey was just "Sinde" to her regulars. She was always on the move behind that stone-marbled countertop that separated her from the unkempt masses. And if the solid counter didn't de-motivate someone from slinging abuse at her, the worn Louisville Slugger she kept underneath was very persuasive.

The Banner Elk Café was conveniently situated halfway between the middle school and my place. The school was about eight miles down the mountain and my place was up at Hawks Lake Drive—about 8 miles the other direction. Okay, technically I lived in Seven Devils. I'm not sure why it was called Seven Devils but I figured it was named after at least three of my ex-girlfriends. Booyah! Nailed it. I hope you're reading this, Rachel Lynn, you backstabbing meth head.

Anyway, nestled right there between home and work was Banner Elk. And this time of year the town looked as if the Mayor of Whoville had brought his ornament spewing gatling gun and vomited decorations upon every rafter and light pole and shop window. Every hall was decked. Every bough, holly'd. In fact, the only thing this mountain town lacked was the one decoration they needed the most for a successful tourist season.

Snow.

That could be why the Town Council had gone overboard turning the whole town into an TikTokker's wet dream. They needed those seasonal tourists and their bratty influencer teens. Or at least their money. But for the rest of us it was kind of nice. I could get off work at the school and pop in for a pint and not have to elbow my way through a bevy of hipsters ordering craft beers. Yech.

I jumped when something slithered across my ankles, but it was just the Café cat, Gandolfini the Grey. The fuzzy little hobo was making the rounds, looking for handouts. "Ugh, I thought I smelled brimstone," I encouraged him along with my foot. "Go away. Get a job."

Instead, he plopped onto the floor and turned his attention to licking his toe beans. "Gross," I frowned at him. "You are violating so many health codes right now."

Sinde had been bartending at the Banner Elk Café since birth. Or shortly thereafter. She knew this town, all the customers and everyone's drink orders before they even ordered. She'd heard all the angles of all the stories and nothing ever rattled her. Once, she'd even run out a black bear that had wandered into the place accidentally. Rumor had it the bear was fine for his first two beers but then he got handsy so she gave him the option to become a rug or get. So he gat. Sinde was one of life's constants. As dependable as Pythagoras theorem. Except the triangles were love triangles. Ha. Okay, see, to get that joke you have to know that the theorem states… you know what? I'm not explaining it to you, go take a math class.

Sinde scooped some ice into a silver shaker. She counted in some nectar of the gods I liked to call Aviation Gin and then topped it and shook it vigorously. "Imagine you could wave a magic wand," she mused at me, "and become anything you—"

"Actuary!" I blurted out, startling her so badly she froze mid-shake.

"You mean, you mean, with the numbers and the, uh—"

"Oh god, yes. An actuary. All day long. Insurance reports and excel spreadsheets in my own cubicle with no distractions by myself for eight hours?" My heart raced just thinking of it. I closed my eyes and exhaled blissfully at the thought, "Pura vida, mamacita."

Sinde just stared at me like I had sprouted a third head. "Spreadsheets and corporate cube farms? That juices your snowblower?"

"I don't know what that means, but I am a little turned on by statistical software, so yeah—"

"Eh, back to that therapy thing, you shouldn't write that off just yet, darlin," she finished pouring out the martini and dropped a plump, skewered, blue-cheese stuffed olive into the middle. "I have a nose for crazy."

"Crazy accurate data statistics," I said, attempting to oversell it.

"Nope. The base-line few-baskets-short-of-a-picnic crazy," she winked as she handed the drink to a passing waitress. "Thanks, Amanda Panda."

"I feel like we're saying the same thing," I finished off my drink and chased an ice cube around the glass with my finger, stalling while I tried to figure out the delicate wording of my next question. "Speaking of crazy, how's that, uh, old roommate. Jan, was it?" I knew perfectly well her name was Jan. I knew it. Sinde knew I knew it. And I knew she knew I knew it. Check mate. "She still fighting crime in the big city of Hot-lanta?"

Sinde's mouth twisted into a smirk. "Again, it's Raleigh, not Atlanta…"

"Tomato, potato," I dismissed it with a wave. "It's all the same once you get down past Blowing Rock."

"Well, you can ask Jan all about it," she leaned in closer just to intimidate the hell outta me like that TV Detective Sipowicz. "She's coming home for her Christmas break this weekend." Her NYPD Blue skills were working.

I gulped audibly. Or maybe it was a burp. Hard to tell if it was going up or down, I was too distracted. "Oh? Little, uh, Janeane coming home for Christmas? Not that I care what she does. She's a big girl. Takes care of herself. Probably has like three or seventeen boyfriends in the big city…"

Sinde raised an eyebrow and shook her head slowly. "Nope. Single as a pringle."

"Ah. A p-pringle? Once you pop you can't…stop —I am so sorry I don't know what I am—is it hot in here or is it…?" Sinde enjoyed watching me flail around like a hooked bass in the bottom of a canoe. I couldn't turn it off. "What time is it? Look at the watch I'm not wearing, I am late to Orphan Fight Club."

Sinde lowered her voice sexily, "I'll let Jan know you said…*hey*."

"Nope!" I protested a little too loudly. Duck Dynasty looked down our way. I waved politely and continued. "Ahem, no, I mean… it's cool beans, or whatever, I wouldn't wanna trouble you and did I just say 'cool beans'? Ugh, my heart itches all of a sudden is that a thing? Spotted mountain dengue fever, maybe, or leprosy—? Thank you, Sinde. I'm around. You're around. Jan's around. And I bid you, adieu," And I exited quickly before I could embarrass myself. Well, any further, that is.

Holy crap-cakes, I was a full-blown babbling mush brain at the mere thought of Janeane Abigail Switcher. Okay, look, I promise you she's no one. I mean, sure, it's cool our names rhyme: Dan and Jan. Jan and Dan. Dan and Jan. And, yeah, so what if she's got these hypnotic blue eyes on her Instagram pics and a new blonde pixie haircut like if Orlando Bloom and Liv Tyler had a supermodel elf baby. And maybe she was my first kiss in 7th grade and maybe she wasn't. Frankly, it's none of your business. And what she does with her Christmas break and who she does with her Christmas break, is none of my business.

Anyway, as a professional professor I'd like to think of myself as a hunky, yet resourceful Dr. Indiana Jones-type but lately when I looked in the mirror I was getting some strong Ichabod Crane vibes. Nothing a little Keto diet, a couple of pushups and some TaeBo couldn't fix. Sadly, not by this weekend though.

You can't come home yet, Jan, I'm not show-ready! I screamed into the void.

Where were we? Oh yeah, Orphan Fight Club. That's the name of a game night I host at the Sylvanian Home. It's an orphanage at the edge of town that I wanna say was built by some Freemasons or Knights Templar back in the day? I might be getting that part wrong. It might have been the Baptists. Anyway, it looked like a miniature castle nestled into the mountainside. This massive stone estate overlooking Boone's lush Valle Crucis had the biggest, creepiest basement-slash-dungeon so our Fight Club met there on Thursday nights.

To be fair, the only fighting we did was dice fighting. As in boardgames. As in we loved to get primal on some *Settlers of Catan* or some *Lord of the Rings Monopoly* or sometimes some really aggressive *Yahtzee*. The nun wouldn't let us play D&D. To her it didn't stand for *Dungeons and Dragons* it stood for dark and demonic. And no *Ouija* boards or *Tarot*, either. Hell to the no. We were just trying to have some fun bonding time not summon Rosemary's baby.

This particular Thursday was gonna be our last meet up before the Christmas break so we incorporated a little holiday party into it. The orphans obviously weren't old enough for my world-famous Gummy Bear Sangria but the culinary school lent us their slushee machine. Muy delicioso! We mixed in some wild flavors like Mountain Dew Code Red and chocolate espresso shots. We all got so buzzed we could smell the color green.

Currently, there were nine kids all together at Sylvanian Home. The four older ones played in the Orphan Fight Club. The younger four stayed upstairs with Sister Marguerite. And, well, Charlie was Charlie. As it happened, we had two older kids in the orphanage that were twins—Jada and Juan Marquez. They were both some kinda tech geniuses. It was probably all those Baby Einstein videos they used to watch. Jada was physically older by two minutes; emotionally older by a good couple of years. Her brother had adopted his nerd-moniker years ago and wouldn't respond to anything other than Obi Juan. Yes, as in Kenobi.

Obi Juan had set up his camera drone on a shelf with a view of the whole table and wore a VR headset the whole time. He fed the signal to Jada's laptop who streamed our games on Twitcher or Despacito or whatever dark web they were into. They explained it to me so many times but, honestly, I just tuned them out. You have to. But the twins seemed really excited about having a 'record' twelve viewers tonight.

Thanks to a challenge issued forth by one of those viewers—StankMonkey98—Obi Juan drank an entire blue raspberry straight from the flavor packet. The whole night everyone made fun of him saying he'd french-kissed a smurf. Orphans could be mean like that. Okay, technically, I had made the joke first. But they didn't have to keep repeating it.

Anyway, tensions were high, sugar levels were spiked and the title of Grand Emperor Supreme Commander of Catan was on the line. Yeah, these juvies were so blitzed they weren't gonna sleep for a week. Especially Liam. Not my monkeys, not my problem, though. Plausible deniability. If it was good enough for Tony Soprano, it was good enough for me.

"Okay," I said passing the Catan box lid with a couple of dice sliding loosely across the bottom. "Play goes to Liam. Liam, try to keep the dice off the ceiling this time and inside the box, capiche?"

Liam had a retainer that made him sound like a cartoon squirrel with a lisp. "I don't know what capish meansh but what I do know ish the Catan godsh have shmiled upon me and the day of reckoning ish at hand," he scooped up the box with one hand and the dice in the other shuttling them back and forth vigorously.

"'Capiche' is Italian," I said trying to throw him off his game. "It means bratty little jackass."

"Ohhhhhhhhhhh!" the whole table erupted as they covered their mouths and chanted at me like the children of the corn. "Cuss bucket! Cuss bucket! Cuss bucket!" I caved to the pressure and ever so dramatically snatched a dollar from my wallet and added it to a couple dozen others in the little mason jar.

"Oh by the way, jackass is a bible word!" I held up another dollar bill and dropped it in just for good measure. Then I set the cuss bucket back on the shelf behind me and waved my hands dramatically over it. "Is the moral turpitude of society once again copasetic? Can we puh-lease finish this marathon game before Obi Juan reaches puberty."

"Hey," Obi Juan objected, thumping his chest with pride, "I already got pubes, bro."

"Ew," Jada scowled.

"Sick!" the others giggled.

"Whoa, TMI! I need a restraining order for my ears," I made a sour face back at him.

"Wait, you're the one without any chest hairs, Mr. Dan," Jada challenged mischievously.

I smirked back, "that's because grass don't grow on a playground, amigos!" They all slapped the table and busted out laughing. "Liam, please roll the dice, some of us have to teach mañana."

As they settled down, Liam shuttled the dice, "Big money, big money, big money." He released the sticky cubes into the cardboard container and they ricocheted from wall to wall until they finally settled. "Nine! Yesh!" He pumped his little fist. All three players that had resources adjacent to the number-nine spaces collected from the 'bank.' Liam's eyes lit up as some evil plan came to fruition in his snot-nosed, terd-muffin little brain. He started cackling and wiggled his butt back and forth in the chair like a golden retriever pup that had to take a whiz.

"All right, all right, Mr. Poker face," I rubbed one of my tired eyes with the palm of my hand. "Stop your gloating and just carry forth your dastardly plan."

Liam handed me a ridiculous handful of cards. Bricks and woods, mostly. "I'd like to buy four roadsh. I'm going to finish paving Liam Lane! Heheheheh!" He cackled some more. Everyone watched intently but I'd already done the math. I knew exactly where we were headed and started returning my resources to the tray.

Liam laid out the roads, end to end, across the board. Yup, the two roads that I had been building the whole game to converge into a full-fledged interstate Catan super highway had now been interrupted by this much inferior Liam Lane. "Take that you little capish!" He laughed and held out his grubby little paw. "Longesht Road card, pleashe!"

I begrudgingly picked up the 'Longest Road' card from my pile and handed it to him. Along with two victory points. Along with the game.

"That makesh eleven victory pointsh for me," he announced standing up and then he climbed even further onto the seat of his chair. Towering above us all, arms outstretched he bellowed, "Which makesh me your new, Shupreme Emperor of Catan." Now, finally, some of the slower members caught on and their faces dropped. They searched the board, this couldn't be true. You could see the little math wheels helplessly spinning in their heads. "Bow peasantsh!" his Supreme-ness commanded.

"Okay," I said rising to collect game pieces. "Well, this has been a dense slice of Mordor. Let's get this mess cleaned up."

A chorus of "Nooooooo!" and "Not Fair" and "Let's play again!" peppered me from the orphans but I was prepared for their little revolt. I had learned this life hack from Sister Marguerite. I plastered a very serious look upon my face, glanced nervously to the hallway door and then dropped my voice really low. "I'd love to play another game, guys, you know that…but you know the house rules. We have to be outta the dungeon by 10pm and back upstairs—we have eleven minutes—before the Wookalaars come out."

I really added some menacing zhuzh to the word "Wookalaars" and tapped the the top of my wrist where a watch should be. The make-believe monster had exactly the chilling effect on them I had hoped for. Wordlessly they set about in fast, efficient motions collecting the pieces and bagging them up and sorting the cards and packing the drone tech away. Even Supreme Pain-In-My-Ass Liam jumped down from his high horse to pitch in his royal assistance. He trashed a couple of empty pizza boxes and red solo cups. We gathered up the leftover drinks into the ice cooler and less than five minutes later we were all packed when a loud clanking sound and a grunt came from the hallway. I froze. The children froze.

"Wookalaar," Jada gasped aloud.

I counted the kids but no one was missing from our troupe. They all looked up at me. I smiled and calmly held my hand up, "Probably just a sewer gator," I lied. "I'll check it out. You get your stuff together."

I went to the big old wooden door, swallowed nervously and opened it slowly with an ominous creeeeeeeeeak. I poked my head into the hallway. This place gave me the willies. The freaking light situation didn't help. A couple of the overhead flourescents were on the fritz and the sparse, stone hallway flickered in and out of darkness. I gave it a second to let my eyes and ears attenuate. There was something down there I didn't remember seeing when we'd come downstairs earlier. Looked like a small garden shovel. But, was it rocking back and forth a little bit or was my mind fully playing tricks on me now?

Obi Juan held his VR visor aloft and whispered loudly, "I-is it a w-wookalaar?"

I held a finger to my lips, imploring him to silence. "Quiet, Obi Juan! Have you never watched a horror film before? Characters with ironic nicknames get eaten first." I pointed straight at him. His eyes went wide as I turned back around and chuckled to myself. It was so much fun to mess with their little orphan heads. I turned to check back up the other direction and suddenly a small trollish figure in a cloak stood before me.

"Ahhhhhhhh!" I jumped back.

The orphans all screamed, too. But then the lights flickered back on and I saw that it was just that weirdo girl, Charlie. She might have been 14 or 15 or 22 years old. I dunno, she was smaller so it was hard to tell. She was like the love child of Halle Berry and Eeyore. Her full name was Charlotte Summers but of course she had to butch it up and go by Charlie.

"Oh good grief, it's just Charlie frown!" I said holding a hand out to soothe the others. "It's just Charlie, guys. It's just… Liam are you crying? Supreme Emperor's of Catan do not…"

"No, I'm not crying," Liam said angrily wiping tears from his eyes. "What you did was not nice."

"Me?" I asked innocently and thrusted a finger at Charlie, "tell it to Charlie! She's the rude one."

Charlie stood there, silently. Her face betrayed nothing. A complete blank. Now that was a good poker face. In fact, she never really talked. Never played with the other kids. Had the personality of a tombstone. The color palette of her entire wardrobe ranged from Stormy Gray to Black Despair; what I liked to call Tactical Grunge. She rarely joined us for Orphan Fight Club. If she did she just sat in a corner and watched us all. Or read one of her dusty ole medieval books. The kid's nose was always in a book. For some unknown reason tonight, she had speckles and lines of neon paint on her pants and boots.

"Hey Banksy, did you get any paint on the actual canvas this time…" Charlie brushed past me and headed upstairs. The rest of the kids quickly scooted past and followed her up. "Y'okay. Good talk."

I took a deep breath and turned the basement lights off. And even though my adult scientific math mind knew grownup statistics about the general impossibility of monsters and serial killers and sharks in that basement, when the hairs on the back of your neck stand up math needs to shut up and let your legs scramble to freedom. So that's what I did.

We all made it out of the basement to the first floor a little winded but alive. Victims only of our horribly overactive imaginations. Once again none of the kids had been murdered so that part always looked good on a LinkedIn profile… finishing with as many kids as you started with. No terd left behind. Ha.

Upstairs was a whole other world. Cozy. Christmas lights blinked rhythmically to some Bing Crosby music crooning from an old record player in the living room. Cinnamon-y pastry smells wafted from the kitchen. They mingled with pine scents from the freshly cut Christmas tree they still had to decorate. I think that was this weekend's planned orphan activity.

Sister Marguerite came out of the kitchen rubbing her floury hands on a "Baking Spirits Bright" Christmas apron, shadowed by little Phoebe. Sister Marguerite was a nun but not the kind you'd want to imagine, like Whoopi or Gidget. No, this nun looked to be 147 years old. Possibly older. In fact, she might have been here when the Baptist Freemason Knights Templar built this home shortly after Columbus had landed. Alls I know is she was a sweet old cuss who took no guff from me or the kids and gave them everything they needed until they graduated to their forever homes.

"Very good, so who won the big game, Love?" she spoke like a Downton Abbey character with a big, warm denture-commercial smile. The lenses of her glasses were thick as a Hubble satellite. She couldn't see worth squat diddly but we could see, grotesquely magnified, every hairy mole and eye booger.

"Well," I said avoiding eye contact, "we're all alive so I'd say we're all winners here tonight, Sister Margaritaville." My thick flannel jacket hung on the rack beside me. I pulled it on and punched into the pocket for my car keys.

"Not true," Liam bragged, "I won fair and shquare."

"Oh, I'm so glad you all had such a fun evening," she beamed. "I sent Charlie down to tell you we had some freshly baked cookies ready."

"Uhhh, yup," I looked up to see Charlie seated at the top of the stairs peering through the bannister at me with those unblinking serial killer eyes. "Yup, she told us and that's why we ran up here to gobble 'em right up. Carbs don't count at Christmas," I said, poking at little Phoebe's stomach to gain a giggle. She did not disappoint.

Now the Orphan Fight Club crew was emerging from the kitchen, each one with a large molasses cookie with Christmas sprinkles on top, still steaming inside when they broke it in half. I reached out and grabbed a huge chunk of Liam's cookie as he passed by.

"Hey!" he protested. "Taxation without represhentation."

"Sharing is caring, your Majesty, go grab a new one," I told him and then shoved a piece into my watering mouth hole. Mmm. So good. Seriously, it was like a Michael Jordan Gatorade commercial on your tongue. Pure poetry.

Liam dragged himself back into the kitchen in a huff. I grabbed the front door and pulled it open, "Okay, y'all have a great evening. Remember to say your prayers to Santa. Good night and Merry Christmas and God bless us every one. Especially you, Tiny Tim." I pointed up at Charlie.

Crickets.

Echoes of "Good night, Mr. Dan" and "Merry Christmas, Mr. Dan" rang out from the others but with mouths full of warm winter pastry deliciousness. Little Phoebe hugged my leg and I patted her pigtails. Then I closed the door behind me and instantly let out a huge sigh of relief. The cold mountain air bit into my flannel but I did not even care. It didn't matter. People time was over. That's what mattered. And now it was me time. Quiet time. Just me and Sméagol, a steaming cup of ramen noodles and some Gilmore Girls on BluRay.

I high-fived an overhead oaken beam as I passed beneath. It was a well worn spot with the words "Dan the Man '95" etched in. I practically skipped back to my Forerunner and climbed up inside the matte black off-road tank. Once seated, I stomped my boots against the running board to knock off some dirt and gravel before shutting myself in. Then I savored another huge bite of molasses cookie. Mmm. Seriously, these cookies were so good I could just kiss Sister Marguerite right on her crypt keeper mouth. I cranked the engine. Some Taylor Swift Christmas tunes and stale air blasted me simultaneously.

As I backed the truck into a sloppy 3-point turn, I kept my bumpers from kissing the low stone walls lining the gravel driveway. As the headlights swung around, I glanced up to the arched, chiseled windows on the second floor and caught a brief glimpse of creepy Charlie before the curtains fell closed. I smiled and said, "See you later, Chuckles," and wiggled my pointer finger at her, adding a gravelly, "RedRum. RedRum."

Turns out I would be right about Charlie. Not the part about her wanting to wear my face like a mask, but the dark and simmering rage concealed within her. As much as I wanted to disassociate, I'd find out soon enough that these *were* my monkeys, and they were very much my problem.

The bedtime routine at the Sylvanian Home was akin to herding cats. On a roller coaster. In a Category-5 hurricane. Sister Marguerite had her hands full every night policing up all of the orphans—especially the little ones—who busied themselves with bath time, clean up and bedtime stories. "Liam did you brush your teeth? Then why isn't your toothbrush wet? Erika, no one wants to see your *Hello Kitty* underoos, cheeky monkey. Wrap it up. Obi Juan, is this your lego bat-plane in the hall," and on and on she'd nip along behind them like a border collie.

Amidst the distracting melee, it was easy for Charlie to slip back downstairs, unnoticed. She passed the warm blinking Christmas lights in the living room windows. The record player was still playing the rhythmic static of the innermost record ring. She picked up the needle and placed it on the hook and powered the whole thing off. She turned off the lava lamp beside it and then continued down through the cellar door; down into the dark, dank basement.

At the bottom of the creaky stairs, she stopped, clicked on a small, tactical flashlight with her thumb and raked the beam across the inky black stillness ahead. The only things moving were the dust and asbestos flakes swirling in the light stream. She listened carefully, straining every sense. She heard the tiniest scrape far up ahead. Eyes forward, she bent down and retrieved the trowel—speckled with the same neon paint as her sleeve and shoes. She moved down the dark hallway without a sound. She passed the rec room—aka Catan headquarters—and continued further. On the ground the flashlight beam illuminated more of the neon paint drippings. She followed them. As she did so, the gritty, scraping sound was getting louder. Closer.

The neon trail disappeared around a corner. She paused there, clicked off the light, took a deep breath and then eased around for a look. A soft red glow was cast about the whole alcove. Antique pictures and junk dressers and broken chairs were piled high along the walls like a garage sale had exploded here, but a hundred years ago. The red light was coming from a large, oval, wooden frame mounted on the wall next to some other worthless storage junk. It looked like it could be a mirror, but there was no glass. No reflection. Just a red, pulsating portal with some sort of membrane across the face of it.

A few feet in front of the portal was a half-dead Hell hound, still squirming, still clawing its way towards the portal. It was disgusting. Not of this world. Like a long, skinny boar that had been turned inside out. It was panting and dragging itself along the floor. The veiny, leathery skin had multiple punctures that bled out the same neon streams Charlie had been following. She drew closer.

"Now, where were we?" she asked.

It craned its head feebly in her direction and let out a sound that was part hiss and part squeal and all horrible. Charlie flipped the trowel around expertly in her hand to a reverse grip. The beast watched her, helplessly, with yellow burning eyes.

"Vaya con dios," she crossed her torso ceremoniously. Head to chest. Left shoulder to right. She spoke with neither excitement, nor remorse. It was just another day at the office. She might as well have been stapling papers together. Then, swiftly, she slashed down with her full weight and plunged the weapon deep into the heart of the beast. The pig monster kicked at her, almost throwing her off and then huffed once and collapsed, dead. Suddenly the whole creature evaporated. Neon blood exploded everywhere. She stood up with the shovel in hand. Neon gunk oozed off the sharp edges. The whole front of her black hoodie now looked like a paintball target.

Charlie flicked the trowel like a samurai and excess viscera flew off of the blade. She stabbed it down into the dusty dresser beside her and it wobbled there on its own. "Lights out," she observed as the portal light slowly dissipated into nothingness until the room was dark. Charlie ignited the flashlight and checked the magical space in front of her but it had reverted into a plain old, dull mirror again. She ran her fingers across the surface. So strange. She saw her own reflection. A waif of a gypsy warrior with dark eyeliner and messy gunk all over her hoodie stared back at her, frowning. The sweatshirt was ruined. Paint flecks even in her short, dark hair. Ugh. What a disgusting mess. She peeled off the top layer and then bent down to mop up the trail, obscuring most traces of the evening's gory struggle.

The whole house was dark and quiet now. Charlie finally slipped back into her own bedroom and sat down on the edge of the bottom bunk. An electric Christmas candelabra from the window cast a multicolored haze about the room. She lifted her t-shirt up to reveal a bloody claw mark on her left rib cage. She affixed the shirt into her teeth and then dug quietly into her bedside table and retrieved a small can of Dermoplast. She shook it a couple times and then blasted the bloodied area to stave off infection.

"Sssssssssss," she and the can both hissed; she, through gritted teeth at the stinging pain. Her eyes welled up but she choked back the tears. Next, she lifted out a box of Kotex MaxiPads. She pulled one up and tore it open. She peeled the protective layer off the sticky wings and then slapped it against the wound. Mushing it all together stung almost as bad as the Dermoplast. She let her shirt drop back down. Not her best triage, but it would have to do.

Charlie collapsed backward into the bed with a sigh. Her bunkmate up top stirred sleepily. It was little

Phoebe. The nun liked to partner the older kids with the younger kids. Kind of a buddy system. Phoebe was all of seven years old, if that. She reminded Charlie of that Little Cindy Lou Who kid from the Grinch story. Only the Grinch wasn't trying to devour the little kids and suck their souls out through their noses. He just stole a few toys. How bad of a villain could he have been? His crime was hating the commercialism of Christmas? Hell, he might have been the hero.

Phoebe squeaked softly, "Good night, Charlie. Sleep tight. Don't let the bed bugs bite." She yawned and was back asleep before Charlie could reply.

"Yeah," Charlie whispered. She reached into the wood slats overhead and pulled out a pencil. On the cardboard layer she scratched off another hash mark alongside thirteen others. Fourteen in total. Then she returned the pencil to its little cubby hole. She rolled onto her good side—facing the bedroom door—and clutched her pillow and withdrew a trowel from beneath it. She held the pillow and weapon close. Each day brought its own terrors and triumphs. She expected tomorrow would be no different. Her breathing slowly settled into a long, gentle pattern of inhales and exhales. Finally, a deep weariness overcame her and she closed her eyes and fell into a restless sleep.

CHAPTER 2

Knock. Knock. Knock. Ding-dong.

My front door was blowing up for some reason. On a school day, too. Made no sense. I pulled on my oversized Grove Park Inn bathrobe and unceremoniously dumped my cat Sméagol off the big Wookie slippers which he'd mistaken, again, for a bed. He flipped me off with his tail.

"Coming, Dear. Keep your pantaloons on, Guv'nah," I sang out like Ms. Doubtfire. I opened my front door and there on the other side was a huge crate the size of a commercial refrigerator. "What in the—?!" *Clang.* The thing was so big it blocked the screen door. I looked past it down to the driveway where two hulking UPS drivers were climbing back into their brown van. I tried to push the screen door open but it would only go about four inches. "Wait! Hey, wait! Is this the Panini press I ordered? Guys...?"

They just waved, cranked the van and then drove merrily on their way.

"Son of a biscuit," I tried to get out the door. No matter how hard I pushed or prodded or tried to wiggle through the opening, I couldn't squeeze through. *Damn you, broad shoulders and big head!* I went to the window, unlocked it and slid it open. Could I have used the back door? Sure, if I'd wanted to slough my way through the fire swamp like a freakin Dread Pirate Roberts.

So, I climbed through the window, trying to avoid the spider webs and dead bug carcasses lining the sill. The robe and Chewbacca feet made it more awkward than it needed to be, but I finally hopped free. Sméagol just leapt right out like some sorta fuzzy Olympian. He was a gray, oriental shorthair with ears the size of a bat and a spicy Samuel Jackson temperament.

"Show off," I said. "Brrrt brrt," he chirruped back with another flick of his tail. So rude. I went over to the large wooden crate. I'm gonna be honest, I didn't love the radiation hazard signs spray-painted on every side. A little unnerving. I found an envelope with the shipping manifest taped to the back. I peeled off the pouch and opened it. It was all in gibberish. The only word I recognized on the whole page said, "Romania."

"Great, another family heirloom," I angrily crumpled the paper back into its envelope and frisbee-tossed it inside the window. I tried to run at the box, I tried to put my back or my shoulder against the box. Nada. Bupkiss. That thing was heavy as a Buick and it was not moving. And my shoulder was starting to give out. "I am late for work, ya ding dongs!" I yelled out to the already long-vacated UPS bros as I rubbed my sore arm.

I shuffled back over to the window, put a leg through the sill, caught my robe on a corner and fell inside onto the floor. "Ow! Son of a country bear!" Sméagol jumped up to the window ledge and sat there perfectly balanced, like some sort of Flying Wallenda.

Today already sucked. I hated today. And my Santa outfit sucked. I hated Santa. Not the real Santa. No, he's a magical saint that smelled like peppermints and baby giggles. I'm talking about Dennis Holberman. Standing outside the Banner Elk Café and Lodge Espresso Bar and Eatery in his used, mangy Salvation Army Santa suit ring-a-dinging that annoying bell. *Well, I guess we are doing this thing,* I thought, climbing out of my truck. I stepped up to the sidewalk and the second he saw *my* Santa suit his bell froze, mid ding-a-ling.

He looked me up and down, and not in the appreciative way. See, it was the last day of classes at Cranberry Middle School. That meant some hapless teaching schmuck was volunteered to don ye merry ol' Santa 'fit and pass out goody bags after class. Despite many protests and threats to quit or die or relocate to the Adirondacks, I had won by default for the past three years simply by being the closest body size to fill the suit. The up side here was that the Santa suit I now wore was way newer and fancier than Dennis's flimsy Spencer's

Gift special from the mall. And he knew it, too. I had Santa superiority.

"Holberman," I said, casually moving past him on my way inside the bakery; never turning my back to him.

"Helsing," he sneered back and spat some chewing tobacco juice onto the sidewalk. Oh yeah, hate to burst your bubble, but mountain Santas always have a chaw of Copenhagen. It's like redneck candy canes.

"There can be only one, Holberman," I whispered loud enough for him and no one else to hear.

"Sure. Anytime you wanna dance off, Helsing, we can f—" I couldn't hear the rest because I'd already stepped inside the store and let the screen door slap his trap shut. He shook his head and then went back to ringing that incessant bell of his, but a lot less jolly.

"Well, good morning, Santa," beamed Gladys Griffin, the portly granny behind the counter. With the salt and pepper hair and twinkle in her green eyes, she could have been the real, live Mrs. Claus. "You want your usual table or you gonna belly on up to the bar?"

"Ho ho ho no not today, Mrs G," I began, affecting a deep, resonant Santa voice. "This Santa has to be to school early today because his boss is an Ebenezer Scrooge-head and she needs to have her halls decked with—" I stopped myself short because Mrs. Griffin had formed a little "yikes" face and cut her eyes to the corner of the room where some of our lovely students sat at a table. The little eavesdroppers and their moms were keenly noting my every move.

"Ahem, that's real nice, Santa," one of the frown-y moms reprimanded me.

"Ho ho ho boy, this really is the most wonderful time of the year," I said, but not meaning it in the least. "Remember boys and girls, Santa is not on the clock right now so everything is off the record. Ho ho ho."

I turned my back to them and moved quickly over to the baker's display before they could answer. "Yeeeesh," I whispered to Mrs. Griffin in passing. "Muggles, amiright?"

Having no clue what a 'muggle' was, she donned a fake smile and changed the subject. "Would Santa care for a drink?"

"I'll take a scotch on the rocks. Yeah, and if you could sprinkle in some cinnamon and deep remorse that'd be delightful," I said, making sure those nosey brats couldn't hear me.

"Ha," she wiped her hands on a frilly apron and turned to prepare my sugar beverage. "One large salted caramel mochaccino with triple shots coming right up."

"Mmmm," I smacked my lips appreciatively, "You had me at salted, Gladys," I winked and then turned my full attention to finding the perfect pastry soul mate for my coffee. They had everything in there and it was all homemade and fresh and scrumptious. Danishes, bear claws, pumpkin muffins, tartlets, cakes, pies, you name it they had it. I was about to go for the flaky, delectable strawberry and cheese danish until the Christmas muffin caught my eye. I crouched down to inspect it closer. "Red velvet muffin?" I read the little sign. "So naughty. Oh ho, you're coming home with me," I ogled it lustily.

Okay, technically it was a cupcake but I didn't care. It was red velvet cake with white cheese cake frosting and a single candy cane on top. Confectionery perfectionery. It was glistening there under an angelic toplight like that golden fertility idol in the beginning of Raiders of the Lost Ark. You know, just before Indiana Jones grabs it and all hell breaks loose? I picked up the muffin and I'll be damned—

"Jan Switcher, I didn't know you were back in town," Mrs. Griffin just radiated warmth as she maneuvered around the counter to hug her long lost buddy. My head swiveled back and forth to peer through a stack of holiday cronuts and there she was: Janeane Abigail Switcher. In the flesh. You know those cartoons where the wolf's eyes pop out into hearts and his tongue unfurls and he's like "Aoooooogahhhhh!" when Jessica Rabbit walks in? Well, here she was, my Jessica Rabbit, and my heart was doing obnoxious cartoon cannon balls into the pit of my stomach. I couldn't hear Jan's reply because she was being lovingly smothered by one of the premiere huggers in the Appalachian mountains.

This was my chance. My big meet-cute. Hadn't seen Jan in two or three years now. I had to make an impression. I looked down at my muffin and—*ding*—got this inspired idea. What I did was, I stole a little candy cane from another muffin and then lay the two candy canes side by side in a perfect mirror position of each other atop the frosting which made an adorable little Christmas flavored heart. Or close enough.

This was gonna be so perfect, I was giddy. I took a deep breath and popped up from my crouched position a mere four feet away from my long time girl-crush. Gladys was still there gushing over Jan's outstretched hand. No, not her hand, it was a huge diamond ring that Jan was showing her on that finger. Yeah, you know the one. Who did it belong to? Hm. I dunno, maybe it was the hunky blond—what I assumed was probably a—playboy billionaire behind her kissing her neck and drowning her in PDA. *Seriously, get a room you two.* Oh god, they probably had gotten a room. And here I was, like an idiot, presenting them both with my love cupcake. Ack. I quickly spun around hoping she hadn't recognized me in the Santa suit.

"Dan? Dan Helsing," her sweet, melodic voice enchanted my earholes. I clenched my eyes closed trying to will myself to vanish but that didn't work. Time for Plan B. I panicked and stuffed the whole cupcake into my mouth to get rid of the evidence and then I turned around.

"MmfffMMMffMmf!" I tried to look casual as I spoke with a yap full of frosting and ended up just spewing a lot of little crumbs everywhere. I'm not gonna lie, it was pretty horrific. Not the suave, Ryan Gosling impression I had hoped.

"Dan, what are you—" Jan was smiling but, you know, a little concerned at the same time. I held up a finger as I chewed and chewed and chewed as fast as I could and then swallowed.

"Gladys!" I put a hand on the proprietor's shoulders, "A-plus on the muffin, ma'am! Hey, the muffin ma'am! That'd be a great name for a food truck. Or a porn star," I turned to Jan and held out my arms. "And Jan Switcher! Get in here, you!" I pulled her into a hug which I wanted to prolong so I pulled in her Euro-Chic fiancé, too. "You, too, Sven or Björn or whatever your name is, there is no such thing as a stranger in Banner Elk." I released them both but my hand kept patting Jan's shoulder like a psychopath. "Unless we don't know you."

"Dan, this is Brodie," she motioned to the norse god behind her. "My fiancé. He's from Sweden." She smiled a little sheepishly, gazing into Brodie's sparkling blue eyes. "We met at the Farmer's Market two months ago, but it feels like we've been in love our whole lives." It was so adorable I wanted to stab him with a pumpkin.

"Two months! Wow, and look at him, it's like Mufasa and Abba had a baby together. Somebody must need a green card, ho ho ho!" I shook his hand with a smile but hated him. Hated him deep within my heart and pancreas.

"Nice meeting of you," Brodie said, genuinely, with his fun and deliciously quirky accent and then added with a wink, "Mr. Santa Nicholas."

"Oh ho ho I am—yes, I am, I forgot about—it's for the kids at the school where I teach—math," I swallowed hard, looking back and forth between this stupidly handsome couple.

Jan began to ask, "So, you're still at the middle school?" At the exact same time I was speculating aloud, "Oh, your kids are gonna be gorgeous!"

"What?" She asked, not completely hearing me.

"What?" I echoed, feigning ignorance. "Oh, yes, still teaching at the middle school for now but fingers crossed the real Santa brings me…" I lowered my voice for the next part, "…a job interview at Blue Cross Blue

Shield so I can finally be delivered from those pesky little demon spawns." I leaned past Jan and Brodie to my students who were still over there eating breakfast. "Not you two, you are both a gift from heaven's sour patch. Also, we're still off the record."

Jan and Brodie laughed awkwardly and then Jan turned towards me, warmly. "Well, it's great to see you, Dan," she rubbed my arm. "We need to catch up while I'm back in town."

"We just did. Haha, I am kidding, no seriously, that would really chuff my goat, yeah, I would love that. We should do that. Then I can learn more about those cool little knives your people make," I gestured to Brodie. "With all the little tools in it."

"Ah. Those are *Swiss* Army knives. From Switzerland," he politely corrected.

"Oh, I am so sorry, I knew that… Swiss knives and Swiss chocolates. The Swedes gave us, what again, girls with dragon tattoos and Skype?"

"How do you do that?" Jan's mouth hung open, a little smitten by my pop culture prowess.

"You know I just love me a good trivia, Jan Switcher," I nodded sagely and wrinkled my nose.

Brodie perked up at that, "Well, we also invented the GPS."

"Whaaaaa—? This guy! We would just be lost without the Swedes, wouldn't we, Jan?" I gently shoved past her so I could wrap an arm around Brodie's sculpted, herculean shoulders. "Wow, forget Sugar Mountain you can ski down these trapeziuses. Trapeziums? Trapezii? Anyway, what is the secret? P90x? I mean look at the two of us side by side just a couple of the most eligible bachelors in town and equally as manly."

"Salted Caramel Mochachino, triple shot," Gladys chimed in outta nowhere. She had one hand on her hip and held the drink straight at me with a sly smile on her face.

"Ho ho ho, triple shot through the heart, Gladys," I gave her the stink eye. "Yes, my coffee… for the, uh, Missus."

This was obviously news to Jan. "Oh! Are you— do you—?"

"Missus Claus, darling, ho ho ho, no I am happily and tragically single. As a Pringle. Look at me, I'm my own secret Santa. But you're skipping ahead! We'll catch up later. I promise, okay, buh-bye now," and I bee-lined for the door and threw a last warning look at my students in the corner, "If you're late for class you'll have a Civil War book report due! Ho ho hooooooooe!" I pointed at their mom when I said the last hoe.

I ducked out the door as fast as I could but Jan was hot on my tail, "Wait, Dan, hold on. Hi, Dennis," she said, not really able to avoid Salvation Army Dennis, awkwardly standing beside us.

"Hi, Janeane," Dennis smiled really big. When she turned away he winked real big at me and made kissy faces.

"What are you doing tonight? After school?" Jan asked me.

"Tonight? After school?" I repeated like a dumb ass, my mind completely toasted. Verbal skills jumping ship like Titanic extras.

"Yeah, are you free tonight? We could all grab dinner, maybe. You, me, Brodie and Sinde. I'm sure she'd love to hang out with us and catch up. She doesn't even know about this," she said wiggling her ring finger. "Gonna surprise her."

"What about next week, we could—"

"Oh, God no, we'll be long gone," she smiled, looking out over the town with a hint of disdain. "I just get claustrophobic when I come back here, you know? Like this place just sucks the life outta you," she saw the surprised look on my face and quickly added, "I mean it's a great town for some people. You're doing great, here. Are you doing great here? Don't answer that," she put a hand on my mouth. "We can talk about it at dinner tonight, right?"

I should have just yelled, "Hell, no!" And palmed her gorgeous little perfect unicorn face and shoved it out of my life forever. I should have. I know that now. But I didn't. I said, "Okay, sure. Sounds exactly like something I definitely want to do with you. And Brodie. And Sinde."

"I'm free tonight," Dennis whined, more to himself than anyone.

"Shut up, Holberman," Jan and I both said at the same time, never breaking eye contact. "Tonight, then," Jan smiled with her perfect mouth lips while her gorgeous blue eyeballs grabbed me, threw me in a headlock and body-slammed me into the ground. "Pick you up? Say, 5:00-ish?"

"That ish sounds perfectly perfect," I hoped I wasn't having a stroke. "Well, haha, I had better get the Elf outta here."

"Oh, of course, one more hug," she jumped me before I could decline, throwing her arms around my neck and then she pulled away and slipped past Dennis who thought maybe he also had a hug coming his way, but was dead wrong. Ha. She was back inside the store before I could even blink. My god, was her perfume made from mermaid ovaries? She smelled like a rainbow.

Dennis pushed into view and shouted, "Shame! Shame! Shame!" And with each word he rang, rang, rang his annoying bell at me. I quickly retreated to my inner-truck sanctum and cranked it up. See? I told myself. Life's not so bad. Just because I wanted to be run over by a sleigh full of reindeer didn't mean it couldn't be an absolutely extraordinary Christmas.

Ho ho holy isosceles triangles, Batman.

My phone rang through the truck's bluetooth. I meant to send it away but accidentally answered. Grimacing, I said, "Mayor Doug, what is up, buddy?"

"If I didn't know better, Dan, I would think you're avoidin' me," he drawled on like Boss Hog adding extra syllables to words like "Day-un".

"Haha, no sir, I have not forgotten about the thing," I lied.

"It's just a fundraiser video for the abandoned hospital. You know the town needs a win here," he laid the guilt on thick. "Or stuff's gonna get bad."

I looked up the street where a couple of Greyhound busses debarked a couple hundred uniformed marching band kids. I shook my head, "Well, Doug, if money was so tight, maybe you should have just cancelled the Christmas parade instead of shipping in a platoon of… where did you dig up this poor marching band, anyway?"

"App State, look, never mind about them," he brushed it off. "If the fundraiser works, Dan, there will be more than enough money in the town budget to pay for Christmas and revamp the hospital."

"Yeah, of course. The, uh, haunted hospit—"

"It's not—," he boiled up and then quickly contained himself. "It's not haunted." He whispered the word 'haunted.' "I wish you would take this seriously, Dan, I really do."

"Oh, speaking of serious, Mayor Doug, I just ran into your ex-girlfriend, Jan, at the café," I was still tracking her and Brodie through the shop window.

"Well, I doubt very much Jujibean is gonna wanna have squat-all to do with our, quote, redneck GoFundMe campaign, unquote," he opined, angrily.

"No, forget the dumb video—look, I'm just saying I saw her. Jujibean looks great. Maybe you two could bury the hatchet and act like real humans so she'd stick around longer than a weekend," I said testily.

"Yeah, sure, and if frogs had wings they wouldn't bump their asses when they jumped. Goodbye, Dan," he said and hung up.

"What?" I yelled into my phone. "Naughty list! And stupid, stupid asshat list," I looked up and my students and their moms were walking by. The moms were suitably horrified, of course, and covered their kids' ears, herding them out of earshot. "Sorry," I waved apologetically. "Telemarketers." But they had scooted around the corner.

Holberman smirked back at me. "Worst. Santa. Ever," he dinged his bell with each word, gleefully.

Ugh, maybe Jan was right. In the words of one famous Arkham Asylum inmate, "this town needs an enema."

Everyone was so happy to see me at school, but I was not happy to see anyone. I just needed one minute to myself. Ninety seconds max. And a Xanax. "Santa," some kids squealed as I walked past. "Nope! Not yet. Still off the clock," I answered in rapid succession to each kid as I quickened my pace down the hallway. A couple more students tried to address me and I dodged them, too. I don't recall but I may have even stiff armed a little kid that was coming in for a hug. I'm telling you it was all an obnoxious blur. Everything was getting on my nerves including these clown shoes squeaking all the way down the damned asylum floors. Squeak, squeak, squeak. I got to my classroom and there were already students in there, too. *Those ridiculous brown-nosers. Give it a rest, nerds!*

"Santa is here," a couple of them chimed in.

"Nope," I said and turned on my heel and walked back out closing the door behind me. I stepped quickly across the hall to the art room praying it was empty. I didn't see a soul. I closed the door behind me, took off my Santa hat, held it firmly in front of my nose and mouth and screamed a muffled, primal scream that lasted several long seconds before I ran out of breath.

A mason jar smashed into the sink behind me. Apparently old Ms. Lennings, who I had not seen at the back of her room, had been a wee bit startled.

"Ms. Lennings, I am so sorry," I said, literally hat in hand.

"Are you out yo damn m-mind," she stammered. She clutched her heart and balanced herself against the counter's sturdy ledge.

"I—maybe. Look, I didn't realize anyone was in here. You're not having a heart thingie are you? Do you see spots? Smell toast? Taste aluminum? I mean if you did flop over dead that would be very on brand for me today, but I would appreciate you not going to the emergency room on my behalf."

She finally stood upright again, adjusting the gray hairs to lay them flat behind her ears. "Mr. Helsing, would you please just give me a moment of silence to compose myself."

"Go for it," I nodded contritely. "Take your time. You want silence, I can be silent. Silent as the grave. Okay bad choice of—"

She gave me an exasperated look, left eye twitching. I took a deep breath in and out and refocused my attention on the gallery behind me. There were dozens of paintings up there, all had the Christmas theme, of course. All painted by the students. Sera, age 12, had painted a janky ass tree with what appeared to be a gold Komodo dragon but was probably the family dog. How quaint. Buddy, age 13, painted Santa riding a T-rex. Well, Universal Studios would have something to say about that blatant copyright infringement. And so on and so forth.

All of them were passable attempts at holiday kitsch. One even had drawn a Santa kneeling at a cradle of Baby Jesus in a manger. Not very original, Sean, age 13, but I liked where his head was at in terms of commercial appeal. Very Norman Rockwell. If he'd had Tourettes. And then I got to one that was unlike any of the others. Abstract. A real doozy. It was a black fabric canvas with hundreds of green and yellow neon splatters all over it. That was it. That, and a tiny, white blob down in the corner. Oh, not a blob. That was a skull.

I checked over my shoulder at Ms. Lennings who appeared to be recuperated and not dead. "Which, uh, little Salvador Dali did the crazy ink splatter?"

Ms. Lennings, now fully composed, ventured closer. She tilted her head back to squint down her nose through her spectacles, "Ah, that was Charlie, of course. She called it 'Christmas Visitor' but that's all she'd say about it. Very avant-garde that child."

"Yeah, in a Jack the Ripper sorta way," I nodded appreciatively, studying it closer. This looked a lot like that sweat shirt she was wearing last night. What a weird, but somewhat resourceful kid. Ms. Lennings shuffled away and so I turned and asked, "May I assist you in cleaning up the broken glass?"

"Honey, you think it's a good idea for you to be anywhere near sharp objects?" She looked at me with a beleaguered expression on her face. A look that only a teacher four hours away from a much needed Christmas break would understand.

"I'm fine," I lied through my teeth, "that primal scream was just a little drop of holiday stress that leaked out. I should be—"

The school bell rang, interrupting our little tete-a-tete.

"Oh. Saved by the bell. Back to class, Screech. Thank you, Ms. Lennings. Good talk," and with a wave, I was back out the door.

"Damn fool," I heard her mutter under her breath.

"Santa heard that," I held a finger high in the air as I crossed the hall to my own classroom. Squeak, squeak, squeak. We just had to make it a few more hours and then we were all free for a week. But, I couldn't focus on any of it. I was too distracted by my throuple date with Jan and Brodie tonight. And our court-appointed chaperone, Sinde.

I'd been at the school entrance for almost thirty minutes. Behind me were two folding tables that had once been filled to overflowing with gift bags. Now, we were down to the final few. My arms were tired, my feet were sore. My throat was hoarse from six bajillion "Ho-Ho-Hos" and frankly I was over all of it.

Santa needed a drink.

The Sylvanian Orphan van pulled up out front. It was the last of the carpool line so all my chatty, little orphans gathered around me like park pigeons.

"Well, Liam, a Merry Orphan Christmas to you, Supreme Catan Commander," I said mustering the last ounce of merriment I had on tap. I handed him a goodie bag. He looked skeptical.

"What'sh in it," he frowned.

"Well, let's hope it's some deodorant for all of our sakes, ho ho ho!"

Liam sniffed at one of his pits and said nonchalantly, "Seemsh fresh to me," and walked off.

"My Lord, Liam, they can smell you at the North Pole, ho ho ho," I yelled after him but he ignored it. Jada and Obi Juan stepped up next.

"Feliz navidad, Señor Helsing, er, sorry, Señor Santa," Obi Juan corrected himself.

"Ho ho hobi Juan, you are too smart. You've learned too much from this school. Take the rest of the semester off, you've earned it," I handed them both their gift bags.

They smiled and Jada said, "No school for a week! En serio?"

"Si," I said ruffling their hair, "Mucho serio. Vamoose."

"Gracias, Señor Santa," they both said in unison and ran off to join Liam who was climbing into the van. The sign on the side said "Transport for Sylvanian Home" in big letters. But when they pulled the sliding door open it overlapped and truncated the words which now seemingly read, "TranSylvanian Home."

Haha, strange, I thought.

I turned back around and Charlie had snuck up so silently she spooked me. "Cheese and rice on a cracker,

Charlie. Why haven't they put a bell on you." She was about to ignore me and walk right past. "Ho, ho, hold up a second, little miss sunshine." I put my arm out to stop her and she walked into it, wincing when it hit her ribs. "Santa has a bone to pick with you." She looked up at me with that blank Charlie expression on her face. "All the other good little boys and girls spent a lot of time on their art projects. Santa could tell. Santa appreciated their efforts. But not you, did you," I poked her and she winced again. This time she looked up at me angrily. It caught me off guard, but I leaned on her harder, "Oh you want a piece of Santa, tough guy? Do you? You're the one that took, what, all of three seconds to splash some colors onto a sweatshirt and turn it in for a grade? Humbug, Charlie," I scolded her as I handed off her gift bag. "Humbug. I don't know what's in here but probably a lump of coal."

She snatched it from my hand and marched off. Maybe I'd gone too far with her. There was something in those eyes. Like, pain. It was there for a second and then gone again. I couldn't figure this kid out. I swear, you could practically see the dark clouds hanging over her head with lightening like in the cartoons.

Principal Marsha Bean nervously fidgeted with her large, gaudy Christmas necklace with one hand and swirled an iced tumbler in the other. It was probably eggnog. Or a White Russian. Either was in character for her. She tsk-tsked after Charlie, "That goth girl is something else. What was that all about, Dan?"

"I dunno," I said honestly unsure. "I don't think she likes Santa."

"What? Everyone loves Santa," she punctuated the idea with a slurp of her milky beverage.

"Yeah, not Charlie. I think she is, ahem, *Claus*-tro-phobic." I held back a laugh, until I couldn't help it any more.

It took a few seconds but Marsha finally caught it. "Oh. Oh, very clever. Santa Claus. Claustrophobic. Con-gratulations, you just volunteered to be the non-denomi-national springtime fertility bunny."

That sobered me up real fast. "Noooooooo ho ho ho hoooooooo!" I wailed as she turned on her heel and walked off, whistling a Christmas tune as she went. "Very humbug!" I yelled after her.

Santa needed a Cadillac margarita at the B.E. Cafe. But, Santa didn't have time for such holiday self-care. No, I had to run home, get showered and feed Sméagol before he reported me to the CPS—cat protective ser-vices. And then, of course, I had to get ready for the most awkward group date of all time. The one where Jan Abi-gail Switcher would just simply exist and the rest of us would all sit there making googely eyes at her; falling deeper in love.

CHAPTER 3

There was no "ish" about it. 5:00pm on the dot, Jan and her beau, Swedish Delight, were pulling up my gravel driveway in a navy blue Outback Forester. I perched next to my window—the one that was also the door to my home now—and watched them share a kiss before climbing out of the car. Sick. Brodie even opened the door for her and helped her out. What an absolute cad.

"Oh, it's just you two lovebirds," I shouted at them as they sashayed up the walk holding hands. "For a second there, I thought it might be a lesbian fire fighter. Because of the lesbian SUV. A lez-u-vee."

Jan didn't even spare me a pity laugh on that one. She just pointed to the huge obelisk in front of my door, "Whoa! What's in the boooooooox?" she dragged out the word "box" like Brad Pitt's infamous line in "Se7en" before his world (and ours!) is shattered. Now, she laughed. At her own joke. Weirdo.

"Beats the hell outta me. Could be the Russian bride I ordered from Victoria's Secret. The secret is that inside every Russian bride is a smaller Russian bride. And then another. Incredible craftsmanship, lotta mouths to feed. Anyway, you'll both have to come in through the window like a Duke Boy." I motioned them my way. Jan looked adorable in the skirt and sweater top. With her leggings and boots and scarf she was quite the little Snow bunny. Minus the snow of course. She accepted my hand through the window and ducked through with an ease and professionalism that caught Sméagol and I by surprise. Maybe it was a pilates thing.

"How long's it staying out there you reckon?" she asked once she was upright again. Brodie needed no assistance. It was a tighter squeeze but he managed just fine. So, yeah, apparently I was the only spazz about it.

"Oh, you know, maybe a day or two or a month. Tops. Great anti-theft device. I think the whole neighborhood's gonna want one. Keeps the grizzly bears out," I put my hands on my hips to match Brodie's whole Mighty Mouse pose he had going on. Jan bent down to wiggle her fingers at Sméagol and gave a little pspspsps.

"That doesn't work on him," I warned her.

"Oh, yes it will, won't it Sméagol-beagle. Look at you, you little chunky monkey," She used a little baby voice that Sméagol never could resist. I didn't blame him. He sauntered right over and flopped down right beside her to allow her some pets.

"Okay, but don't be fooled. He's a killer. Leaves bird heads and squirrel tails right on the pillow where I sleep," I pointed a thumb over my shoulder to the bedroom, "like living with Don Corleone."

"He's just a good whittle kitty-witty sharing his trophy-wophies wiff his daddy," Jan continued running her hands from his head down to the small of his back. Sméagol was in heaven. I was jealous as hell.

Brodie bent down to join in on the fun, but Sméagol was less certain about him and skittered away. I've never been more proud of that dumb cat in my life.

"Oh, no," Brodie said a little hurt. "Come back and be friends."

"Mm, that's not really how cats work," I said smugly. "While Jan and I both know you're a sweet angel of a man, from a cat's perspective you're like a giant hairless baboon so give it some time. He'll warm up to you," I lied convincingly.

Jan and Brodie stood up again. Observing the living room area, she said, "I am obsessed with the matching furniture, Dan." She ran her hand over the brown leather sectional. "You've come a long way from refugee flood victim or whatever you were doing before."

"Ha, ha," I laughed off her little jab. "Well, Jan, there comes a point in every man's life where he can finally walk past a dumpster couch and just leave it there to die."

"Hmm," she conjectured. "Bedbugs?"

"Oh, it was awful. I found this deeply discounted Persian rug. In an alley. I know, I know, but I brought it home and the next two weeks were hell on earth. Complete infestation. Sméagol almost divorced me. Life lessons," I conceded with a sheepish smile, "were learned."

Jan laughed along with me. Brodie had moved over by the door and was pondering the mystery box. "You know, you can keep with the shit-shat but I think that if you have crow bar, I can open box for you."

"The shit-shat," I echoed, looking to Jan slightly amused.

"Don't," she warned.

"You wanna work on the box *now*?" I asked glancing at my watchless wrist, "don't we have reservations at Stonewalls?"

"Are you kidding," Jan scrunched her face up at me. "Sinde has the owner eating out of the palm of her little hand. For her, they'd hold a table for a week. So, if it means we can liberate your front door, let's do it. I mean what if some Christmas carolers come a-wassailing?"

"A-wassailing?" I scowled back at her. "Humbug."

"Okay," now she got really animated, "what if a cute, Hallmark-y New York City stock broker comes to buy a Christmas tree and, whoopsie, ends up needing roadside assistance and also…your penis?"

I laugh snorted. "Alright, alright, sweet baby Jesus, okay, I'll go, uh, find an axe," I said and left the room to go rummage through the hall closet.

"Crowbar," Brodie corrected.

"Or a hammer and chisel might work?" I yelled to them, head deep in the closet.

"Crowbar," Brodie said, again. Jan nodded at him and patted his shoulder.

"Not sure I have a thing for this. What about a hacksaw or a drill?" I spitballed some ideas back at them.

Brodie stepped over to the window, lowering his voice so only Jan could hear, "I think the car has a crowbar in the spare tire kit. I will check on this." He ducked back out the window. Sméagol stood up with his front paws in the window, curious to see where the hairless baboon was going.

"How do we feel about dynamite?" I shouted back at them.

"Daniel Archibald Helsing, we are not blowing the front of your house off!" Jan stormed into the hallway and pulled me up by my arm. "Brodie has a crowbar in the trunk. Let's go."

"Okay, okay," I said getting dragged along behind her. I loved the fact she was holding my hand. Super protective of her. Like I was a goat, and she was T-rex.

Five minutes later there was a loud crack and splintering wood sound and the crate peeled open and light poured inside. Brodie manhandled the side facing the driveway and forced it all the way open. "Good job, baby," Jan rubbed his shoulder enthusiastically and peered around him. As the dust settled, we were a little disappointed to see another box on the inside. A black, shinier box but another box none-the-less. Light glinted off of its sleek, carbon fiber exterior. It looked like some gun safes I'd seen before in some friends' homes. But, like for bazookas.

"Ugh, a box within a box," I said.

"Like, who sent this thing," Jan said, badly imitating my deeper voice, "Christopher Nolan?" She smiled at me expectantly.

"I don't—that's not how I talk," I kept a straight face. Brodie stepped forward, raising the crowbar with some intent to use it. "Whoa, whoa, whoa, Cameron Crowbar. This one might need a little more of the Dan Helsing touch," I wiggled my fingertips at him. "At least let me check the edges before you go all scorched earth. They usually have a thingy."

"A thingy?" Brodie asked and stepped back to give me space. I began to slide my hands all over the surface and down the sides. Jan helped by feeling down the left side. My fingertips brushed against a small, raised square area the size of a postage stamp. When I put my finger on it to check for a keyhole a blue light scanned my finger pad and beeped twice and the door cracked open with a long hissing decompression noise. Jan and Brodie took a cautious step back.

I grabbed the edge intending to slowly maneuver it open, but the whole door suddenly slung wide open and before I knew what was happening, a decomposed body slumped out on top of me. There was a loud screeching sound that originally I thought was this attacking mummy but later Jan confessed it had been her. I fell backwards off the porch steps with the decayed eyeball holes staring right down on top of me. Okay, I might have been screeching a little, too.

"Ahhhck, get it off, get it off," I pawed at the monster but the more I did, the more we entangled, it seemed. It got weirder. As soon as we hit the front yard, the sunshine hit Skeletor's remains and he (or she?) just evaporated into dust particles. I laid there in the grass with an entire sack of brown powder exploded on top of me. Brodie and Jan recovered from initial shock and ran off the porch to help me up.

"Dan, Dan, oh my gosh," Jan grabbed one arm and Brodie grabbed the other. I coughed a couple of times and ashes puffed out of my mouth.

"Agghh, sarcophagus guts in my mouth," I spat and spat. "Blech, great I probably have a medieval tongue plague now." Once I was upright, they tried to brush me off, but I waved them away irritably. That dirt was everywhere. I was gonna have to shower and change clothes. Again.

"That was wild," Jan looked from me to the box and back again. Then she bent down to the ground and brushed some ash aside revealing a footlong sharpened stick in there. She held it up to inspect it. "This was stuck in its back; like some sort of primitive weapon. Dan, you may have a 250-year-old unsolved mystery here. How cool is that?"

"Not cool. Not cool at all," I was still too dazed to elaborate. Brodie was still brushing off my pants leg when something caught his attention in the ash pile. He lifted it out and it was a very ornate man's ring. Very gothic stylings. He inspected it, cleaning it off really well while Jan helped me back to the porch stairs.

"Come on, just sit here a sec, that's good, you're fine, that's it," she coaxed me down. Something slithered past my hand and I jumped again. "Jesus!" I yelped, but it was just Sméagol.

Jan looked over to Brodie to see what he was so distracted with. "Babe," she asked, "what is that?"

"Huh. A super cool ring, babe," he answered holding up the small treasure. "Look at this." Before anyone could object, he slipped the ring onto the index finger of his right hand. "It fits. Haha." Suddenly, a shockwave burst forth from it like a gust of wind in all directions. Brodie was unphased at the epicenter but it blew Jan and I back a little bit as it washed over and through us and then was gone. In the distance, birds jumped into the air from the treetops, frightened at the outburst.

A click and a clang arrested our attention back to the opened, but seemingly empty, box behind us. Two doors in it folded aside after the shockwave passed over it, activating something within. The doors opened and a dozen weapons spilled out onto the porch. Swords and knives and axe-thingies. A spear almost whacked me on the head when it fell. Jan and I dove to either side to get clear. The rest of the weapons clattered down the stairs until they finally came to a rest.

I was face down on the grass and my hands covered my head. When I slowly looked up I was staring down the barrel of a loaded crossbow that had landed on the last stair aimed right at my moneymaker. I gulped and crabbed quickly to the side and out of range.

"I'm sorry," Brodie said helping us both back to our feet. "I had no idea."

"Okay, let's try not to trigger any more catastrophes, agreed?" Jan grabbed both our shoulders. We both nodded. "Until we figure out what all of this stuff is, we don't touch anything, we don't move anything, we don't breathe anything. The last thing we want is Tom Cruise showing up with a C-130 and a horror franchise."

"She's not wrong," I added, looking suspiciously at Brodie's ring, "you should probably take that thing off. Slowly and gently and—"

"I can't," Brodie winced, giving it a tug painfully. "It's stuck."

"What?" Jan yanked his hand over to inspect it closer.

"Easy," I said, pulling back. "We don't know what it will do if we—"

She stuck Brodie's whole finger in her mouth, ring and all, and sucked and slurped it for a good five seconds. I'm not gonna lie, it was a little hot.

"Uh, babe," Brodie's voice warbled a little. Oh, he was enjoying this.

She spit the finger out and tried to twist the moistened ring off. "Okay, let's try it now because the extra juices—"

"Owww, ow, ow!" Brodie screamed. "Hold on, babe. It's not… stuck. It's, I dunno, latched on."

The three of us looked closer and it was true. There was no space between ring and finger. In fact, the tiny spiked edges of the ring had actually bored into his finger holding it firmly in place.

"Does it hurt?" Jan asked.

"Yes, but only when you yank it," Brodie confessed sheepishly.

"Phrasing, you two. Phrasing. But, yeah, you'd literally have to cut his finger off to remove it," I shook my head sadly. "Hey, maybe that's what the axe is for."

"För fan i helvete!" Brodie cursed in Swedish.

Jan put a comforting hand on his shoulder. "It's okay. It's okay. We'll… figure something out. Meanwhile, maybe we, uh, put these weapons inside the house while Dan goes to de-powder his nose."

"Yeah, wouldn't want to leave the weapons out here," I added, sarcastically, "in case some carolers come a-wassailing. Or, hey, a cute Hallmark-y New York City stock broker might need a—."

"Go, get in the shower," Jan pushed me up the stairs. "You're dumb."

"I'm just glad Brodie and I have a big-time Atlanta police detective here to save the day," I couldn't help myself.

Jan lifted up a mace that had an ugly spiked ball at the end and waved it right in my face, "First of all, not Atlanta, not a detective, not the police."

"But something with law enforcement, right? That's the big rumor Sinde has been spreading for years," I needled some more. She looked down at the ground, considering something and then turned back to me with a sigh.

"I am a security guard," she said quietly, almost confidentially. She was hiding something else. I waited her out and she finally 'fessed up, "At Crabtree Valley Mall." Before I could respond, she brandished the mace again, "Tell anyone and I shove this right up your yankee doodle."

"Aye, Captain Blart!" I saluted with a smile.

"Ugh," she growled and shouldered past me up the stairs.

Charlie lay on her bunk reading a book on "Practical Alchemy." With her free hand she absent-mindedly flipped the trowel back and forth from handle to blade, without ever cutting herself. She stopped for a second tuning her ear to the bedroom window. She could hear a lot of birds chattering excitedly as they flew past. Then she felt a small shockwave pass through and she dropped the trowel and the book.

She was on her feet in an instant, curtain pulled aside, fearful eyes searching the skyline. She backed away, horrified. Breathing heavily. She scrambled for her black tactical pants and boots and pulled them on. She attached some leather wrist coverlets to each arm and latched them into place. She climbed into a clean, black hoodie and a utility belt. She tucked the trowel and flashlight in her belt and let the hoodie drape over it; the bagginess hid everything. Her pants had two long skinny pockets down each thigh and she inserted a sharpened wooden stake carved from chair legs into each one.

Charlie rushed into the hallway and pitter-pattered down the staircase with a trained ninja stealth. She stopped at the edge of the living room and peered in. Most all of the orphans were decorating the tree with various and sundry homemade decorations. The Grinch was playing loudly on TV and the younger orphans would stop to watch between decorative clippings and giggle. She could hear Sister Marguerite banging around in the kitchen. She moved quickly past the room's opening, completely unnoticed, and then disappeared down the basement stairs.

Even though the basement was mostly underground, it had long, dirty windows to the outside laid out horizontally up at ground level. Some daylight filtered into the hallway so it wasn't nearly as dark as the night before, but still just as creepy. She made her way down the hall, past Catan HQ and only slowed when she got to the last corner before the alcove. She could already see the red light from the reactivated mirror which cast undulating shadows on the walls and ceiling. She could hear movement around the corner. She pulled out the trowel in one hand and a stake in the other and stood with her back against the corner, clutching them to her chest.

Luckily, she'd done this enough times now she had it down to an art form. Pun intended. When she got down there early enough she could catch the beasts coming through the portal from whatever hellscape they'd originated. Each Level-2 Hell hound, though small as a German shepherd, was still an aggressive pain to wrangle and took a while to kill, but she'd gotten better and more efficient at it over time. Her older sister would have been proud of the slayer she'd become.

Charlie listened intently, trying to time this perfectly. Finally, she heard a heavy thump as if the creature had made it all the way through the portal. She could hear its raspy breaths as it acclimated to our atmosphere. She could smell that sulfurous, burnt-matches smell. She smiled. This was when she was most and truly alive. Moments just like this when her adrenaline coursed through her veins and her pupils dilated so her eyes no longer looked brown, but completely black. Game time.

With great resolve, Charlie stepped out from behind the corner and struck a silent, defensive pose, squaring off to the beast. And then she froze. She almost gasped which would have given her completely away, but she forced herself not to move, not to blink. Yes, there was a thing in the hallway coming through the portal just as planned. And yes it was a Hell hound just as planned. Except it was a Level-4, the size of a Suburban. Not as planned. The others she'd fought were the size of small boars. This one was like a Kodiak bear that had been blackened and scorched by a wild fire. With no fur, you could see its huge muscles rippling under the black and red, slimy surface of its hide. Its head was turned away as it pulled its long, spiked demon tail through the portal along with it. It hadn't noticed Charlie. Yet.

Charlie scrambled back for cover around the corner. She took two seconds to catch her breath and then she moved away as quickly and silently as she could. What was she gonna do? She couldn't handle this nightmare on her own. Not with sticks and freakin garden tools. And certainly not cornered down here in the tight confines of the basement. She passed by the Catan HQ and arrived at the base of the stairs to the first floor. She couldn't allow that thing to go upstairs, either. That's where all the children were. Her pseudo family. Innocents. She would die before she let that happen.

Think, dammit, Charlie cursed at herself. *Come on, think!*

She searched all around for ideas. Further down the hall she saw the fading afternoon sunlight spilling through cracks in the cellar doors. And suddenly she had an idea. It was not a good idea. It might not even work. But it was all she had. She tucked the stake back into its thigh pocket. With the trowel's sharp edge, she dragged the blade along her sweaty palm. Blood formed immediately and she squeezed some drops onto the ground. Then some more a little further up. She reached under her shirt and pulled off the triage-tampon keeping her previous scratch clean. She dropped that on the ground at the base of the five concrete stairs that led up to the cellar doors. For good measure, she dripped out a few more drops of blood. She turned around to check behind her when she heard the soft, low chuffle in the distance. The beast could smell the fresh blood. And she knew it was now hunting her.

She stood on the third stair and grabbed the rusted door bolt over her head and tried to shove it clear. It wouldn't budge. She tried again. Nothing. Charlie could hear the beast moving closer and closer. She pulled out a wooden stake and used it as leverage and with a mighty heave, jerked the latch open. She put a shoulder to the left cellar door and shoved it open and then flipped the right one wide. The big wooden doors slammed open and settled in a cloud of dust. Charlie climbed out and drove the stake into the grass, her bloody handprint would be the last of the trail. Then she crouched down under the lip until she could make out the beasts shadowy shape downstairs.

The Hell hound stopped at the bottom of the stairs leading up to the orphans. Craning its neck to hear and to smell. *No, no, no,* Charlie thought. *This way you big dumb moose.* Then it caught a fresh whiff of the blood trail and continued towards the cellar doors. *Yes!* Charlie sighed, relieved, until she remembered she was the lunch ticket. She scurried back to the garbage bins, pulled out the top bags and climbed inside. Her nose crinkled at the awful smell of spoiled food and other nasty ingredients. She ripped the top stinky bag open and poured it all over herself and then crouched down and closed the lid, peeking out just underneath.

It was just past sundown. Charlie was happy about that. Any orphans that happened to look out into the backyard would most likely have missed the huge creature emerging from the cellar. Especially with its dark topography. Charlie held her breath. Partly from fear and partly to keep from gagging. It was rancid in there. A combination of spoiled milk, rotten eggs and lawn clippings. Coming from a house with teenaged boys, she realized it could even be worse.

The beast was even larger out in the open. She was right not to tangle with it. She'd have easily been torn to pieces. The Hell hound turned and she could swear it was staring right at her with those golden eyes. Then, suddenly, the thing caught wind of something else and bolted off into the darkened tree line. It was definitely hunting something. And that something was not Charlie, fortunately.

She tumbled the garbage bin over and rolled out. She shook free of banana peels and coffee grounds and all the other gross crap clinging to her which she swatted off, irritably. She stood there sucking in the fresh air around her. And then she had another bad idea. She couldn't believe she was doing this. Shaking her head at her own idiocy, she pulled her hoodie up to keep her head warm and then she leaned forward and began a slow jog in the exact direction that the Hell hound had escaped.

It was time to hunt the hunter.

CHAPTER 4

Yellow, glowing eyes cut through the darkness disappearing in and out of the tree line as it darted this way and that. Finally, the shadowy beast ground to a halt on a gravel driveway triggering the security lights which flicked on illuminating not a Hell hound, but an Outback Forester loaded down with some very inebriated passengers.

"You ran over my rotodumdrums, my rhodo—you ran over my bush, dude," I complained way too loudly at Brodie and punched playfully at his bicep. "I'm the only one allowed to kill plants at my house. How are you this bad a driver? You didn't even drink."

"I'm sorry, my friend. I did have one Fireball," Brodie stage-whispered loud enough for the whole neighborhood to hear. "But don't tell Yaneane. She's a cop and she'll send me to yail."

"Is she *hic* is she though," I countered rather sloppily. "Mall yail. Hey, did she never, hey did you never tell us why Atlanta kicked you out of police school?"

Jan had her head down in the back seat comfortably rested on Sinde's lap. Sinde was curled up sideways. Both of their eyes were closed but Jan slowly raised up a middle finger. "You have the right to go fork yourselves pew pew pew," she slurred as she shot us with her middle-finger gun.

"Okay, to be continued, then. Thank you all for a rememborable, memberable, for an evening I won't forget," I said. I turned around to the back seat and patted my hand awkwardly on Sinde's face, "I'll Venmo you for the drinks. Take the rest of the *hic* rest of the night off, Barkeep, you deserve it."

"Shut up your face and go, damn Helsing," Sinde said, annoyed by my fingers on her face.

"Yeah shut up your damn Helsing face, haha," Jan giggled which got Sinde to giggling with her.

I patted Jan on the head, "Nighty night, Mall Cop. Welcome home."

"Pssshhht," she said and then blew a raspberry.

I patted Brodie's face, "And good night to you handsome prince, parting is such sweet swallow." I cracked up laughing, too. Now we all had the giggles. "Sweet swallow. Holy slit I am blintzed."

"Good night, Blintzen," Brodie said throwing the SUV into reverse.

"Take care of my dumb family ring, it's a hair loom," I slammed the door behind me and waved again over my shoulder. They began to back up slowly, winter tires crunching over the loose gravel. As I reached the porch they were pulling away down the street. I took a minute to watch their tail lights recede into the night. All around was crisp and clear and quiet; stars twinkled above and a full moon slowly crested the blue ridge mountains.

The wind blew through the trees and gave me the shivers. I could smell a wood fire from one of the neighbors. This weather was actually really nice by North Carolina mountain standards. Usually we'd had snow by now. Not that I was complaining, mountain snow could be a real dick. Fresh snow was maybe fun for a day or two but then the snowboarders arrived and we were over it and ready for Spring. Did Banner Elk tourism and general commonwealth depend heavily on the snow each year to pay its bills? Yes. Just ask Jan's ex, Mayor Poopyface.

"Good night, moon," I said and turned to go in my front door and almost walked into the huge black coffin that still stood there blocking the doorway. "Ugh. You again? Good night, box. Do not be here on the mañana." Even without the weapons inside, it had still been too heavy for the three of us, so it sat where it sat. I patted it on the way to the window. I paused when I heard something moving out there in the bushes. Snap. Crack. Rustle. Rustle.

I moved to the edge of the porch to inspect the darkness. My warm breathy exhale hung in the moonlight. The tree line was beyond the reach of the flood lights. Besides they were motion sensitive which meant that since the driveway was clear—click. Yup, the flood lights turned off after sixty seconds. Snap. Crack. Rustle. Rustle.

Suddenly, there was movement. Then, a small grey blur. "Meowr," Sméagol fussed at me, running across the lawn.

"Sméagol?" I looked at him confused, "What are you doing outside, you nut?" I turned to look at the window and it was wide open. Sméagol joined me on the porch and rubbed against my pant leg. "Okay, buddy, alright, let's get you inside. Why don't, uh, why don't you go first."

I pointed in the house. Sméagol looked at the window then back at me.

"Fine," I said mustering up some courage. Truth is, I probably would not have done this sober. "I'll go first." I peeked in the window but the house was completely dark. I could have sworn I'd left on a lamp or two. Luckily the moonlight filtered in so there was some light to go by. Even if it looked all murder-y inside.

"Mrowr," Sméagol was getting annoyed by the delay.

"Shh, I'm going," I shushed him again and tried to climb through the window as gracefully as Jan and Brodie. How had they done it? I'd forgotten all about the weapons we'd brought in; they were stacked there and I tripped and sent them all clanging and banging to the floor. Real smooth. After they'd settled, I picked myself up and grabbed some sort of ornate half-spear. I aimed it into the dark and moved forward. Sméagol hopped onto the window sill and remained there, skeptically.

Abruptly my ears picked up a scraping sound in the kitchen. I lifted the spear higher. Creeping forward as stealthily as possible, the floorboards were not helping. They creaked and moaned with each footstep. Screw it, I decided. And I braced myself and ran headlong into the kitchen with a war cry that sounded more like a war yo-del.

"AhhHHhhhhHHHahhhhhh," I warbled as I rounded the corner.

Whack.

The next thing I remembered I was flat on my back looking up at that serial killer Charlie who had a very concerned look on her face. *Wow, so she can emote*, I remember thinking. The alcohol still wasn't doing me any favors. Charlie had a stick in her hand that she quickly slid into some sort of thigh holster on her pants and then offered me a hand.

"Dude, are you okay," she asked, helping me unsteadily to my feet.

"I... maybe, I dunno, what happened," I flipped on the light switch and sat down on a barstool at the kitchen counter.

"You attacked me so I hit you," she said matter-of-factly, "with a stick."

"Yeah, that checks out," I said as my fingers touched a fresh lump on my forehead, but I was still a little disoriented. "Isn't this my house?"

She nodded, watching me carefully. I looked over on the kitchen table and my big box of board games was opened and several manuals stacked up beside it. Along with some weapons from the mystery porch box that had been laid out on display.

"Did you come here just to play Parcheesi?" I asked still trying to piece it all together and failing miserably.

"Of course not," Charlie backed up and paced around, scratching at a bandage on her palm. "I need to tell you something and it's very, very important that you don't freak out." I was still a little wibbly-wobbly so she moved closer to grab my shoulders and make sure I would focus. "It's a matter of life and—ew, have you been drinking?" She was finally getting a better look at me. And smell. Her nose wrinkled up.

"Santa is off the clock!" I shouted in my defense. "And you don't smell so hot yourself, Chuckles."

"Ugh," she backed away with a hand to her forehead, exasperated. "We don't have time for this."

"Time for what? Look," I stood and grabbed my 'Math Counts' mug off the fridge and set it in the Keurig and pressed the button.

"Um, don't you need a k-cup," Charlie looked at me skeptically.

"Don't you lecture to me Charlie frown. That's what Big Coffee wants us to think. You can get three or four coffees from one k-cup, you trust me on the math because I'm a math-magician," I weaved back and forth to grab a spoon from the sink. "You never talked to me before because you hate me so, one, why are you talking to me now and, b, why are you perturbing my cat and bonking me with sticks? On my day off?" I took a gulp of coffee as the Keurig spilled onto the counter and then put the cup back under the spout. "Remember, I don't have to care about you right now, Charlie, I'm on vacation."

Charlie's brow furrowed. I could see something was bothering her. A chair could see that. She leaned against the kitchen table, staring down at all the gaming stuff and weaponry she'd laid out. But she didn't say anything. I softened a little and added, "Look, maybe start with the big stuff, like, have you…killed somebody," I hazarded a wild guess and then watched her reaction very closely for a tell.

"Yeah, that's probably the best place to begin," she admitted, finally.

"What," I said. That's not what I'd expected to hear.

Charlie pulled a seat out from the table. "Maybe you should sit down."

Instead, I chose to perch on the barstool and keep some distance between us, "No, no, here's fine. Go ahead. Spill it. And don't lie to me. Because I'll know. I mean I probably won't know; you're pretty good at it, but I will suspect if you are discontinuous. Discontinuous," it felt like my tongue was a wallet. I tried again slower, "Disingenuous."

Charlie rolled her eyes in frustration and just blurted it out, "I am a slayer."

"I knew it," I stood up. "I'm calling the Mall cops."

"Stop!" she commanded in such a strong tone I froze immediately. Who was this 12- or 14-year-old drill sergeant? "Sit," she ordered and I sat. "Listen," she continued, "I am a monster slayer but you are, too. It's in my family, and now I finally know it's in your family, too."

"Pfffft, I think my family would have told me if our family was monster slayers—"

"Listen," she said, again. She motioned to some leather bound books on the table, "At first I wasn't sure why the middle school math teacher had authentic hunter-slayer handbooks mixed in with all the board game stuff at Sylvanian Home but then tonight a Hell hound came through the portal way bigger than the others and I tracked it all the way over here and you had the freakin Weapons Chamber right there on your front porch which means we finally have the Piscatory Warrior Ring and can begin your training, defeat the Hell hound and any familiars that came through with it and hopefully shut the portal down for good."

It took me a moment to process all of those words. Charlie waited patiently as I thought it over. Finally I spoke. "Okay, good, I think I got most of that, I just have one question and that is what the hell are you talking about?!"

Charlie picked up one of the old, dusty books from the table and flipped it open to a picture of the Piscatory Warrior Ring. She handed it over to me saying, "Okay, Dan…"

"Mr. Helsing," I emphasized.

"Dan," she continued, ignoring me, "forget the weapons and Hell hounds and all the other stuff. That can all wait. What I need to know is: where is this ring?"

Janeane and Brodie had dropped off Chrissinde and were now settling into their own luxurious AirBNB; listed online as the "Glass Treehouse." A remotely located cabin, surrounded by lush Appalachian forests and an adjacent waterfall, most of the exterior walls of this modern-luxe rental were floor-to-ceiling glass for the couple that loved to commune with nature. It was quite the cozy little love nest.

Accent lights and Christmas decorations all over the house and yard made this place glow like a Thomas Kinkade painting. Jan and Brodie had left a trail of clothes along the deck and the two were now tangled up in the jacuzzi making out. Steam rose off of the bubbling water as well as their exposed skin in the chilly mountain air. Outdoor speakers pumped out some Christmas party jams.

Brodie pulled away from Jan's hot embrace. "Baby, baby, baby, hold on, hold on. If we're doing this right here and right now I need to go grab a little blue pill."

Jan circled him in the water like a shark. "Oh we're doing this right here and right now, butter nuts, so you go do what you gotta do to get that yule log ready for this Christmas chimney..." she made a face, knowing her Christmas-themed sex talk was... just terrible. Yet somehow she couldn't stop the train wreck, "So, Santa can leave some presents tonight in the stockings with care."

It didn't make a whole lot of sense to Brodie, either, but he didn't let that deter him. She was drunk and horny and he was willing and able. Or soon to be able once the miracle of modern weiner science kicked in. He climbed out of the Jacuzzi, grabbing a towel as he did so.

"Wait, wait, I need some Swedish sugar upon my lips," Jan slurred, completely relaxed, her eyes at half-mast.

Brodie gave her a suspicious look and then began to slowly unwrap the towel from around his waist. "A kiss, dummy," she quickly explained, "I need a kiss on my lips. Jesus!"

"Oh, of course," Brodie replaced the towel and then leaned down to give Jan another long, wet kiss which melted her further into the swirling waters. He shivered, and then retreated back to the house. "I love you, Yaneane," he said over his shoulder as he tip-toed across the cold deck. She closed her eyes dreamily and stretched both arms out to the sides of the tub as she leaned back. "Mmm, and I love you, too, Dan," she murmured with a smile, not realizing what she'd said.

Brodie stopped and turned around, not sure what he'd just heard. "Walkin' in a winter wonderland," she sang along obliviously to the music. Brodie shook his head clear and pulled the sliding door open and continued on into the mountain home. When he closed the door behind himself he was surprised at how very soundproof it was. Like, he couldn't hear Jan or the music anymore at all. He tucked his towel in better to free his hands and then stepped into the bathroom. Unzipping his travel bag with all his medicines and toiletries, he pulled out a prescription bottle of pills.

Suddenly something caught his eye. The bathroom windows beside him were large, frosted glass. And the outdoor lights were casting a shadow from something on the other side. Probably a weird tree or boulder, he thought. But then the tree boulder moved.

"Yaneane?" he asked, although that made no sense to him even as he said it aloud.

The shadow turned when he said that and now he could clearly see two golden yellow eyes through the opaque glass. Then, whatever it was launched itself through the glass knocking Brodie back into the hallway. He looked up to see a hideous monstrous beast with red and blackened skin stalking toward him. The low, throaty growl was even more horrific. Brodie was paralyzed with fear as he lay on the floor.

"Wait," he said out of desperation and the thing actually stopped. It almost looked like the creature was scared of Brodie. Or at least the ring on his outstretched hand. But after a beat with no followup, that little standoff ended and the beast bared its fangs as its lips curled back and then its rippling muscles tightened to pounce on top of Brodie.

"What's this Episcopal Water Wing have to do with me," I asked, studying the picture in the book.

"Piscatory Warrior Ring. What it is, isn't important," Charlie snatched the book away from me. "Where is the ring, Dan?"

"Don't worry, it's safe. That bonehead Brodie put it on his finger and couldn't get it off," I snorted derisively. "Dumb ass."

Charlie was doing a little math in her head, "Would you say that was about 5:15 this evening?"

"I guess so, yeah, look at you little Enola Holmes. Little Scrappy Do," I joked, trying to lighten the mood.

She snapped her fingers. "That's what time the portal opened," she said, more to herself than me. She spun on me with great urgency, "Look, your friends are in significant danger. Do you know how to find them?"

"Of course. Those two blabbered on all night about their little AirBNB love shack, made me sick," I grumbled. "It's Belinda's old place. She got to keep it after the divorce when she found out Clint was taking hookers up there."

"Why would you—I don't care about that," Charlie went back over to the table and lifted up a couple of stabby looking weapons, "Do you know how to use any of these?"

"Charlie, ya don't have to orphan-splain how knives work," I said, not amused.

"I doubt that very much," she said with such disdain I started to protest. She immediately picked up the crossbow and tossed that my way, "Here."

"Hey," I said, barely catching it. "Careful."

She came over and pointed out the five bolts in the tray. "Pull this lever back and it locks in place." Ka-chunk. She pulled it back for me. "And when it's locked, it's loaded and lethal. So try to be very—"

Sproing! I barely touched the hair-trigger and a bolt flew across the room and buried itself in the fridge. Splak!

Charlie gave me the stink eye. Then she took a deep and measured breath. "As you get more familiar with your family weapons, some of your instincts and genetics may start to kick in. I pray to God that happens before we're all dead."

"Question…" I started to say.

"Shut up, we leave now or your friends die," Charlie busied herself attaching all sorts of weapons to her person. She stopped suddenly and looked me up and down. "What are you waiting for? Keys! Crossbow! Kevlar if you've got any!"

"Why do you get to be in charge?" I challenged her.

She came right up to me, grabbed my lapel and yanked me down to her level. "Because while you're a clueless middle school math teacher, I've been training since I was two years old. While you were playing board games in the basement, I was fighting my ass off trying to keep you all from being eaten alive by Hell hounds. Now, I'm the only one in a thousand miles that has any idea how to kill one of those suckers. So for the last time, get your damned keys!"

I gasped, "Cuss bucket!" She whipped a wadded up $5 bill out of her pocket and stuffed it in my shirt pocket. "Keep the change," she said through gritted teeth. I pulled my car keys from my pocket and jingled them in her face. "I'm driving."

"Nuh-uh," she said sourly, "You're drunk." She snatched the keys so quickly it took a second for me to stop jiggling my hand and realize they were gone.

"I am the adult," I said mustering some righteous indignation.

"Then act like it," she turned on a boot heel and walked out. I wanted to strangle her. Or shoot her with a crossbow. Not fatally, mind you, just like in the butt cheek or something, c'mon.

Michael Bublé crooned on the radio with that buttery voice of his about Santa Claus coming to town. Jan dreamily watched the stars glistening like tiny water droplets in the night sky. All of a sudden, she sat bolt upright when she heard the sound of breaking glass inside the house. "Brodie?" she called into the night air. She wasn't answered by her fiancé, the reply came in the form of a low, beastly growl. An unnatural growl. Like, no bobcat or bear she'd ever heard and she was from the mountains.

She quickly climbed out of the hot tub wrapping a towel around herself snugly. She paused, holding the edge of the hot tub until the world stopped spinning so fast. Then she walked along the deck and bent down to pick up her black clutch from their night on the town. She twisted the latch open on top, reached in and drew out a pink SigSauer P365 and an extra magazine. Then, lithe as a panther she moved to the back door and peeked through the glass.

The pristine, white interior of the glass treehouse was now completely splattered in blood. She couldn't even see Brodie because she was wholly distracted by the gigantic Hell hound tearing at a chew toy with its teeth and claws. More blood splattered the window as it violently shook its head. Jan suddenly realized that the chew toy was what was left of Brodie. Shock gave way instantly to rage.

Jan yanked the sliding door open, stepped inside and immediately unloaded ten rounds into the body of the beast. It had some effect, but it wasn't as lethal as Jan had hoped. More like it was just pissing the thing off. It turned around and scanned her with those hateful, yellow eyes. Jan took that instant to eject the clip, pop in the new mag and racked it back ready to go. No more body shots, she thought. Next she'd go for the head. The monster leered at her, blood dripping from its fangs. And that's when Jan discovered the thing in its mouth was an arm. With a very distinct gothic ring on the finger. Her eyes teared up, "No, no, no," she said but determined to remain absolutely resolute. She was ready to die there if necessary.

The thing took a step in her direction and suddenly a tiny arrow flew through the air and hit it in the back haunches. Right in the butt cheek. Time slowed to a trickle. The Hell hound recoiled in agony and turned its attention to the front door where a short spear flew out of nowhere and buried into its rib cage. It must have punctured a lung because the beast faltered to its knee and dropped the arm. The bloodcurdling roar became a raspy, wheezing sound.

Of all the crazy things Jan could have imagined next, she saw little Orphan Charlie who ran into the room straight at the beast. And Dan appeared, too, pulling back the action on a crossbow and shouldering it again as he made his way over to Jan's side. He let another bolt fly and it scored a direct hit in its throat. Neon green demon blood sprayed everywhere.

"Good shot," Charlie yelled. "Aim for the heart!"

"I am aiming for the heart," Dan yelled back at her.

Running full speed, Charlie dropped to her knees and leaned back, sliding beneath the crippled beast and as she passed underneath she raked two long knives across its belly opening its gut. Jan took that moment to unload her mag into the thing's thrashing, howling head. She took out one eye that exploded green goop everywhere. Dan landed another shot under its chin and the thing fell back to the floor, barely missing Charlie who flopped out of the way just in time.

Jan's pistol racked open after her last shot. Empty. Smoke danced off the tip. Charlie circled around the monster, yanking the spear from its side and repositioned herself near the underbelly. Jumping with her full weight she plunged the spear into its chest and through its heart. The Hell hound thrashed once, its tail whipping around and batting Charlie away, and then it howled once more, shook violently, and died. There was a moment of complete silence before the whole creature disintegrated in a tornado of smoke with an explosive force that also sent more neon goop onto every surface and window in that living room.

"Are you okay, Jan," I said scrambling over to her and checking for injuries. I tried not to notice that she looked sexy as hell in her towel holding that pink gun still aimed at the Hell hound. Hands shaking. What? I'm sorry, she did.

"No, Dan, I am very, very not okay," was all she could muster, lowering her arm and taking in the whole grisly scene before her.

Charlie, who'd been bowled over a couch when the Hell hound whacked her good, raised an arm, "I'm okay by the way, guys. Don't worry about Charlie." She struggled to her feet, brushed herself off and got a full look at the damages, letting out a long slow whistle. "You are definitely not getting your deposit back," she added, but Jan wasn't paying attention.

Jan had a thousand yard stare as she sank down onto the edge of a footstool beside her. She was now cradling the gun in both hands. "We've got to f-find Brodie," she said weakly.

I knelt down beside her laying the crossbow aside. Then I gently worked the spent SigSauer out of her trembling hands and laid that down, too, but not before burning myself on the muzzle. "Jan, ow, Jan, Brodie is gone. That Hell hound, that's what we call that terrible thing, it got him. Got him good. I'm so sorry we didn't get here in time."

"Found the ring!" Charlie stood up holding the Piscatory Warrior Ring. "Now we need to torch the place and leave in case they send any more."

This got Jan's attention. "There's more of those… those things?" she folded her arms across her body, holding herself uncertainly.

I put a comforting hand on her back and spoke softly, "Let's get you dressed, Jan, and then we'll all go away and figure out what to do next."

"Okay," she said softly. She allowed me to help her to her feet. She leaned into me unsteadily as I walked her towards the bedroom. "We should leave a note," she said hoarsely.

"A note?" I said looking at Charlie who was collecting weapons. Charlie shrugged back at me and shook her head. We were both lost.

"Yes, a note," Jan insisted, rallying now. "We'll leave a note in case Brodie comes back. Then he won't be worried."

"O-okay," I stammered, not really knowing what else to do. Charlie winced, too. Jan's hastily erected wall of denial was painful to watch. I mean, whose arm did she think that was on the floor? But Charlie and I had no other choice at the time. We had to participate. "We'll, uh, we'll leave a note for Brodie," I reassured her.

Charlie crawled into the back seat of my truck with a duffel bag of our weapons over her shoulder. I slid Jan's purple paisley suitcase into the trunk and latched it closed. The car ride back to my place was only eleven actual minutes but to this day it's still the longest road trip I've ever taken in my life.

As we drove away, I watched in the mirror as the fire in the glass treehouse blazed higher and higher. Charlie watched, too—that little pyro—and turned back around when she was satisfied that our tracks would be covered. Our eyes met in the mirror. We both peeked over at Jan who rested her head back, staring out the window into the night. And then without even turning her head, Jan reached over and grabbed my hand where it rested on the gear knob and held it. I pressed in the clutch and shifted into third gear. Jan's warm hand stayed with mine the whole time.

"Mm, that smoke smells nice. Somebody's got a fire going," Jan said, fogging up that part of the window.

Charlie looked at me wide-eyed and slowly circled her ear with a finger. I frowned back at her. She wasn't wrong, but still. Then Jan let go of my hand and turned all the way around in her seat towards Charlie.

"Charlie, you seem to know more about that angry moose than anyone," Jan said chewing on her bottom lip, thoughtfully, "wherever it disappeared to, is that where we'll find Brodie?" Charlie stared at her blankly. So, Jan rephrased the question, "what I'm saying is, if we find out where that thing lives, will we find Brodie?" She asked without a trace of irony.

"Look," Charlie exhaled deeply, "we don't know much about the other side of the portal. We only concern ourselves with this side. We deal with the things that don't belong on our side. When we kill them, they go…"

Charlie searched everywhere for a good answer, but came up short,"… well, I'm not sure where they go, they're just gone."

When she looked back up, Jan's eyes danced with an eagerness that caught Charlie off guard. "There's a portal?" Jan said excitedly.

"Oh my god," Charlie said, more like an apology to me than anyone.

"There's no portal," I said as deeply sympathetic to Jan as I could and then I stared icily at Charlie, "Is there, Charlie?"

Charlie caught my angry look, "I was probably mistaken about the portal."

"Tomorrow, we need to go to the portal," Jan turned back around ignoring us both. "We'll see if we can find a way inside. I'm sure something from that weapons box could help us, right Charlie? You mentioned the ring with all the powers?"

"There… is a family ring," Charlie admitted.

"Dammit, Charlie. Stop talking," I admonished her.

"Cuss bucket!" Charlie and Jan said at the same time. And then pointed at each other, "Jinx!" Then Jan laughed. What the hell was happening?

"Charlie, you are too much fun," Jan giggled and then patted my arm. "Do you think the ring caused the angry moose to come after Brodie?"

Back to reality. "Yes," Charlie said, "whoever puts on the hunter's ring receives some special power, but at the same time the ring issues the hunter's challenge and the, uh, fire mooses and other stuff comes to fight the challenger. More or less."

"So this ring," I said, "doesn't *repel* evil it attracts it."

"Yeah, it lures things in," Charlie explained. "To kill or be killed."

"Fantastic," a shiver ran up my spine.

"Hm," Jan mused aloud, "Dan you should put on the ring; seems to be your family legacy."

"Hell to the no," I said emphatically. "I will do no such thing. I'll call the city tomorrow and have them remove that stupid box from my porch. The police can have the ring and all that junk inside. It's cost us way too much already."

No way, I thought. *That ring is as bad as a cursed monkey paw. Nope. Not happening.* I downshifted to second as I pulled into my own driveway and the tiny rocks crackled against the treads all the way up to the house. I stopped the car, threw on the parking brake and turned off the ignition. The whole Toyota frame rumbled to a halt and we all sat there in an awkward silence.

I looked over and Jan was staring at me, sadly. "It's gonna be okay, Dan. We'll find Brodie. We have to. We've got the ring," she pointed at the back seat, "we've got a dwarf."

"Hey," Charlie protested.

Jan continued, "…and we've got the clumsy, naive hobbit with the heart of gold and the big smelly feet." She patted my arm.

"Ouch," I said. She gave me a reassuring smile and then climbed out of the truck.

"We're gonna need a bigger cuss bucket," Charlie said and then popped her own door open, slung the duffel strap over her shoulder and slid out to the ground. "Oh, and Dan? No cops. Civilians can't ever know about our...," on this part she added air quotes, "...family business." Then, she took a pensive beat and added, "Just, trust me on that." She slammed the door and followed Jan inside.

She was right about the cuss bucket, though. F*ck. Me.

CHAPTER 5

I awoke the next morning with a start. I don't remember the dream I was having and I wouldn't trouble you with it if I did because that's annoying and dreams are dumb. But I do know that there was falling involved. And possibly Nancy Reagan. But more falling. An endless falling, in fact, with an abrupt halt at the end. I gasped once and then I was awake. When I opened my eyes, there was Sméagol staring down at me. "Brrt" he chirruped sweetly. This was odd because he wasn't usually this respectful. Normally he'd teabag my face like some Johnny Knoxville "Jackass" stunt until I'd wake up and feed him.

We heard a little yawn, smack, smack and he and I both turned to find Janeane Switcher snuggled up with her pillow in the bed beside me. Oh my god, that's right. Janeane. Her eyes were still closed and her beautiful cheeks pressed against the white satin as peaceful as a poem. I couldn't see what time it was but there was enough light in the room that I knew it was well into mid-morning. It was all so perfect, to be honest. Well, perfectly dreadful. The wine from last night was still tap dancing on my frontal lobe. And my muscles were twisted and achey from that battle with the Hell hound.

What I needed was a handful of ibuprofen and one of those super greasy chili cheese burgers from Cook-Out. But I didn't want to rouse sleeping beauty just yet. I already knew from the prescient gnawing sensation in the pit of my stomach that today was gonna be a disaster, too. That wasn't some voodoo prophecy, either, it was just simple math.

And this was supposed to be my Christmas break. Full of shopping and prime rib and egg-nog and yams and white elephant gifts and awkwardly drunk relatives and nostalgic holiday movies like *Miracle on 34th Street* and *Die Hard*. Instead it was full of weird, gothic jewelry and medieval weapons and family curses and Hell hounds and fire and death and half-naked, forbidden temptresses in my bed. I wanted a do-over. A mulligan. A stunt double.

I felt my pillow shifting and realized Sméagol was walking across the top of it. He stopped when he got close to Jan and reached out a tentative paw and touched her nose ever so slightly. "Sméagol!" I whispered at him but he ignored me and booped her nose again, the son of a bitch. Suddenly, she stirred. I held my breath anxiously.

Jan's eyes flittered open and she saw Sméagol looming next to her and smiled. "Hello, cat," she practically purred herself. She reached up and scritchscratched him behind the ears which sealed Sméagol's loyalty to her forever. Didn't take much. He pressed into her rubbing hand and she giggled and then her eyes refocused and landed on me for the first time. And she erupted.

"Ahhhhhhhhh! Dan, what the hell are you doing in my bed? Get out of here," followed by some less coherent yelling sounds as she scooted back away from me, pulling the covers around herself like a cocoon. I ejected myself from the bed with a single pillow to cover myself and headed for the open bedroom door almost running smack into Charlie who ran in the room brandishing what looked like a garden shovel in her hand. This caused Jan to yelp again.

"What happened," Charlie gushed, blood-shot eyes a-frenzy looking for a monster attack and finding only two half-naked adults, scrambling to opposite ends of the bedroom. "Sick, did you two—"

"Stop, stop, everyone, calm down, relax," I waved my arm in surrender. Sméagol stood on a pillow with his back arched and tail fluffed out also trying to decide if he needed to bite someone or run or both.

"What is going on," Jan asked, gathering her bearings. "Where's Brodie?"

"Brodie is—" Charlie began and I cut in before she got too far ahead.

"Missing. Brodie is missing," I said. "Charlie and I brought you here last night just to be safe. Do you remember last night?"

Jan looked from me to Charlie to the floor searching for a clue. "Fire moose," she answered.

"Yes, okay. Fire moose," I said watching her slowly remember things.

She adjusted the bedroll around her and her eyes lit up, excitedly, "Portal!"

"Sh*t," I mumbled softly.

"Cuss bucket," Charlie whispered aside to me.

"Ring of power, open the portal, kill the fire moose, find Brodie," Jan answered. She nodded to me and Charlie, "That's it, right?"

"Great," I exhaled loudly. "Yeah, something like that."

Sméagol was done with all of us. He jumped down off the bed and walked out of the room flicking his tail with short, agitated strokes. "Maybe some coffee first," Charlie suggested, lowering her weapon. "And, ahem, pants. Then we need to decide some things." She tapped the shovel against her palm a couple times then looked back and forth between us. We gave no objections so she headed back out of the room.

I looked down to see my knobby knees just flapping in the breeze. I quickly found my jeans wadded up on the floor and pulled them on. Jan turned to see all of her own clothes laid out in the chair from the night before. She pulled on her own pants awkwardly under the covers. "I'll put some coffee on," I said excusing myself and left the room.

Charlie was folding up the blankets that had made up her bed on the couch. She waved me over and we talked in hushed whispers. "What happened? I thought you were gonna sleep on the floor," Charlie said, keeping an eye on the bedroom door.

"I was," I said as I pulled on a baseball cap to cover my outrageous bedhead. "But it was uncomfortable. And I missed my big bed. And she's tiny."

"She's already in a deeply precarious emotional state," Charlie jabbed a finger into my chest. "Why didn't you just wake up early and go back to the floor?"

"I forgot," I said, equally agitated. "Look, I didn't ask for any of—" we both stopped abruptly when Jan walked out of the bedroom. "Ask for any of the cream and sugar with your coffee? Is that what you wanted?" I covered weakly.

"No cream. You got any Stevia sugar? The green one?" Charlie asked.

"What does this look like, Cracker Barrel? No, you get regular sugar sugar or Equal if you prefer a little cancer with your coffee," I continued into the kitchen.

It was Jan's turn to come over and whisper with Charlie, "So what's the deal, Slayer, when are you gonna make him put the ring on? The sooner the better right?"

"Actually, no," Charlie recoiled at the idea. "None of us are ready to fight another, uh, fire moose. We got lucky last night."

"Is that what you call it?" Jan rolled her eyes as she leaned against the fireplace mantle.

"Lucky," Charlie repeated. "We need to do some training first. Planning. Or we're all dead. Ring part comes later. Once we've got a solid flow."

Jan didn't look like she loved the idea. "So we just sit around and hope Dan gets the Helsing mojo back?" she gestured at the large family portrait hanging above the fireplace.

"I saw that last night. The Great Van Helsing," Charlie moved closer to the painting. There was a rugged man standing there wrapped in furs and black leather armor with swords and weapons hanging off his belt and strapped to his back. Except for the wide brimmed slouch hat, he looked like a Lord of Winterfell. The brass plate on the bottom of the frame simply read "V. Helsing."

Jan looked closer and gasped, "I'll be damned. Look." She pointed up at Helsing's right hand.

"Whoa," Charlie said, somewhat amazed. "Dan, come check this out."

I walked out of the kitchen with my hand buried in a box of Fruitloops and joined them at the painting I'd passed a hundred times in my life and never paid any attention to at all. Just one of those family heirlooms you keep on your wall because your parents kept it on their living room wall and on and on back. "Yeah, great, great, great grand-pappy Larry Van Helsing. What of him," I asked, nonchalantly scooping cereal into my mouth.

"What about that?" Charlie snapped on her tactical flashlight with a super tight beam. She pointed it at Helsing's hand. Sure enough, there was the gothic ring that Brodie had worn, that had signaled the Hell hounds and gotten him killed. "Oh, you have gotta be kidding me," suddenly, my head was swimming again.

Charlie reached in her pocket and pulled out the ring and held it up. Identical. She inspected the painting again. "Does that crossbow look familiar?" she asked. She knew it did.

"No way," I couldn't believe it just yet. "That's not possible."

"Possible is a funny thing," Charlie said.

"Where did you say the big box was from?" Jan asked, studying the image closely.

"Uh, Romania," I answered. "That's all I could read. The rest was gibberish."

"Well," Charlie said, smugly, "I find it all very, very interesting indeed."

"I do not," I said. I was not happy about this whole thing. "I was just gonna put that dumb box with the other one and be done with it. And now this."

Charlie and Jan shared a look with each other and then turned on me at the same time. Charlie blinked a couple of times and then clarified very slowly, "There was… another weapons box?"

"I don't know, I never opened it. It showed up back in October around my fortieth birthday and I just threw it in storage with all the other dumb family junk," I shrugged.

"Oh my god, you turned forty on the last hunter's moon. That's when all this started," Charlie smacked my arm.

"Ow, what was that for?" I winced.

Charlie squared up to me. "For the past three months I've been fighting these things with garden tools and chair legs that I sharpened by hand like a prison shiv and all the while you've had god knows what gear and books and maps I needed all packed away like it was a stamp collection."

I exhaled slowly as I considered my answer. "How was I to know? After my Uncle died last summer, stuff just started showing up."

"Yeah, Hell hounds started showing up," Charlie said. I took a step back because she was crowding me a bit. "And stuff to fight the Hell hounds... stuff passed down from the greatest monster hunter of all time: Van Helsing."

"Take it easy," I raised my hand to fend her off a little. "It's just a bunch of hyped up faery tales to scare the kids. That's it. It's not true."

"I'm gonna strangle you," Charlie angrily swiped my box of Fruitloops and then sulked away to the kitchen mumbling under her breath.

"How did I never put that together? Van Helsing. Dan Helsing. That is crazy," Jan laughed at the revelation and then headed off toward the smell of the fresh coffee. "I can't wait to tell Brodie. He is gonna flip out," she said over her shoulder.

"Yeah," I gave her a thumbs up and flashed a big smile til she left the room and then let it melt into despair. Whatever was in those boxes was not gonna bring Brodie back. I knew that much.

Thirty minutes and three sausage McMuffins later we pulled up to the Banner Elk Self Storage on Silver Springs Drive. It had been three months since my last visit there. I had to look up the paperwork on my phone just to remind myself the unit number and access codes. I punched them into the front gate and it beep-beep-beeped incessantly while the black barriers slid apart. We drove around to the back and parked.

My key still worked on the outer door, too. We walked in and the motion lights detected us and all the fluorescents flickered on with a steady buzz. "Tah-dahhh," I threw my arms open proudly welcoming them to the warehouse. Charlie just scowled and waved for me to hurry up. I lead them all the way down to the end of the narrow corridor past row after row of roll-up doors locked down tight. Finally I got to my space, #327. I cracked the lock and hung it off to the side. Grabbing the bottom lip of the door, I heaved it up and the metal clangity-clanged all the way to the top.

"Whoa," Jan summed up all of our thoughts succinctly.

The 10x20 space was deeper than it was wide. And, yes, there was a tall box like the one on my front porch at the back of the shed. But between us and the box was a love seat, five broken chairs, a comic book collection, stacks of books and VHS tapes, half a foosball table, a full-sized Stormtrooper and a couple dozen boxes of Helsing family documents and photo albums and assorted junk.

"Hoarder?" I said jokingly, "I don't even know 'er! Haha." I laughed and wiggled a pretend cigar at them. I was the only one laughing. "You get it? It's like 'Liquor? I don't even, oof—"

Jan shoved a box into my arms rather forcefully. I took it down the hall a little ways and then set it down. Item by item we slowly emptied out the whole dusty space, cobwebs and all. The love seat was the last big ticket item in the way but the angle was awkward. We had all stripped off our coats and as many layers as we could. We were a sweaty mess as we tried to force the oversized furniture up and out.

"Pivot," I said, cracking myself up. "Pivot!"

"Dan, so help me God," Charlie said, letting the unfinished threat hang in the air.

"You're too young to remember *Friends* on TV. But Jan gets it," I explained. "Right, Jan?"

"Less talky talky," Jan said curtly.

We shoved and adjusted and wiggled and finally got the love seat out of the way and into the hall. Jan and I flopped down on the small couch to catch our breath. Charlie moved in to inspect the weapons box.

"So, how did you open the last one? Incantation? Secret family amulet?" Charlie asked, anxious to peek inside.

I held up a single finger, like E.T., and stood up. "Step aside, amateur," I said maneuvering past her. I felt down the right side of the box and there was another fingerprint ID. I pressed my finger pad on to the square and it scanned me and clicked unlocked. This time I stood back. I wasn't gonna get bum rushed by another dead crypt keeper dude.

The door began to swing open by itself, pressed from the inside by what looked and sounded like a thousand green and blue glow-y marbles. They just kept pouring out as the door swung fully wide open.

"What the hell," I said moving my feet trying not to slip on them all as they cascaded past.

"Careful," Charlie said picking one up to inspect it closer, "if I'm not mistaken those are like nitroglycerin modules."

I froze in fear, "N-nitroglycerin?"

"Relax," Charlie smiled, "if they were gonna blow, we'd be dead by now."

"Wow, you've got the bedside manner of a rattlesnake," I said through gritted teeth.

We looked back into the weapon box and leaning there against a rack was Van Helsing's amour and outfit exactly like the one he wore in the painting in my house. Charlie stepped forward, careful not to crack open any orbitals. She reached into the box and pulled out a black, wide-brimmed slouch hat. She smiled at us and then gently placed it upon her own head as if she were crowning a Duke or Dutchess. She turned around and showed it off appreciatively.

"Actually, yeah, that looks pretty badass on you, Charlie," I had to admit.

She grinned from ear to ear. It might have been the first time I had ever seen her smile. She was wearing her man-crush's signature hat and loving it. She looked over at Jan and her smile suddenly faded away. "Stop!" she shouted. I turned to see what was happening.

Jan stood by the love seat. She had Charlie's coat in hand and had pulled the ring out of the pocket. There were hundreds of little nitro-rounds at our feet, there was no way Charlie or I could get to her in time. She held the ring up poised to slip it onto her finger.

"Jan," I tried to sound calm. "What are you doing? Are you crazy? You put that thing on and another monster comes through the portal. To kill you."

"Exactly," Jan said. "The portal will be open. Look at all this fire-power we now have. No more wasting time, guys, it's time to get Brodie back."

"No," I started to say but it was too late. She slipped the ring onto her finger. There was a pulse of massive power that flickered all the lights and almost blew Charlie and I over as it washed across us in a massive wave. We both held our arms in front of our faces to block the surge. And as quickly as it began, it was over.

I turned back to Charlie, panicked. "What do we do, Charlie?"

Her face was ghost-white, but resolute, "We have to get back to the orphans before something comes through that portal."

We both looked at Jan, sadly. Mind you, she was not sad. She was exuberant. In her own world. The ring was now an indelible part of her hand. There was only one way that thing was coming off now. She'd sealed her own fate. Here we had just had our teeth kicked in by our first fire moose and now the clock was ticking til the next one arrived. Yes, our funerals were imminent. We had to move and move fast.

CHAPTER 6

"Holy traffic jam, Batman," I groaned as I peered through the truck windshield.

"Mm," Charlie grunted from the passenger side, as she watched the same thing.

"I'm confused," Jan said leaning up between us from the back seat. "Why are all these cars here?"

"Annual Orphan Christmas Dinner Theater," Charlie and I said at the exact same time. I had completely forgotten about it. And given the past 48 hours no one could blame me. AOCDT was a big part of how the Sylvanian Home raised their operating funds each year. One big $1000 a plate Christmas dinner where the who's who in town showed up, opened up their wallets and their hearts and their off-shore accounts in exchange for some lukewarm lemon chicken and rubber green beans—the gross kind from the can that squeaked on your teeth when you chewed them. But that was really the least of our worries. Somewhere below this posh gaggle of party-people a Hell hound would be portal'ing through any minute. And not in the cool Dr. Strange or StarGate-y way, either. More Jurassic Park-y. I mean, if JP had portals.

The front lawn looked like a CarMax. Vehicles everywhere. And not haphazardly. This wasn't Coachella. No, Sister Marguerite would never approve that music or glitter bra situation. Obi-Juan and Liam were outside directing and organizing traffic. But since everyone was mostly inside, at this point, they were just messing around using their flashlight/traffic wands as light sabers to act out movie scenes.

"And now, Emperor of Catan, I killed Snoke and you shall taste the blood of a thousand—Charlie!" Obi Juan saw us first and ran over as we climbed out of the truck. He'd withdrawn from what was about to be a finishing deathblow to Liam who lay on the ground with one hand pulled into his sleeve like it'd been chopped off in battle.

"Where you been, Charlie?" Liam jumped up nimbly to join us.

Charlie switched back into silent, brooding mode. Having experienced the real Charlie, this other persona was now funny to me. The kid had created an elaborate alter ego like Batman or Deadpool or Hillary Clinton. Only Charlie's cover was that she would just wallflower into the background, unnoticed and underestimated. She just answered Liam with a bored shrug.

"Work detail. For talking too much," I answered for her. "Where's Sister Marguerite?"

"I dunno," Liam answered, looking back toward the house. "Inside, I guess."

I ruffled his hair, "Just a fountain of knowledge, aren't you?"

"Hey," he protested as he combed it back in place with his fingers.

Obi Juan piped up, "I saw her in the kitchen talking with Mayor Doug."

"Doug's here?" Jan said, clouding up a little. "Maybe, I should go in there and punch him in the nu—"

"Nope! Absolutely not," I pulled out my wallet and gave the boys a $5 bill. "Okay, listen up. I want you two to go on a top secret mission. I want a plate full of the best cookies—the best, I'm saying, no peanut butter, no lemon, and no fruitcake or the deal is off. I want them all saran wrapped and placed on my dashboard. To go." I looked them right in the eye. I had their full attention. "Think you can handle that? Oh, and another $5 when you finish the job if you tell nobody a single word about us or about your secret mission. Capiche?"

"Capiche," Liam winked and threw us a finger gun and clicked his tongue twice.

"Come on," Obi Juan said and they both ran off towards the house.

"Remember, no fruit cake!" I yelled after them. They both shot me a thumbs up.

"Dan," Jan looked a little agitated, "shouldn't I just go talk to the mayor for, like, five seconds?" She held up five fingers and then balled them into a fist.

I put a loving hand over the fist and eased it back down. Then I looked into those shimmering, hypnotic pools of sapphire blue and simply reminded her: "Portal?"

That sobered her up real fast. She nodded her head, "Portal."

I smiled and kissed Jan's forehead and then went back over to the truck to grab our weapons duffel. Charlie followed me over and smacked my arm. "What are you doing," she lectured, "keep your hands and your lips to yourself."

"Ugh, it was an innocent, uh, fatherly type gesture," I argued. She was not buying into it so I quickly kissed her on the forehead, too. She jerked back and held up a warning finger. "See?" I said nonchalantly, "Fatherly affection, it's just kinda my deal. That's all."

"I will bleed you out if you try that again," she warned without even the hint of irony. And I believed her.

"Don't worry, ptui," I spit a dirt fleck off my tongue. "You taste like a shower drain." She just glared back. I pulled the black bag over my shoulder which made me feel like a scene in every Schwarzenegger movie ever made. I closed the door and said in my best Arnold voice, "Be careful, or we'll be molested murdered and mutilated, auhhauahhauhh. Head to the cellahhhh."

"What…was that?" Charlie asked dryly.

"Arnold," I was a little offended she even had to ask. "Come on, really?"

She stared at me blankly and shook her head.

"Schwarzenegger?" I asked, incredulously.

Still nothing.

"Ugh, you are such a zygote. If we live through this we are all doing an 80s action movie marathon with all the orphans because this," I swirled my finger around her face, "is unacceptable."

Charlie rolled her eyes, then ducked into a crouching run and lead off toward the darker tree line. Jan followed and I brought up the rear with the duffel bag smacking and clacking against me with each step. "Ow, ow, ow," I protested.

So much for my action hero moment.

Christmas music echoed loudly down the stairs. The dinner party was in full swing. That was actually providential because that sound would drown out whatever happened down here in the basement. Unless we were unsuccessful and then the Hell hound would get past us, go upstairs and have its own Christmas buffet.

Jan, Charlie and I moved in a tight delta formation down the cellar steps. Thanks to her training, Jan had shown us a Mall cop breaching maneuver in a little 10-second demo upstairs. The fluorescent bulbs flickered on and off eerily. Charlie was on point with her new short swords and that cool slouch hat. Jan was next carrying a slingshot rifle with seven rounds of nitro-rounds locked and loaded. And I had my trusty crossbow. We'd also divided up some of the Helsing armor so Charlie had the wrist and arm guards, Jan had the long black leather overcoat and I had a breastplate with the family crest emblazoned on it—a gryphon or a dragon or a winged otter, I wasn't really sure, but it was inlaid gold and pretty badass to look at.

"We need a safe word," I realized aloud. "In case, you know…"

"That's dumb," Charlie moved forward steadily, "If something jumps out, we're all gonna see it."

"Just in case, like 'Tapioca!' or no what about 'Sea Biscuit!'" That sounded right to me. "Yeah, if anything goes sideways, 'Sea Biscuit!' Yeah?"

They just groaned. Well, it would serve them right if they got eaten because they were not prepared like I was. I almost tripped on a bucket and they both gave me the saltiest look as it rolled loudly in a circle. I stopped it with my toe. We pressed on.

Down at the end of the hall we could see the red glow pulsating. "Portal's open," Charlie whispered. "Head on a swivel."

"Okay, GI Jane," I chided, "Head on a swizzle… what is that even supposed to—that's not a thing."

"A *swivel*. And it absolutely is a thing, Navy SEALs say it all the time," Charlie snapped back.

"Oh," I laughed quietly, "Okay, so fourteen year old junior monster slayers do a lot of training with the SEALs, do they?" They both glared back at me, but I just shook my head at them and added a *psshhht*.

"Yes, our people train a special unit of SEALs for unorthodox warfare, now will you please shut up," she hissed at me.

"I call bullsh*t," I mumbled.

"Cuss bucket," Jan and Charlie said at the same time pointing to the Catan HQ door as we passed.

"Ugh," I complained and broke formation to enter our game room. I froze halfway to the money jar when I saw little Phoebe sitting at the table munching merrily on some milk and cookies. A pale, but very striking man dressed all in black, flowy leather sat with her as if he were waiting for someone. Or some *thing*.

"Who the heckballs are you," I asked.

The man turned to me and eyed me up and down disdainfully. He sniffed the air and then leered, "Well, it's about time, Helsing." His deep, Eastern-bloc accent would have been cool if it hadn't been so menacingly aimed my way. "I am Count Victor Von Lichtenstein."

"The dude from *A Knight's Tale*?" I asked, confused.

"What?" he said, but it sounded more like, "Vut?"

"What?" I kept my crossbow trained on him but took one step back toward the door, "Psssst, guys. Back here. Sea Biscuit. Stat. On a swizzle. Tapioca." Then I took a step around closer to Phoebe's side of the table. "Phoebe, darling, what, uh, whatcha doin'?"

She smiled up at me, delighted. "Just having some cookies and eggnog with my new friend Mr. Victor," she beamed. With the big chair, her little legs didn't even touch the ground and she swung them merrily back and forth humming as she chewed.

"If you hurt her, I swear to God—" I started to say.

"Don't bother," Victor grimaced at me, "As long as that silver abomination is around her neck this little one is protected."

I looked back at Phoebe and saw her beautiful necklace with the cross pendant. Jan and Charlie entered the room behind me. "What are you blabbering—" Charlie froze when she saw Victor.

I gestured to Victor and whispered from the side of my mouth, "Sea Biscuit."

Victor's eyes lit up when he saw the Piscatory Warrior ring on Jan's finger, "Oh interesting," he said. "Helsing, you put your family challenge ring on a… peasant?"

"Hey," Jan and I said at the same time. I didn't like the way he ogled her. Or her hand decor. Charlie stepped forward, her voice low and raspy, "Let the little girl go, she has no part of this."

Victor looked surprised, "Oh, Phoebe? She's free to go whenever she likes. She was just keeping me company until my friend arrived."

"I am not your *friend*, pal," I seethed and then quickly added, "and I'm not your pal. I just said that platonically, bud. Dammit." I needed to quit while I was behind.

Victor leaned over to Phoebe, "Sweetheart, you're free to go back upstairs now if you'd like. Enjoy the party."

"Thank you, Mr. Victor, so nice to meet you," she slid off her seat, gathered up her leftover cookie and headed for the door. "Merry Christmas, everyone," she sang over her shoulder. She even hugged Charlie's leg as she passed. "Awwww," everyone cooed at Phoebe. Even Victor. Charlie backed out of the room with her to watch her go upstairs, then she came back in and locked onto Victor again. "Don't even think about moving."

"Oh, I'm not going anywhere. It's not my time yet," he took out a fancy pocket watch from inside his suit coat and clicked it open. "As I said, I'm just waiting for a friend." He snapped it closed again with a flourish. He was enjoying himself. Suddenly, from down at the portal end of the hallway we heard a low and ominous growl. "Hm, there she is now."

The three of us shared a look that was equal parts surprise and fear. Charlie poked her head back out into the hallway. She looked at me and then checked on Victor. "Go," he said with a dismissive wave of his hand, "I'll be here when you finish." He reassured us with a crooked grin and added, "if you finish."

Jan and I joined Charlie in the hall. If anything, the Christmas music upstairs was louder. Good. Meanwhile, nothing was visible at the other end, yet, but that wouldn't last. We could hear more and more movement and scraping around. "Form up on me," Charlie ordered. "And stick to the plan."

The plan. Yeah, right. Don't die. That was the plan. By my calculations we had a 1 in 3 chance of survival. And that was if I ducked out and ran while they distracted the fire moose. But, I couldn't do that to them. I mean, I could, but I wouldn't. Charlie would come back from the grave and haunt me if I did. She was spiteful like that. Together, we moved down the hallway to close the distance. We looked cool, too. If it was a movie it would have been one of those slow-mo Armageddon hero struts that Michael Bay loved to do.

"Hot headed," Jan whispered to me out of nowhere.

"What," I looked over at her, confused.

She sighed and rolled her eyes, "You asked why they kicked me out of Police Academy. They said I was hot headed. Too quick to draw down on the bad guys."

"Oh, so you were too good at your job?" I summed up perfectly.

"Their job is not—you know what, never mind," she took a couple more steps in silence and then added, "And also I punched my Sergeant when he got a little handsy."

"Hell yeah," I held a hand up to Jan. She high-fived it lightly while trying to suppress a half smile.

Charlie glared back at us, "Would you two focus!"

We cleared the last corner with Charlie as the tip of the spear. The Hell hound was down there and appeared to be waiting on us. It looked just as big and ugly as the last one.

The thing scanned us with its creepy yellow eyes and seemed to recognize Jan's ring. That really pissed it off and it roared, hatefully. Maybe it was the small space, but he even looked like he was getting larger.

"Okay, Jan," Charlie signalled.

"This is for Brodie," Jan said, raising the slingshot rifle into position on her shoulder. She fired three orbitals at its body. They all exploded with the force of a dyna-mite blast. Dust exploded from cracks in the ceiling joists. The beast growled in pain, thrashing about as the flames licked its skin, creating dark blackened patches in its tor-so.

"Okay, Dan," Charlie said over the noise.

I raised my crossbow and aimed right at the head, but never got a shot off. The Hell hound whipped its tail and flung an antique dresser down the hall at us. Drawers flew out and knocked us all down like duck pins. Jan's rifle skittered across the floor. I hit the back wall and might have been crushed by the full force of the dresser but the family armor protected me.

Charlie was the first one back up to her feet and she didn't wait for Jan and I. She ran headlong towards the monster screaming her own battle cry. She veered left at the last second and ran up onto some furniture and boxes and leapt over the creature's angry jaws that snapped at her in mid air. She landed on its back and began hacking and slashing with her short swords as the thing bucked and rolled and tried to bite at her.

I was finally able to shove the dresser off. Blood was running down my arm. I helped Jan to her feet. She had a scrape on her forehead but nothing broken. We collected our weapons and aimed them into the fray. Things were moving so fast we were hesitant to pull the trigger.

"What are you waiting for," Charlie yelled at us.

"We don't wanna hit you," Jan yelled back.

"Would you idiots shoot something down here among us? One of us has got to have some relief," she screamed.

The huge creature batted another piece of furniture our way and it splintered along the wall beside us but missed. Finally it craned its head back and grabbed hold of Charlie by the arm. Fortunately she had the armored gauntlet on but the thing shook her back and forth and then slammed her into the wall of boxes.

"We've got to lead it away from Charlie," I said. "Come on."

I fired an arrow at the beast and got its attention all right. It was pissed and headed our way. I helped Jan limp along back down the hallway. We ducked into the Catan HQ room and shut the huge wooden door behind us. Victor just stood in the back of the room, browsing some books on a shelf, humming like nothing in the world was going on.

I sat Jan in the chair at the table and told her, "Be as hot headed as you want." She nodded.

Then I went back over to brace my back against the door. It was sturdy, but not impregnable. It wouldn't last long against something that size. *Dammit, Charlie, you better not be dead. You hear me*? I roared at her but from a safe space between my ears. What were we even doing here? I mean this was a helluva way to die. I wiped a trickle of blood and a rogue tear from my flushed, panicky cheek.

WHAM! The growly, ferocious Hell hound was throwing itself bodily against the other side of the oaken chamber door—WHAM! WHAM!—and these scrawny little chicken legs of mine weren't gonna hold out much longer. WHAM! The door began to splinter.

"Jan, I can't hold it any longer. Get ready," I yelled.

I could tell one of her shoulders was hurt, but she swung the gun up and steadied it using the table. She aimed it right at the door space over my head. The next time the Hell hound smashed into the door, it splintered down the middle and I dove out of the way. Dodging door fragments, I brought my crossbow up to the huge monstrous head forcing its way into the room. That thing wanted us dead so badly. But we weren't gonna be that easy to kill. I aimed for the soft spot of the creature's clawed foot. Right between her toesies. And fired.

Thwack.

Direct hit. Charlie was right, maybe I was starting to feel that Helsing mojo. The shot really hacked the thing off and it turned and screamed at us baring its long razor sharp teeth.

"Now Jan!" I screamed.

She took a half second to course correct and then fired a round straight into its big mouth. Bingo. Its whole head exploded. Then a tornado of neon blood flew everywhere as the thing evaporated and the whole room fell silent except for the buzz of the fluorescent lights and my heavy gasps for breath.

Jan sprang to her feet and I limped quickly over to her side. "Hell yeah," she pumped her rifle in the air. "We did it, Dan."

"Well, we couldn't have done it without…," I remembered suddenly. "Charlie!"

We both supported each other as we limped up the hallway and around the corner. The portal was inactive once more. Just a large antique mirror of no note whatsoever. Puddles of fire from the nitro explosions still danced on the walls and furniture. Nothing moved in the alcove for a few seconds and then we heard a groan.

"Charlie!" Jan yelled with great concern. I left Jan propped there with her hand leaning on the wall and ran to our injured slayer.

"Charlie's not okay," Charlie croaked dryly from under some boxes. I quickly dug her out. She helped kick off the last box and stood to her feet. She was a little wobbly and had a new limp thanks to a gash in her left leg, but who didn't.

"Not bad for bull riding a Wookalaar," I said. "Not smart, but not bad."

"So, did your kill shot into the mouth plan work?" Charlie asked with a painful wince.

"It was a helluva shot," I smiled down at her. I couldn't resist a little end-zone celebration at her expense. "And I was right, Charlie. You were so wrong and I was right. Booyah, slayaaaaaah!"

"Gawd, you're the worst," she pushed me away and limped off up the hall to lean on Jan instead. As they hobbled along, Charlie only had one sword, I bent down and picked up her other one. When I did, I saw a stack of black, painted canvasses. I looked through a few of them. These were exactly like the one from Ms. Lenning's art class. Neon splatters and an enigmatic white skull in the bottom corner. On the back was a date and time for each one.

"Charlie?" I said.

She and Jan stopped and turned around. "What," she nipped back.

I held one out in each hand, "You did… all these by yourself?"

She gave a tired nod. "And those," she said matter-of-factly, pointing to the other wall where a bunch of others were stacked up. "I liked to leave them out here as a warning to the other trespassers."

I walked over to her and before she could refuse, I pulled her into a hug and kissed the top of her head. "Ow," she said, but she didn't fight it this time. Without another word, I handed her sword back and we all three hobbled down the hall to reckon with Victor Von Lichtenstein.

We walked into the room looking quite bedraggled. Still, Charlie and I steadied ourselves ahead of Jan who was the worst of us. I picked up my crossbow and we trained our weapons on Victor. He stood with his back to us, regarding one of Charlie's paintings on the wall. He sniffed it closely and then grunted out a very displeased, "Hmm."

"Next!" I said, trying my best to sound authoritative. Victor turned around and looked us over. He was not impressed.

"I could kill you all now," his head tilted sideways as he regarded us thoughtfully. "But then Helsing gets off too easily. Where's the torture in that?"

Charlie shuffled uneasily. She struggled to keep the tip of the sword aimed true. "I don't like this, Dan," she said to me.

"Eenie, meenie, miney, moe," Victor counted.

"What do you want?" I asked.

"Oh, nothing. I'm trying to decide who will die and who will live," Victor said ever so smugly.

"That's it," I'd had enough. I aimed the crossbow at Victor's arrogant face and pulled the trigger. The arrow flew straight at him but right before it found purchase, he shifted into some sort of ethereal shadow cloud.

The arrow passed right through him and harmlessly struck the painting on the other side.

His black, smokey form moved swiftly across the space between us. Before I could even get off a second shot or respond, Victor materialized behind Jan, opened his mouth baring two horrific, gleaming fangs and clamped down on the carotid artery in her neck. Her eyes went wide as her knife dislodged and clattered to the ground. Charlie and I spun around but it was like we were moving in slow motion. I aimed point blank at his head and pulled the trigger. Again, he dematerialized into a mere shadow and flew back across the room to the painting. He formed up again, long enough to spit Jan's blood all over the painting with the Hell hound guts. "Eye for an eye," he grinned evilly at me. "Hurts, doesn't it?" Then he clouded up and flew from the room and out towards the cellar doors.

Jan's legs buckled and she began to fall. I caught her with one arm as I dropped the crossbow. Charlie moved alongside us, too, and together we lowered Jan to the ground. Blood was gushing from her neck. Charlie tried to keep pressure on it.

"Dan! What's happening to me, Dan? I can't feel anything," she said with a panicked look in her eyes.

"Jan, it's gonna be okay, Jan. Don't worry, it's just a little—it's a—you're gonna be fine," I said getting blood all over me, too. "Charlie, what do we do?"

Charlie shook her head slowly, helplessly. Jan convulsed and her eyes rolled back and her breaths turned shallow as the area around the bite spread a blackened vein-y pattern that spider-webbed across her shoulder and face. And in the next instant, she was completely still. Eyes wide. Vacant.

Charlie and I looked at each other in complete horror. "No, no, this can't—she can't be—" I sputtered. Jan's lifeless arm flopped down and the Piscatory Warrior ring slid off her finger and clattered to the stone floor. Charlie and I sat there hugging her close, just rocking back and forth and back and forth. But it was no use. Janeane Abigail Switcher was dead.

It was after midnight when I dragged back home. I crawled wearily through the porch window, set a plate of Christmas cookies on the ottoman and plopped myself right down on the floor face down into the hardwoods. Sméagol sauntered over to nuzzle and nip playfully at me. I had no emotional energy left. I rotated a hand palm up. If Sméagol wanted pets, he'd have to do all the work himself. I just wanted to lay there and wait for rigor mortis to set in.

What the hell kinda Christmas was this, anyway? Charlie and I had given our statements to the police. As she had instructed, we'd left out all the 'family business'—Hell hounds, magic portals and douchebag vampires—and very simply claimed that some sort of homeless vagrant had overtaken us in the basement and stabbed Jan and escaped before we could identify him. We also suggested the AirBNB fire might have been his handiwork, too. It couldn't have been more neatly wrapped in a bow for the B.E.P.D.

The Mayor had come down, outraged, and then left completely distraught. The Christmas celebration was cut short. They took Jan away on a stretcher and taped off the Sylvanian Home basement as a crime scene. I'd managed to sneak out our weapons duffle and it sat in the back of my Forerunner. So far, Charlie and I weren't suspects but if they found all this weird goth gear, it would definitely invite questions.

The living room lamp clicked on, startling me. It was Charlie. She'd been sitting there in the dark. Her eyes were as red and puffy as mine. I didn't even move off the floor, just craned my head sideways, "Mmf. You're supposed to be in your bunk bed fast asleep with visions of sugar plums and unicorns and all that."

"Screw that. Victor is still out there. Growing more and more powerful by the minute. I can feel it. His portal is still active, Dan, our job is not finished," she said plainly. The gash on her leg had been wrapped by the medics and she adjusted the bandages now, grimacing at the pain.

"Oh, we're finished," I corrected her, my voice cracked a little. "We don't stand a chance against that… dick."

"You're right," she conceded softly.

"Thank you. I know it hurts for you to finally admit that," I couldn't turn the assholery off. Somehow, I knew Charlie was the only one that would understand.

"Not without this," she slid the Piscatory Warrior Ring across the floor near my face and it tumbled to a halt.

I hated that ring. Just seeing it again made my blood boil. "That stupid ring has killed two people already, or did you miss that part?"

"Because it wasn't *meant* for them. It's meant for you. All of this, the weapons, the books, it's all for you to fight and—"

I rolled up onto an elbow with a grunt. "I fought," tears mixed with my dirty, sweaty skin and stung my eyes. "I fought, Charlie... I fought and they still died. And I was there. And there was nothing I could do to stop it." I sobbed. "Nothing. You can't fight a smoke cloud."

"Dan," she said softly but sternly. "This ring unlocks your power, your family heritage, your destiny. Who knows? But it was made for you. Not them. And every second you don't put it on, more people will suffer and die."

I shook my head at her, incredulous. "You are a child. A chi-yuld. Do you understand that?"

She held my gaze steadily. "Have I been wrong, yet?" She raised her eyebrows defensively and awaited my answer. "Hm?"

I took extra time thinking through the premise of her question. I was gonna prove her wrong. One way or another. She was a dumb kid drawing dumb kid conclusions. And I was the adult. And a mathematician. Solving difficult math postulates was my job. But in every instance I considered, I found that her figures—her logic—had unfortunately been sound.

"You…" I pointed an accusatory finger at her, and then relented, "You said the new Taylor Swift Christmas album was 'not her best.' And that was a bald-faced lie."

Charlie almost cracked a smile. Almost. I picked my rickety bones up off the floor, my muscles and joints cursing my name, scooped up the ring and joined her on the couch. Setting the ring down on the coffee table both of us stared at it. Even Sméagol jumped up and pawed at it before discovering a much more interesting prey: a moth flittering near the lamp.

I sighed heavily. "Charlie, if I put this ring on, I will die," I said, finally.

"You don't know that, Dan. What we do know is that if you *don't* put the ring on, everyone else will die," she argued. "Monster hunting is literally in your blood."

"That is so dumb," I grabbed my head in both heads. "Aaaargh, and say, just say on the long shot that I am a hero then I don't even get to tell anyone I'm a hero? Because we can't talk about 'family business' with civilians. What the hell kinda deal is that?"

Charlie put a reassuring hand on my arm. "I'll know you're a hero," she said.

I pulled my arm away. "Oh my god, it creeps me out when you're nice."

"Yeah that felt weird," she admitted sheepishly.

"Look, can we just decide tomorrow? I am so exhausted my hair hurts." I turned to Charlie but she avoided my eye contact. I could tell she was holding something back. "Whaaat is it now?"

She rummaged through the backpack at her feet and pulled out one of my family Helsing books. "Hey, that's mine," I protested.

She ignored me. "I found this part," she opened it to a specific page she had marked. It had gory vampire pictures preying on young, despairing maidens. "Obviously we can't read this language, but look at these pictures. See? Male vampires don't kill the young women. They turn them."

She'd lost me. "Turn them?"

"They recruit them," she clarified. "To Team Vampire. Against their wishes."

She held up the pictures again. It was a progression panel. I shook my head, "No, what are you saying? Jan died. I saw it, you saw, the Watauga Medical team confirmed it."

"Yeah, she got bit. She went under the spell or died or cocooned or whatever. And according to this book, she will awaken as a brand new baby vampire hungry for her first kill," Charlie explained rather dramatically pointing out the last frame of the picture which more or less showed the same thing.

I stood up and paced the floor, anxiously. "Cocooned? That's the story you're going with? You are out of your depth here, Charlotte Summers."

She flinched at the full name. Then she stood up and squared off to me. "Do you know why Victor didn't bite me, too? He had the chance. He was faster than we were. He didn't bite you because you're a Helsing. He wants you to suffer. Why didn't he kill me, too?"

"Because you taste bad?" I smirked.

She reached into her neckline and pulled out a necklace with a silver cross on it. "Legally, he couldn't. Because of this."

"Legally?" I wasn't buying it. "Sorry, but this ain't Matlock or People's Court, kid."

"Legally," she insisted. "Look. Math has to follow certain laws. Like, name one math law."

"Uh, well there's the associative law of multipli—"

"Nobody cares!" she waved a hand in my face. "The point is there's laws. Laws of nature, laws of math, laws of physics and laws of Monsterology. Or 'Cryptozo-ology' if you want get all technical about it."

"You're serious," I folded my arms across my chest and scowled down at her.

"Yes, look, the power vortex when a person puts on the ring creates a lawful challenge. It's a challenge for dominion. Winners talk and losers walk." She was quite animated now as she explained the process, chopping one of her hands into the palm of the other. "Brodie lost. Nobody cared."

"Hey," I interjected.

"I'm talking the monster world didn't care about him, of course we cared about him, but he was a nobody. Jan's obviously not a nobody. And so Victor used a legal loophole to get her."

"Glove don't fit you must acquit," I nodded like I knew what I was talking about.

"I don't know what that means. But technically she died, so she lost. And the ring fell off. But now, by vampire law she belongs to Victor which makes him very happy because he knows that—more than her death—her living as his love slave will torture you far more in the end." She now had my full attention. "And, as a bonus, he gains a foothold in our world."

"You are so just pulling stuff out of your…gluteus maximus aren't you," I studied her skeptically.

"It's a working theorem, professor, but it has merit. And there's a very, very easy way to find out if I'm right," she leaned down and picked up the ring off the table.

"Oh really," I said.

"You put this damn thing on and we go down to the morgue and ask Jan herself," Charlie held the ring out to me.

I turned away and leaned against the mantle. I looked up at the Van Helsing portrait. "You suck," I told him to his face. "This sucks. Fuuuuuuuuuu—" I yelled and then saw Charlie winding up with the tired old 'cuss bucket' rebuff.

"—uuuuuuuuun!" I finished. Charlie put her finger back down. "See? You don't know me."

She stared at me with that damnable poker face. I exhaled heavily and Charlie offered the ring up again. I took it from her. My fingers trembled. I studied it carefully. You couldn't even see the nasty little spikes. Looked like any ol' ordinary punk rock Bauhaus swag. Until it latched onto your finger like an alien face-hugger. And, get this, I'd have to wear it for the rest of my life. Which might only be sixty minutes long once the ring doxxed me and the Hell hounds and vampires showed up. Charlie knew enough to keep quiet and just let me wrestle with it.

"Whatever, dude," I said resigning myself to my dark fate. I took a deep breath and then slid the ring onto the pointer finger of my right hand. I braced for cosmic fireworks. Nothing. Charlie watched me, wide-eyed at first, and then with a growing sense of concern. I took it off and slid it on again. Nada.

"Maybe it's a left-handed ring of power," I said and fit it onto my other hand. Still nothing. Every single finger. No vortex of energy. No shaft of light from heaven. No angelic voices. No Van Helsing hologram outlining a new personal quest. Not a damn thing.

"Huh," Charlie said, dumbstruck.

"Here, maybe this," I struck a pose and raised my fist high overhead, "BY THE POWER OF GREYSKULL!" I stood there for several seconds. Still nothing. I relaxed, again, shaking my head, "thought for sure that would spark something."

"I was afraid of this," Charlie said with some gravitas. "You broke it."

"I—" I held up a warning finger. "I did my job and now—"

"Well, don't take it off," she stopped me from removing it. "Just give it some time."

"Oh, okay, yeah, maybe it's sleeping," I said sarcastically. "I'm so glad that one of us gets to."

"Okay, well, we still need to check on Jan," Charlie grabbed her backpack and pulled it over her shoulders at the window. "You coming, or…?"

"Ha," I said as I followed after her, "like I have a choice." I stepped through the window and closed it behind us, giving Sméagol a sad little wave good bye.

The best and worst part of these small towns is that everyone knows everybody. Everybody and their 'bees wax' as Bernice over at the Highlander's Grill was fond of saying. Usually with a big old chaw of gum in her yap. She'd say, "that's none of your g.d. effin' bees wax, Doug! Shyoot." She was like a bulldog in Uggs.

Most times the nosiness worked to your disadvantage, but sometimes it helped. Like tonight, I'd heard that my old college buddy Gerald was working security at the Watauga Medical Center. More importantly he owed me a ton of life-long favors for helping him pass Calculus. He was happy to meet us at the loading docks and crack the door open for us.

"If anyone asks y'all how y'all got in here," Gerald drawled as he lead us down to the morgue, "best y'all jist remember to forgit, hear?"

"Trust me, we never saw you, you were never here," I waved my hands in big sweeping motions. "Oh, here," I pulled two tickets from my wallet. "As requested, two 50-yard-line tickets to the App State Boca Raton Bowl game."

Gerald lit up and took them in his hands like I'd handed him a Dale Earnhardt rookie card, "Brochacho, if there wasn't a lady present ida kiss you full on dat purdy mouth, boy. Hooowhee!"

"Oh, yes, let's not make things uncomfortable for Charlie," I maneuvered her closer so that she was between Gerald and I.

"Bidness doin' pleasure witchoo," Gerald reached over her head and clapped me on the shoulder hard enough to rattle my scapula. Then he wandered off down the hallway whistling merrily to himself through his tooth gap. The door buzzed open and Charlie and I entered the creepy morgue by ourselves. We could see our own breath. It was cooler in there to keep the stiffs happy. Charlie said, "pssst," at me and when I turned, she pointed out an ornate wedding dress hanging off to the side. Weird. In front of us was a row of three covered bodies with their feet sticking out. We walked down the row checking toe tags. The last one was Jan.

"Oh, Jan," I said sullenly. "I am so, so, so sorry. This was not supposed to happen, this…" I couldn't continue. I started crying again just looking at her there. So still and so dead. Charlie stood off to the side to give me space. "Jan," I sniffed and wiped some tears away. "I've been the coward of the county my whole life. And I know I blew it. Never asked you out. Brodie won, I lost. I get it. But if there was any other way. Anything I could do or say, I would. You know I would."

Charlie tracked movement in the room. Not Jan. One of the other bodies whose toe-tag read 'Henry.' His foot wiggled and stopped. Wiggled again and stopped. Charlie very slowly moved closer to me. "Dan," she whispered. But I ignored her. Too busy laying my heart on the line. Shooting my shot, like the Prophet Eminem advised.

"Jan, what I'm trying to say is that I have loved you from the very first time you pushed me off the monkey bars in recess. You were king of the hill that day and in some strange way," I continued to gush headlong over her, "you kinda became the king of the hill of my heart."

The not-so-dead man with the twitch foot sat up. Charlie tapped my arm feverishly, "Dan!"

"Jan, if I never have the chance to say—stop it, Charlie—if I never have the chance to say this, I want you to hear it now…"

"Dan! Sea Biscuit," Charlie spoke loud and clear pointing behind me.

"Charlie, would you please just let me—" I began to say and then the dead man let out a spine chilling hiss like a bob cat or an angry mermaid. "Jesus Christ," Charlie and I jumped back. "What the hell, Charlie?"

"Sea Biscuit. Don't put a safe word in play if it's not gonna make anything safer, Professor," she said rather annoyed. She put a hand up like she was reading a marquee sign, "Dan Helsing, Monster Hunter, One-Star."

"Don't you dare fake Yelp! review me. That is my bit," I pointed a finger in her face. She slapped it aside.

The large, naked man hissed again violently. Somewhere along the way he'd sprouted some nasty little fangs. Spittle shot across the room.

"Okay, truce," I said to Charlie, "Code Red, Sea Biscuit. What do we do here, talk to me, Goose."

"Well, look at those neck marks. The blackened veins. Old Henry was clearly another one of Victor's fatalities," she explained as we maneuvered the lab tables between us and Henry. He lumbered in our general direction, staring hatefully at us like we were vegans or New Yorkers.

Charlie pulled two stakes from her pants pockets and handed one to me.

"What's this?" I said a little upset, "What am I supposed to do with this pick his teeth? Where's my crossbow? Or the rail gun? I'm a long distance guy. This is way too personal."

"Nope, lesson one, metal and explosives won't work on longtooths. You need to drive this wooden stake through its heart," she modeled the kill stroke with her own stake, "or it will keep coming after you and rip your throat out and kill you."

"Are you serious?" I said excitedly. "That's just a comic book thing."

"No, Dan, it's a real life thing," she said.

"I thought you said it couldn't kill me," I argued.

"I said it couldn't *turn* you. They can kill you very dead, very fast," she warned.

"Well, excuse me, but you are the expert, you do it," I tried handing the stick back but she wouldn't have it.

"Relax, Dan. Focus. This is the best controlled environment for your first hand-to-hand combat lesson. Couldn't ask for a better first kill," she patted my back and then pushed me out toward the creature lumbering our way.

"Could we find him a bathrobe? Or a kimono. I can't kill a naked man," I whined. "I am a math teacher, Charlie. Math."

"Great, here's math," she said, sarcastically, "one stick plus one vampire heart equals you not dying today. Capiche?"

"Oh my god, I liked you better when you didn't talk," I said holding the shaky stick out in front of me.

"Other end, Dan," she explained patiently.

"I know how sticks work. I was thinking about throwing it like a knife. Like Crocodile Dundee," I kept my eyes locked onto the naked stalker closing in on my discomfort zone. He sniffed the air and growled like a chewed up pit bull.

"Do not throw the stick, Dan. This is not a scene in Commando," she ordered.

"Ah ha!" I turned and pointed at her triumphantly, "you do know who Arnold Schwarzenegger is!"

My smug victory was short-lived because, in that instant, Henry the baby vampire hissed loudly and pounced. And even though he was fifteen feet away, he flew across the ground really fast. I barely had time to turn back around and stab blindly in his general direction. Henry ran full force into the tip of my spear. He and I both looked down at the stake that had skewered him like a shish kebab.

"That's the stomach, not the heart," Charlie sounded disappointed. She stepped forward and grabbed the part sticking out of his back like a handle. She spun Henry around. "Use this, to keep him under control." She let go and I seized the wooden shaft. Sure enough he tried to spin around and grab me but couldn't. I held him firmly in place. He flailed his arms and tried to bite backwards like a snapping turtle, but I was able to keep clear.

"Here," Charlie handed me her stake. "For his heart, this time."

I took it from her, still being jostled by Henry who was very squirmy. "How am I supposed to—hold still, Henry," I yelled at the man. I looked over and around and it was just too awkward to strike. I'd have to lunge around to get a good angle on his heart. But then I'd also be a target risk if he was facing me.

"You just gonna dance with him all night?" Charlie asked. I looked over at her and she was seated up on the counter, just chilling out.

"I'm not—quiet! I'm trying to—," I saw my moment of opportunity and jerked Henry's handle to spin him around. Before he could get his bearings, I grabbed the handle from the front to steady him and then drove the second stake down into his heart. Or where I really hoped his heart would be. Henry went silent; shock and realization overcame him. And then he exploded into thousands of tiny dust particles that spewed everywhere and covered me from head to toe.

"Not again!" *Ptui*, I spat and turned crankily back to Charlie. "A little warning would have been nice," I said as I wiped vampire residue from my eyes and face.

"Good job not dying," she patted me on the shoulder, and a cloud of dust went up. "Mostly blind luck, but results are results. Had our fledgling Vampire been even an half-hour older, you'd be dead because why? Because you took your eye off the ball…to gloat."

"But more importantly, you do know who Arnold is," I stuck to the point.

"Everyone knows who Arnold is," she shouted back. "Little Phoebe knows who Arnold is, Sister Marguerite knows who Arnold is, good grief. Get over it."

I opened my mouth about to say the most amazingly clever reply you've probably ever read but then we heard movement behind us. We both turned around and saw Jan's foot twitching.

"Okay, what now," I asked getting nervous all over again.

"This one is gonna be trickier," Charlie said. "We want her alive."

"Obviously," I replied.

"She's not going to be herself, Dan. She may not even recognize you at first. So don't expect some mushy Gilmore Girls reunion."

I gasped. "How dare you besmirch the Gilmore Girls," I scowled at her, but then smiled. "At the same time I am very impressed, Chuckles. That is a first-rate, top shelf reference. Up top." I held up my hand for her to high-five. She ignored it so I high-fived it myself.

She continued despite my theatrics, "Like Henry over there, she's gonna be hangry," she warned. "Very hangry. But I have a theory."

"Oh great, another theory," I said, watching Jan squirm under the sheet.

"Yes, you remember how you're a Helsing and your monster-slaying bloodline goes all the way back to great, great, great grandfather Van Helsing?"

"Yeah," I said. "Uh-duh."

"Okay, good, so then we're agreed," Charlie said, relieved.

"Agreed on what?" I said, genuinely confused.

"Agreed that you should let Jan bite you," she answered.

"What!" I exclaimed.

"And suck your blood," she added.

"What?!" I said louder.

Jan began to sit up. The sheet fell off her face and Charlie and I both took a step back. There was black all around her eyes like a viking warrior or a goth raccoon. When her eyes opened they were very red. Not like bloodshot, like red. Glowing red. Way worse than Henry's. She tilted her head left and then right, loosening up, and then hissed at us. As she moved, the sheet fell off of her more, exposing her bare chest.

"Oh dear," I said. Charlie reached up and covered my eyes and wouldn't let me peek. "Wait, why do you get to look? That is so sexist."

"Keep 'em closed. It's best you don't watch this next part," Charlie said. She watched Jan stand up and take tentative steps our direction.

"The next part," I said with my arms stretched forward trying to feel for my bearings. "What's the next part?" I shook with anticipation, "Don't spoil the surprise, Charlie, but cough once if she's got any tattoos down there. Or like a hello kitty tramp stamp. Mind you, this is for science."

Charlie ignored me. "Your blood will counteract the vampire toxins," she explained. "It's not a cure all, but if she's lucky we won't have to kill her."

"You're not killing her," I corrected her.

"Yeah, probably won't have to," she conceded.

Jan moved up close to me, silently and curiously studying my arms as they waved and flailed around. She watched me standing there, watched Charlie on the other side of me. Smelling me, her hunger instinct got the better of her. My forearm was right next to her mouth. She gently and tenderly grabbed my arm.

"It's working, get ready," Charlie whispered.

"Oh my god," I whispered on the verge of tears, "she does recognize me. Hi, Janeane. Yeah it's me, baby. I am so happy to—"

She bit into my arm. Hard.

"Ahhhhahahahhhhhaaaaaa," I screamed a high pitched shriek as her fangs pierced my muscle and tissue.

Charlie clamped her other hand over my mouth. "Shhhh! Hold still," she warned brusquely, "or she'll rip your arm off."

"Ahhhahaha it hurts," I wailed. "She's draculizing my blood. I don't wanna be a longtooth."

"She can't turn you, dummy," Charlie said. "Now, shush. It's working."

Jan drank until she got a little woozy. Apparently that Van Helsing blood is some top shelf sh*t. Still, I felt like a used Caprisun. Finally, with a last big slurp she released me with her tiny, beautiful bear trap of a mouth and started to fall forward. Charlie swept across and caught Jan. She helped her onto the closest lab table to lay her down.

"See?" Charlie said. "Blood coma. Already your Helsing juices are counteracting the poisons and—"

At that moment, feeling not so great myself, my leg strength disappeared and my knees forgot how to knee and I promptly passed out and collapsed to the floor with a resounding *ka-thud*.

>— >———< — >———< —<

Forty-five minutes and a nice whelp on my forehead later, the three of us were shuffling down the long hallway towards the hospital exit. The only extra clothes we had was the wedding dress so that's what Jan now wore. It seemed like it was tailored for her, it fit perfectly. She leaned between Charlie and I and it was slow going as her bare feet padded along. We heard some whistling and jangling of keys and Gerald strolled around the corner.

"Howdy. Y'all get what you came—HOLY SMOKESHOW!" he saw Jan and Jan saw him right back. The dark around her eyes and forehead had greatly diminished along with the red eyes, but she was still a fright to behold.

She sniffed at him and he backed up.

"She was—she was—she was—" Gerald stammered.

"Dead?" I offered.

"Now she's—now she's—she's—"

"Not dead?" Charlie asked.

Seeing this large, soft target in front of her shaped like a beer keg triggered Jan's hunting instincts again. Her strength began to return and she stood upright as her hunger roused. She wanted to feed again. Like a light switch being turned on, her face and skin changed from what I called the dark mode of the ravenous wolf to an angelic, seductive thirst trap. Whatever vampire pheromones she was giving off was making us all a little tipsy in close proximity.

"You look delicious," she purred to Gerald.

Gerald, for his part, got over his recent dead/un-dead aversion rather miraculously. He turned red around the gills and slowly flapped his arms self-consciously under her piercing gaze. "Shucks, I mean, I been told by Brenna Lou over at the Studio what a snack I am." He smiled, casually, as if he were flirting in a bar.

"Jan wants a snack," Jan said, pulling away towards Gerald. It was all Charlie and I could do to keep her in check. She was very strong.

"No, no, no," I spun her away from him towards the door. "No snacks for Jan. Stop. Gerald, you best walk away now."

Gerald blinked a few times and rubbed his forehead at the strange sensation which had enveloped him. Without Jan's full attention and eye contact the hypnosis wore off quickly, but left a strong residual desire he couldn't shake. "Seriously, brochacho? We're vibin' hard. Finally got us a chubby chaser and you're gonna deny our sexual congress?" He followed us with a hurt, puppy dog expression on that big face of his. "What if she's my soul mate? My lobster?"

"She's not your lobster! She's a frikkin' barracuda. Walk away, Gerald," I warned, again, "she's still very sick."

"Why, sick because she loves me? No, you sumbitch, she's perfect," Gerald sighed, as he walked through the door behind us. Jan turned back and gave him a sly wink that almost melted him into a puddle.

"Stop that," I shook Jan lightly. "Keep it in your pants, white fang. You're like a cat in heat."

Jan hissed at me, disapprovingly, but walked forward under our firm insistence. She turned her full mojo on Charlie next. "Okay, how about a little baby snack then." She licked her lips and sang sensually, "Baby snack, doo doo, doo doo baby snack…"

In a flash, Charlie had a stake up to Jan's neck, "Try it, lady, and you're dust."

"Easy, Charlie. Just take it easy, everyone. We're gonna figure this mess out together," I said, not fully believing it myself. But it sounded nice. The best lies do.

Jan snarled at Charlie and then lightened up, whining like a petulant teen. "Well, y'all are no fun at all. This is *boooooring*. I shoulda stayed dead."

"No, boring would be a welcomed change of pace with you two," I said. *Chirp, chirp.* I unlocked the truck with the remote fob. "It's 4am. This is ridiculous. I'm tired."

"And cranky," Charlie added under her breath.

Jan looked up at the full moon and tossed her head back, "Arrooooooooo," she howled. Way off in the distance a wolf howled back. She smiled, very amused with herself and then climbed in the backseat of the truck and flopped down in a sea of white crinoline.

I grabbed a water from the trunk and twisted off the top. I took a swallow and swished a couple of times and spit out the last of the vampire dust. I was about to climb in the driver's seat when a large crow landed right on the hood. *Ka-thunk.* It spooked me and I squeezed the bottle so hard that water shot up like a geyser and splashed down all over me. I couldn't tell if the bird was laughing or just caw-cawing obnoxiously. Probably both. Up close, the thing was as big as a teenaged ostrich.

"Go! Shoo, bird!" I waved at it, but it just hopped closer to Charlie's side of the vehicle.

"Stop," she snapped her fingers at me and stepped around her open door to get next to the large black bird. "That's Fitz. I've been expecting him." The bird let her get super close and she grabbed a message canister off of its leg and opened it and there was a tiny scroll inside. "I sent a message to the Hunter Union three months ago and this is the first I've heard back from them with any direction whatsoever," Charlie explained as she unfurled it. "About freakin' time."

"A Monster Hunter Union?" This struck me as very funny, "what, is there like a Local 666 Chapter you belong to? The Fang Gang? Do they have medical with that? T-shirts?" I looked to share a laugh with Jan but she was enamored with the bird. Her head was cocked sideways and she whistled for its attention like a puppy dog.

Charlie shushed us both and then read the paper aloud, "Banner Elk Slayer. Stop. Increased monster activity detected in your region. Stop. Caution advised. Stop."

We waited for more, but that was it. That was the whole message. Charlie looked up at me in complete shock. "That's it?" she checked the back of the paper and re-read the front again but to herself this time. "I've waited three months for them to tell me this? Stuff I already know? Where's the rest?" She frisked the raven all over for another note. Under the wings. On the back. She got nothing but a couple of angry pecks on the arm from Fitz who didn't appreciate being manhandled. Or rather orphanhandled. Although, between you and me, I was beginning to think the whole orphan thing was just a cover story with Charlie.

"And you still want to be paid, you lousy sky trash?" she sighed and dug into her pocket and pulled out a tiny gold coin. I'd never seen one like it before. It was smaller than a penny but larger than a watch battery. She held it out in her hand. The bird cawed again, took the prize in its mouth and flapped off into the night sky.

"Stupid bird," I said using my sleeve to buff out a mark on the hood from the crow's landing. "Dude scratched the paint. That is just the *worst.*"

Charlie climbed back inside the truck and slammed the door closed in an angry huff. I got in my side and cranked it up to get the heat circulating.

"Okay, but does this Hunter Union not have cellphones? Are they Amish?" I asked still flabbergasted by the whole concept. Nobody answered me. "They sent a telegraph. By bird."

"Just drive," Charlie pouted with her chin in hand, staring out the window.

"Okay, not til you tell me what's wrong," I said. I waited patiently. Both hands on the wheel. Just being there. Being available. I learned about that on Dr. Phil, once. After a full minute, Charlie hadn't said anything so I reached down about to put the truck in gear. Just then, she finally took the bait and exploded in a fit.

"Ugh! I didn't even wanna be assigned to this dumb little town," she waved her arms dramatically as she vented.

"Amen to that," Jan snorted.

"There's nothing here. No monster hives. No pet cemetery. No hell mouth. Nothing. One baaaaarely active portal. Ohhh, big whoop. And one…" she gestured to me and then stopped herself short.

"Wait, no, go on," I said replacing my hands on the steering wheel. "I can take it." I wasn't sure I could take it, but it was the grown-up thing to say.

She struggled and then blurted it out, "And one spoiled brat, heir to the Helsing empire who knows less about apocalyptic warfare than, than, than the average crow." She pointed to the night sky and then softened a little. "You need a babysitter, not a battle advisor."

A thick and awkward silence fell upon the whole car. I picked at a small leather fleck on the steering wheel. "That is… fair," I admitted when I could. "Good note. Subtle as a swift kick to the nuts. But fair."

Jan leaned forward between the two front seats, very thoughtfully, "Um, is…any one else hungry at all? I feel like I could just suck a moose dry."

"Shut up, Jan," Charlie and I said at the same time.

Jan held her hands up, apologetically, "Sorry, did not mean to interrupt your little man-baby intervention. Please continue. I'm sure somebody's got another big speech all ready to go."

"There's no speeches, Jan," I said testily. "This isn't a TV show. This is real life." I gripped the wheel so tightly my knuckles turned white. "But I will say this…"

"Called it," Jan mumbled to herself.

I faced Charlie and continued, "…maybe you're not the greatest slayer in the Hunter Union. Maybe Jan's not the greatest cop in Atlanta. Maybe I'm not the greatest Van Helsing. But what we are is a pretty damn good team."

The look on their faces said otherwise.

"Brodie died," Charlie frowned at me.

"I died," Jan added.

"And vampires and Hell hounds are running around town killing people," Charlie said. "At Christmas."

"Look, I didn't say we were the best monster hunters this town has ever not seen, but," I raised my finger to drive home the point, "we are… the only monster hunters this town has ever not seen."

"Oh my god," Charlie exhaled.

Jan clapped unenthusiastically, "Great motivational speech, Coach."

"Not a speech," I reminded her. "Look, is Victor out there draculizing someone right now…?"

"That's not a thing," Charlie and Jan both said.

"Yes, he is," I ignored them both. "But, he now knows how very dangerous we are. Jan? Jan's got some fun new vampire super power. And Charlie? Charlie's got two whole boxes of fun new sharp toys to kill things with. And I've got…chills. They're multiplying. And I'm losing control. Cause the power, you're supplying," I poked Charlie in the ribs and wasn't sure if she was gonna laugh or punch me, "It's electrifying." They say you can't judge a book by its cover but Charlie's look to me was a crystal clear invitation for me to go have sexual congress with myself.

Kaboom!

From out of the dark sky a dead body crashed onto the hood of the car. The front tires popped and the airbags exploded in our faces leaving a dust cloud hanging in the air. We all about jumped out of our skin. The windshield spiderwebbed and smoke poured up from the radiator as the engine seized and then died. Based on the damage, that body must have been dropped from fifty stories up. And we didn't have 50-story buildings in Banner Elk. Barely had 10-story buildings. Through the broken, angular window shards I could see the man's face and two gaping holes in his neck. It was Gerald.

Charlie was the first to recover from the surprise attack. She scanned the skyline for movement. "Victor," she seethed.

Jan was livid, too. She growled, "He stole my snack." She punched the door beside her, cracking it.

I didn't care. I stared at my dead college buddy. He wasn't even bleeding because he'd been drained so badly. "This ends tonight," I pounded the steering wheel. "Charlie? How do we end this tonight?"

Jan chimed in, "You can't start a battle royale tonight, silly, you have to direct Mayor Doug's haunted hospital fundraiser. And I am supposed to marry Victor or whatever."

"No," Charlie spun around angrily, "we've got to declare an Entente. It's a legal monster challenge. Three on one. Victor has to honor it. We name the time, the place, the wager. He has to show. And he can't kill again until it's concluded. We set it for sundown tonight and it gives us twelve hours to prepare."

"What would the wager be?" I wondered aloud.

"Yes, the stakes," Charlie thought it over. "He loses, he dies. Portal closes. The end. But if he wins, one or both of us will die and…Jan becomes his vampire bride for the next thousand years," Charlie shrugged. "It'll be something along those lines."

"Rock solid plan, bro," Jan rolled her eyes.

"Why do you sound like me?" I asked Jan.

Charlie waved a hand at her, "Oh yeah, that's the blood thing at work. You two are like a bonded pair now."

"We're, like, totally Vulcan mind-melded," Jan said. "You, me and Victor are a power throuple."

"We're not a power throuple," I scratched anxiously at the two bite marks on my arm. I noticed they were almost fully healed up. "Hey, look at the spot where Jan draculized me."

"Stop using that dumb word," Charlie said. "You've got Helsing blood. I told you, it's different. Healing properties."

"Mind melding properties," Jan looked at me in the mirror and winked.

"So, will my blood cure Jan," I studied her closely. She blew me a kiss.

"Of course not, and if Jan had fed on a normal human first, and then drank your blood she'd be dead. But she wasn't fully, uh, whatever the word is," Charlie said rubbing at her tired eyes.

"Draculized," I said smugly. "The word is draculized."

"It's not," Charlie said. "Anyway so now she has Helsing powers and Vampire powers—like a halfling."

"Wicked," Jan nodded appreciatively. "Plus, I can do this," she touched the tip of her tongue to the tip of her nose. She was the only one impressed. "Couldn't do that before."

Charlie waved her off and continued, "Like I said, only time will tell whether we get to keep her around or if we'll have to dust her."

"Easy there, Stabatha Christy," I jumped in before Jan could react. "That's not—whatever, but Victor wants her badly, right?"

"He wants to breed," Jan said matter-of-factly waggling her eyebrows up and down.

"Jesus, okay," I steepled my fingers against my lips and took a deep breath, "Then I have a really, really bad idea."

They both listened to the whole plan before saying anything. Finally, Charlie leaned back in her seat and closed her eyes and said simply, "we are screwed. Just shoot me now."

"Just ignore Eeyore," I said to Jan, "Can you get your boyfriend down here?"

Jan grinned at me as her forehead and nose bridge began to darken and her eyes glowed red, "he's already on his way."

"Good," I said, but wasn't totally believing it was. I watched Jan in the mirror. She looked deep in thought. "So Jan, aren't you, you know, still sad about Brodie at all?"

"Mm," Jan practically stifled a yawn. "At first, sure, but that was so long ago."

"It was... yesterday," I corrected her.

Charlie read the confusion on my face and leaned in to explain, "vampires process time very differently with their weird metabolism."

"You're weird," Jan mumbled under her breath.

"To us it was yesterday. It's still fresh," Charlie continued. "For her it could seem like six months ago or longer that—"

"Here he is," Jan clapped and pointed towards the cracked windshield, past the dead body on the hood to the street lamp beyond.

I turned around in time to see a shaft of living darkness shoot straight down from the sky and impact the ground. From the billowy black clouds stepped Victor, smooth as hell. "Pssht," I shrugged, "I mean if you're into cool entrances, it was okay."

"Here," Charlie pulled a small vial from her backpack and grabbed my right hand and dumped a clear, shimmering liquid into it. Then she rubbed it all over the front and back until it dried into the skin, totally undetectable.

"Why does the label have a skull and crossbones on it," I snorted, derisively. Charlie didn't laugh. Didn't even blink.

"When you make the deal," she looked me in the eye, intently. "You have to shake his hand. The radium on this hand will rub off and I'll be able to track him."

"You mean I have to touch him?" I smelled my hand and was about to lick my finger when she smacked my forehead.

"Very poisonous!" she warned. "Keep your hands out of your mouth. Don't touch your face. And don't even pick your nose. It's slightly radioactive so we need to wash it off as soon as possible."

"Nucular—?! Charlie, why would you—you don't —oh god, my nose kinda itches now," I rambled with some concern.

"Go," Charlie insisted, "he's waiting."

"Please itch my nose for me," I begged her.

"You've got two hands," she replied. "Figure it out."

"Oh yeah," I used my non-nuclear finger to scratch my nose.

"Dead man walking," Jan said. A concerned look crossed my face as I opened the truck door and climbed out.

"Stop looking so suspicious," Charlie reprimanded me. "Just—"

Oops, too late. I had slammed the door closed. I went to open it with my right hand, thought better of it and then opened the door with my left hand, very proud of myself for remembering.

"Sorry," I said. "You were in the middle of saying?"

"Put your hand down," Charlie said calmly. I didn't realize I'd even had it raised. I lowered it. She added, "Just act natural."

"He can smell your fear," Jan said with a crooked smile and mischievous gleam in her eye.

That definitely didn't help. I closed the door behind me and walked toward Victor. Me, the one least capable of defending myself against this horror of a man.

The two girls just watched from inside the truck as I went to strike our deal with the devil.

"What's the over/under that Victor eats Dan's face off right now," Jan pondered aloud.

"Shut up, Jan," Charlie said through gritted teeth.

That amused Jan even more and she leaned forward, still in full dark mode, to study Charlie closer. "Interesting," she said softly.

"What," Charlie shot back.

"You're worried about him," Jan leaned in closer. "You like him."

Charlie turned around to look her full in her smug face. "No, what's interesting is how much that man loves you, Jan. He would die for you," she said angrily. "And you—you'd sit there and let him. Just like you did with Brodie."

Jan's smile faded and her brow furrowed. She sat back slowly as her dark energy faded and her natural face color returned. Charlie turned forward again and scrunched up her own face, hiding a look of regret and guilt, "Sorry, that was—."

"No," Jan said. "Good note, Chuckles."

Charlie shook it off and checked out the windshield on the vampire peace talks. Victor and I were gone. She was grabbing her knife about to spring from the cabin when the driver door opened and I crawled back inside with them.

"Hoooohhhhoooohoohoho," I made a bunch of strange, anxious sounds and leaned back, trying to mask the abject terror in my eyes. "That dude creeps me out." I shivered and then added, "But... we've got ourselves a deal. And I shook his hand with the radioactive poison. Poison for Kuzco. Kuzco's poison. At precisely 5:19 tonight—sundown—we, uh, we die."

Nobody said anything. I looked over at Charlie who was deep in thought, chewing on her lip. "Do you think we need more people?" I asked her. She didn't respond in any way. "You think we need more people." I sat back considering how we'd even do that. "Yeah, we definitely need more people." Then, I sat forward excitedly, "OMG did we just have an Ocean's 11 moment right there?" I raised my hand to high-five Charlie but she just ignored it so I high-fived myself, again.

"We need Sister Marguerite," Charlie said more to herself than to us and then climbed out of the truck without another word.

I leaned my head out my door, "What do we need with a three hundred year old nun? This isn't a knitting contest."

Charlie went around to Gerald, the human hood ornament, and searched his pockets until she found what she was looking for. She held his car keys up jingling them for us to see. Then she hit the key fob and a Ford Explorer off to our left chirped twice and unlocked. "Who do you think trained me," she said and pulled the stake from her thigh pocket and as easily as if she were spearing a martini olive she skewered Gerald's heart. He vaporized instantly into a thousand dust particles that settled on the front end almost forming a butterfly pattern.

"Hey, that was my friend you just dusted," I yelled from the car. "And what do you mean she trained you?"

She indicated the whole wreckage, "Phone this in to our guy Greg at the B.E.P.D. Tell 'em we hit a moose."

"That 'moose' had a name, you know," I replied testily, "It was Gerald. We smoked our first doobie together in Boy Scouts. It might have actually been potpourri."

"Let's ride," she said tossing me the keys. She was all business again. "There'll be time to have a good cry later. We've got work to do." Charlie headed over to the other vehicle. I just shook my head at her unfeeling, robot brain.

"Dan," Jan grabbed my arm before I could climb out.

"Yeah?" I said, still mind-punching Charlie.

"Thank you for," she searched for the right words, "for un-draculizing me. With your blood." She smiled at me warmly. "That was sweet."

Her tone, her face…it was a pleasant surprise. I thought she might've been teasing, but she was serious. I smiled back at her, "Of course, Jan, yeah, look hey I've got plenty more where that came from, uh, so if you get thirsty just let me know or whatever." I laughed it off nervously.

"Probably not a good idea," she patted my shoulder, thoughtfully, then climbed out of the truck.

"One and done," I agreed hastily. "Know your limits. We're cutting you off, missy."

What the hell was that, I thought to myself as she crossed the alley to the Explorer in that fluffy white wedding dress and bare feet. No, seriously, I'm asking. What was that? Lady longtooths are super hard to get a read on.

CHAPTER 8

The dank, murdery basement of the Sylvanian Home with its otherworldly Hell hound spout was top of my Buzzfeed list of creepiest places in Banner Elk. No question. But before any of us knew about Sister Marguerite's lovely death dungeon, the old abandoned Cannon Hospital on the edge of town was the scariest, most derelict building around. Being a man of science and math and Twizzlers, I never liked to throw around words like "haunted" or "paranormal." But, for almost twenty-five years, the urban legends had been told from vagabonds to meth heads about the inexplicably heinous goings-on inside its hallowed halls. The Tennessee Wraith chasers even did an episode about it on "Ghost Asylum."

The last fifteen elected town councils had been consecutively unable to solve the riddle of the alleged ghost-infested real estate. Now, it was so run down and vandalized it was no longer even up to code. Nobody wanted to buy a $2 million hobo toilet only to have to tear it down and re-develop it all over again. Not even Lees McRae college and they were next door neighbors. Maybe speculators would've been interested if it had been located in Charlotte or the Research Triangle Park, but not here in the shadow of Grandfather mountain. Not in a town with a population of 1472 people. Oh, wait, didn't the Bryants just have a baby girl named Gigi, so that made 1473. Oh, and I forgot, Gerald and Henry were draculized and dusted, so 1471.

At any rate, that's why the latest Council had agreed to the wild GoFundMe idea that I had pitched them. It was a two million dollar campaign. And, if it was unsuccessful, Mayor Doug had made it very clear, the town would collapse into bankruptcy and despair and unpaid marching bands. Yeah, no pressure. Anyway, so far we'd raised $1125. This was a ridiculously unacceptable amount that caused the honorable Mayor Doug to stop by my house unannounced to yell words at me.

"One thousand one hundred and twenty-five dollars," Mayor Doug angrily spat through the four inch gap in my house's front door. "That's ridiculous. And what's with this giant box blocking your front exit. Do I need to call the Fire Marshall, Dan?"

"One crisis at a time, Mayor," I said as calmly as I could. I was using my body to block his view into my living room which was covered in knives and swords and weapons as Charlie and Jan readied our tactical gear for tonight. "Tonight we're adding that live stream Christmas Eve component that's really gonna drive huge social media engagement."

"It had better," he growled at me. And then more to himself, "This has to work."

"It'll work," I promised.

"It had better or I will make your life miserable," he threatened.

"Oh," I said brushing it off, "speaking of miserable, Jan's here you wanna talk to her?"

He looked at me, disgusted, "Jan is *dead*, Daniel," he backed away from the door. "What sort of sick person jokes about such a thing? Too soon. Even for you."

"I'm sorry, I—"

"Goodbye, Helsing," he glared at me and then clomped off the porch back to his fancy Range Rover.

"But…she's literally right here," I said to no-one because he was already out of earshot. I closed the door and turned and Jan was right beside me, glaring daggers at me.

"Not cool, Dan," she scolded.

"But, you're literally right—" she held up a hand to stop me. Then, she walked off, revealing Charlie, right behind her, also glaring daggers.

"Not cool, Dan," Charlie echoed. Then she stomped away, too.

"Well, thank you, creepy Doublemint twins," I yelled, exasperated.

Our haunted hospital's quiet, off-limits property made perfectly good tactical sense for Victor von Lichtenstein to claim as his unofficial headquarters. I didn't need a nuclear handshake and Charlie's fancy gear to figure that out. But she did. Specifically, she tracked them to the basement. It seemed Victor's ghoulish little rat pack was growing, Charlie reported. She'd reconnoitered their whole hostel situation around mid-day while the sun burned hot and the vamps laid low. As you'd expect, she was quite the versatile ninja and brought back pictures and a headcount. She'd even mapped the layout. What a pro.

I wanted to go right over there and dynamite all the fang-bangers while they slept. When I told Charlie, she just looked at me like I was dumber than a soup sandwich. I got that look a lot from her. She explained, once again, the unbreakable rules of Entente that we were operating under and the fact you don't just dynamite vampires like some Bugs Bunny cartoon. Especially not ones that could shape shift into clouds. "You'd have better luck punching a shadow," she explained.

So we'd spent the last twelve hours prepping an elaborate plan that didn't involve TNT. It was grueling. And we still weren't fully ready, but time was up and 5:19pm—aka sundown—loomed. With most adventure shows like the *A-Team*, *MacGyver* and *Glow* you'd get all of these training and strategy sessions compressed into a nice 30-second montage with some rockin' music and a high-five freeze frame at the end if you were lucky. We were not so lucky. We had not slept in about thirty-six hours, and bordered on delirium. We'd pored through old books, we'd prepped our weapons cache, and we called in a boatload of town favors because we needed all hands on deck if this was gonna work. And I mean all hands on deck.

If the plan worked according to, um, plan then we'd get rid of Victor and the portal, and get our Go-FundMe numbers up for the haunted hospital and save the town and the world and Mayor Doug Douchebag would finally get off my ass. If the plans didn't work out? Well, we'd all be dead anyway so who cared about that?

"T-minus thirty minutes to sundown," I advised into a small Hello Kitty walkie-talkie from my position in the haunted hospital's main lobby. "All units check in." From stations all over the building, everyone reported back.

"All quiet in the hive," Charlie whispered from a hiding spot deep in the basement.

"Super exciting in the ball room," Jan yawned from the large, roofless auditorium, where it was anything but.

"Shishter Marguerite shays boiler room, shtanding by," said Liam. He and Sister Marguerite had snuck into the pump room at the far end of the basement. Glowsticks everywhere cast weird shadows about the whole room.

"Camera Drone and video stream are live," said Obi Juan tucked safely in the cab of the Explorer with his VR headset on. Jada sat beside him with her laptop tracking the stream. They'd turned that whole SUV into a mobile command unit and broadcasting control room. Jada gave a thumbs up to Obi Juan. "Web stream is stable," she confirmed.

Behind me a small video drone buzzed into the air and hung there staring down at me.

"Copy that," I nodded. I took another deep breath, faced the drone-cam and then spoke into the walkie with what some would later describe as the inspiring austerity of a President Whitmore in Independence Day or the Braveheart dude.

"Welcome to what's left of the Charles A. Cannon, Jr. Memorial Hospital," I began. "Some of you have never seen a GoFundMe live stream this elaborate before. Maybe we get funded maybe we don't. That's tomorrow's problem. Today, I promise you this: there will be a lot of action, a lot of noise, a lot of smoke, a lot of scary visual FX. But, it's all part of the greatest Christmas extravaganza this town has ever seen. There will be no second takes. No do overs. No mulligans. Now, it's 25 minutes until sundown and ladies…gentlemen… it's time to bring the thunder."

"Shorry, come again," Liam said over the mic.

"Yeah," Charlie added, "bad reception. Short bursts only."

"What was the part after 'Welcome'?" Obi Juan chimed in.

"Ugh," I pinched the top of my nose, incensed that my glorious moment of inspo was DOA. "Okay, whatever, stand by for the thunder," I whisper-growled into Hello Kitty's face. "Initiate phase one: shock and awe."

I turned around and raised my arms. Behind me in the lobby was an audience. Leading all the way down the front hall of the hospital and out into the driveway was the Appalachian State Marching Band. All 285 members. In their spotless black and gold and white uniforms. The Marching Mountaineers all raised their instruments to ready position.

I pointed at Deion, the drum major, who whistled three short bursts and then the whole unit begin playing the loudest, zippiest Christmas Carol medley you've ever heard. As they did, they march-march-marched through the lobby in a double-file line and on past me into the hospital corridors. The acoustics in there were incredible. It was like a Post Malone concert—if, you know, Post Malone had a ska band and less fog machines and rhythm.

Downstairs, located just outside the hive HQ, Charlie peeked in through the broken glass windows. The music was loud down here, she could only imagine what it was like at the source. The ceiling reverberated with each percussive marching step causing more and more dust to fall. In the middle of the hive was a pile of mattresses and blankets that formed a nest. It practically floated like an island in a sea of creepy white vapors that clung to the floor like an oyster stew. On top of mattress mountain were the bodies of eight or ten vampires. It was hard to tell with all of the intertwined arms and legs as they slept. Victor sat up in the middle of all of them, throwing a leg off of his shoulder.

"What the devil is that noise," he bellowed. The others roused feverishly as well. From the hall, Charlie noted all the wine and liquor bottles laying atop every surface. They were all totally hungover. That would help. The fang-bangers grabbed for clothes and shoes and scrambled around in panicked disarray. More shocked than awed.

Then the floor mists parted. The hairs on the back of Charlie's neck stood up as a dozen level-2 Hell hounds stood to their feet growling and snapping at each other like pit bulls. They began moving toward the door before they were halted by Victor.

"Wait!" he called in a booming voice that froze them all where they stood. "Nobody attacks until sundown or they answer to me. You will remain out of sight until my signal. And *then* you will unleash hell."

Victor buttoned a fancy puffy sleeve shirt and burst through the hive doors slamming them aside. More glass broke from the frames, spilling down and dashing to pieces upon the hard tile floors. Charlie ducked out of sight as he whisked past and disappeared up the stairwell.

In the pump room, Liam and Sister Marguerite had sprung into action as well. They stood on a metal walkway beside a huge, industrial vat. They had a long, sturdy pipe wedged into the latch wheel at the top. In coordinated time with the marching band's rhythm, the nun whacked the pipe with a sledge hammer, attempting to loosen it. Liam stood on top spraying some WD-40 onto the rusty, old turn wheel. Thanks to the band's noise flooding the halls, they'd be able to work in there without detection.

Finally the latch wheel moved. An inch, at first, and then further and soon they were able to remove their leverage pipe and turn it together. Once the seal was broken, Liam jumped down to the catwalk and with a mighty heave they pushed the top door open. *Clang*. Underneath it was a huge cistern filled with decades-old water.

"Disgusting," Liam made a sour face. Sister Marguerite had come prepared. From their backpack, she handed him a clothes pin and she took one as well. They pinched their nostrils closed with them so the work could continue, even if their speech sounded like cartoon chipmunks now.

"Much better," Sister Marguerite said. She pulled out a book called *The Roman Ritual* and opened to a specifically bookmarked tab. "Step one, grab the salt and pour it into the mixing bowl."

"Roger, roger," Liam enthusiastically grabbed a large bag of kosher salt from their supplies and poured it into the bowl. Then, he picked up the container and held it steadily in front of her. Marguerite read aloud from her sacred text as he did so. She had to speak loudly so her prayer could be heard over the marching band's flamboyant, "Joy to the World."

"O salt, creature of God, I exorcise you by the living God, by the true God, by the holy God, by the God who ordered you to be poured into the water by Eliseo the Prophet so that its life-giving powers might be restored." She hovered one hand over the salt as she read from the text in her other hand. "I exorcise you so that you put to flight and drive away from the places where you are sprinkled every apparition, villainy, and turn of devilish deceit, and every unclean spirit, adjured by Him who will come to judge the living and the dead and the world by fire. Amen."

"Amen," Liam nodded. "Whatsh next?"

I was having the time of my life. The Christmas music, the marching band's youthful exuberance, the drone zipping up and down the parade lines, the threat of a painful, agonizing death in twenty-two minutes. It was all so invigorating. Not just for me, I watched the GoFundMe numbers on my iPhone steadily climbing. We were up to $9700 now. A long way to go, of course, but word was slowly getting out about the crazy Christmas fundraiser at the haunted hospital. We had just registered 100 viewers and climbing.

I excitedly waved my arms in time with the trombone section passing by me now. I hoped nobody was contacting me on the radio because I would not have heard it. I trusted, though, that the plan was unfolding without a hitch. How could it not? I was so wrapped up in the music that I didn't even notice Victor materialize out of thin air behind me.

I jumped when he spoke into my ear, "What is going on, Helsing?!"

I stepped away but not too far. Otherwise we couldn't have heard each other. "Mood music," I shouted back at him. I hoped I was smiling cool like Han Solo and that I did not look like I was about to sh*t my pants. Which I was. "Smile for the camera," I pointed up at the drone, knowing full well—and this is according to Charlie—that none of the fang-bangers would show up on camera. Victor ignored the pesky machine.

"You would send these fools to their deaths in," he checked an ornate pocket watch, "twenty-one minutes?"

"They're just—," I paused to let some particularly obnoxious tubists play through, "they're just civilians passing through."

Clarinets and piccolos marched by next. Victor's eyes narrowed at me, "These percussions and these winds won't save you, Helsing."

"No, I don't need a lot of wins," I shouted back, mishearing. "Just need one big win." I held up my fingers in a "W."

"What?" Victor said, confused.

"What?" I said, confused by his confusion. And then my phone vibrated. I held up a finger pausing Victor just as he was about to speak again. "Oh my god," I shouted when I saw the Caller-ID. "This is Blue Cross Blue Shield." I immediately got on the walkie talkie yelling "Cut! Cut! Cut the music!" And then I waved and yelled to all of the band members, "Cut! Cut the music!

Hold on!" And little by little they all stopped playing as word rocketed up and down the line. "I've gotta take this call, quiet please! Shush! Everyone please, this is the big one. Job interview. Blue Cross Blue Shield. SHHHHH! Everybody, shhhhhhh!"

Hundreds of very confused Mountaineers froze in place to help me out. Victor, too, watched the whole thing unfolding with great curiosity. This little chess match kept getting more and more interesting. And less and less threatening.

"Hello? Hello, can you hear me?" I said into my phone, plugging my other ear. I even handed off the Hello Kitty radio to Victor. He looked at it dumbstruck. "Yes, Glenda, this is a great time to talk. Oh, so sorry, Linda," I held up a 'just-a-minute' finger to the whole marching band, eagerly watching me.

On the radio, Charlie called through, "What's going on, why has the music stopped?"

I waved "quiet" to Victor and walked a few more feet away. He lifted the Hello Kitty walkie and depressed the talk button. "Please stand by, Banner Elk slayer, we are in the middle of a job interview."

Radio silence.

"Oh, I love teaching and kids are great I will miss that part of the job," I said, lying as smiley and casually as I could with a wink to the drone cam hovering nearby. "Now I understand there may be some training components in this new job that I'm really suited for but, to your question, the thing I want most from an actuary position is, for one, the growth potential of working with a competitive national company like Blue Cross Blue

Shield. That really floats my dinghy. And the chance to use my love for math and statistics in a more comprehensive way to help you and your department achieve your quarterly goals. " I gave a thumbs up to Victor and the band. Victor shrugged and held his hand out wobbling it back and forth like my answer had been "so-so."

Charlie had moved out from her hiding position and was now at the base of the stairwell trying to see or hear anything from above. She was getting more and more frustrated by the second. She was about to hop back on the radio but when she turned around a Hell hound was standing right there, head-to-head, eye-to-eye. She moved right, it moved right. She moved left, it moved left. And then another one poked its head through the hallway door. They weren't snarling, they weren't doing anything but watching her very intently with those piercing, yellow eyes.

Very slowly so as not to disturb or provoke, she checked her watch and it read, "5:08pm." Eleven minutes until sundown when the Entente ended and the battle began. She then backed towards the stairs and started walking up a flight. Ever so slowly. They seemed to be firmly on Victor's leash but she didn't want to test how far that would go. At the landing, she turned and saw they had paced her a good ten steps back. And there were four of them now. She continued on, leading this incredibly low-speed chase.

>— >——< — >——< —<

In the boiler room, Sister Marguerite and Liam huddled around the silent walkie. "I suppose we should probably continue with our maneuvers," she said.

"Let'sh do it," Liam nodded his agreement.

"Okay, Young Liam, set the basin on the ground," the nun instructed. "And place your hands upon the tankard like so." She laid her own hand upon the water tank and Liam did the same, but both hands further around to the side. Then she read from the ancient texts.

"O water, creature of God, I exorcise you in the name of God the Father almighty, and in the name of Jesus Christ His Son, our Lord, and in the power of the Holy Spirit. I exorcise you so that you may put to flight all the power of the enemy, and be able to root out and supplant that enemy with his apostate angels: through the power of our Lord Jesus Christ, who will come to judge the living and the dead and the world by fire. Amen."

"Amen," Liam echoed. They smiled at each other, but then something in the shadows caught Sister Marguerite's eye. "What'sh wrong," Liam lisped, a little worried.

"Oh, nothing," the old nun said calmly, "we've just received a curious visitor. No sudden movements, now."

Liam turned around and gasped when he saw a Hell hound standing down below them at the base of the catwalk; between them and the exit door. Not hissing, just watching. Very intently.

"What do we do, what do we do," Liam quietly panicked.

"They are under contractual restraint for another ten minutes," she said soothingly. "So we'd best continue our job. It'll be okay. We're fine," then she clarified more ominously, "for the moment."

Liam watched the gruesome Hell hound staring at them both. He wasn't as convinced as the nun that it was not gonna eat their faces right now.

Jan had found an old office chair. One of the fancier ones by Herman Miller. She was sprawled back into it resting, just enjoying the setting sun's color palette in the clouds above her through the collapsed roof. She hummed to herself and swayed back and forth gently, her wedding dress tooling rustled with each movement.

"I know you're there," she finally spoke, without looking over. A Hell hound lingering in the big double doorway stepped into the room, its long nails clickety clacking atop the tile. "That's far enough," she raised a hand and it stopped. "Good boy," she said. "Now sit." The thing just stared at her, defiantly. She suddenly sat up, her face contorting into full dark mode, eyes glowing red and she yelled, "SIT!" And the beast complied. "Relax," she said laying back into her chair. "We're off the clock."

The marching band was getting antsy; their instruments were heavy and their patience wearing thin. Victor stood over by one of the windows. A ray of light painted an orange streak on the wall and as the sun set, that streak was growing smaller and smaller and smaller. He had stepped into the waning sunbeam and his skin smoked and sizzled where the sun line touched. The band was a little horrified but Victor calmly opened up his watch and brought it over to show me the time. 5:12pm. I was more distracted by the half of his face still smoking as it self-repaired.

"Oh, I do, actually, Linda," I turned from him as I paced back and forth. "I guess my question for you is are there any, like, sports teams or clubs that employees can join if we're feeling, you know, extra competitive; like say if it's been a stressful day you know how you just wanna punch someone in the face sometimes?"

Victor and the marching band looked at each other slightly horrified at the oddball question. "What are you doing?" Victor whispered. "Stay the course. The job is practically yours, Helsing."

I tried to listen to him. I really did, but it was still bothering me. "Sorry, not punch someone, that's a poor choice of words, but don't you ever wonder about applied mathematics? Like, say, the geometry of shooting a crossbow into a moving target?"

Now the whole marching band was giving me hand signals to cut the call.

"Hang up," Victor mouthed to me. "Thank her and hang up."

"You know what, Linda, I withdraw the question. Thank you so much for your time and I look forward to hearing your decision soon," I nodded and "mm-hm'd" a couple more times and then finally hung up. Everyone was shaking their head disappointed with me.

Victor handed the walkie back to me. "Do you have this Romanian expression? 'He really threw his boogers in the beans'?"

"Ew. No, Victor," I grimaced at the thought.

He walked over to one of the marching band members and noted the garlic clove around her neck. "How about, 'he's really gone on a raft and diddled the goat this time'?"

"I get it, I get it, not my best work ever," I said as Victor rolled the garlic around his fingers.

"Is this for me?" Victor asked, amused.

"I mean, it's supposed to, you know, ward you off or—I dunno," I trailed off weakly.

"Well," he said, encouragingly, "Please continue whatever this is while I go have a moment with my bride-to-be."

Before I could object, he clouded up and wended his way out of the room and up the hall. Some band members gasped. "Visual FX," I reminded them. "Ha, ha! Smoke and mirrors and part of the, you know, the thing." I pointed at the drone hovering nearby and then raised the walkie and called out loudly, "Marching band needs to double time it out of here, Deion, get this funky train moving."

We heard his distant whistle tweet three times and then the Christmas medley started up again twice as fast as before. The two lines marched forward and the last of the drum line rattled through. I could see through the lobby window the very front of the marching band line emerging from the far end of the hospital in formation up the driveway and away. At least some of them would be safely out of range by sundown.

"Jan," I said into walkie now that I could almost hear again, "Victor's on his way up."

"You're as helpful as Charlie's message bird," she called back. "Because he's here."

"Okay, initiate phase two," I commanded into walkie as I ducked into the stairwell. The drone followed. I skipped two stairs at a time and was halfway down the flight when I froze. Charlie was slowly walking up the other way with four Hell hounds climbing up behind her. She stopped and they stopped.

"Um, Charlie?" I whispered. "I don't mean to be—"

"I see them," she said. "It's fine. We've got another four minutes."

"They're not exactly wearing watches," I eyed them warily. "Okay, I'm gonna check on the boiler room," I told her. "They should be wrapping up down there."

"Copy," she said, now on the same stair flight as me. "Jan and I will hold Victor as long as we can."

She handed me the smaller of her two duffel bags, in passing. I slung it over my shoulder and then pressed up as far as I could against the handrail and wall. Charlie continued on up the stairs. The Hell hounds saw me but stayed with her. They all pushed past me on their way up. Except one. One remained on the landing below. Watching me.

"Here kitty kitty kitty pspspspsps," I said. It stood there like a statue. Unblinking yellow eyes

"Dan!" Charlie whispered.

"It was worth a shot," I snapped back at her. I raised my walkie-talkie to my mouth. "Obi Juan is the camera picking this up at all?"

The radio crackled, "All we see is a dark, creepy shadow in front of you. Three dark shadows behind Charlie," Obi Juan said.

"Okay, stay with Charlie for now," I ordered. Then, I choked down my fears, put one foot in front of the other and slipped… ever… so… carefully… past… the beast. It's hot breath singed my arm hairs. This thing was like a living furnace. Up close I could hear its skin sizzling. I continued past the fire moose and on down the stairs. I moved quicker than Charlie. I had to. Time was running short until the murder moratorium was up.

"Draga mea," Victor said warmly, with a hand to his heart, as he materialized across the ballroom from Jan.

"My darling," she purred back at him, now standing there expectantly. Both of them had shifted into their radiant light mode. Full seduction. As if they were glowing. Victor scowled over at the seated Hell hound and it quickly jumped back up to attention. He returned his loving gaze to Jan as he closed the distance.

"My heavens, I knew you'd look ravishing in that exquisite ensemble," he admired her up and down.

"Don't throw vapors at me, dark lord," she said with a raised eyebrow and flirty side-eye. Finally, they stood face to face. The clenched bosom of Jan's dress raised and lowered with each of her nervous breaths. She leaned in closer, "I know why you're here."

He ventured an innocent guess, "Love?"

"Power," she corrected.

"Same thing," he flashed a charming smile. No fangs, obviously. They were retracted like a cat's paw, until needed. He held up her hand and kissed the back of it softly. "Have you decided whether or not to let me love you for the next thousand years?"

"Listen, Twilight," she pulled her hand gently from his and considered the very spot he had just kissed. Then she back-handed him across the face with it. He absorbed the blow in good temper, although a trickle of blood ran down from his lip. They stood staring into each others' eyes as before, an animal hunger rising. "I have," she admitted. "But, you stole something from me."

"Yes, I did steal something from you," Victor agreed. Then he backhanded *her* across the face. As she straightened up some blood ran from her nose, but she was still smiling. "Weakness." He moved even closer to her. Inches from her face. Lips close. Very breathy. "Though the Helsing stench is within you. Come my darling, let us purge your bloodline once more. Then you can be free from grief. Free from the torture and the pain of mortality's insipid tedium. You can be pure."

"Oh, Victor, that freedom is not yours to give and it's not mine to have," she withdrew a smaller slingshot gun from the folds of her dress and pushed the end against his temple. He was not expecting this and opened his mouth to speak and she pulled the trigger. A tiny marble sized blue orbital hit him point blank and exploded.

Victor's head disintegrated into a thousand, dark cloud particles as his body stumbled two steps back. Then the clouds pulled back together and his head re-materialized, only he was now quite irate. "That bloody hurt," he scowled at her, ramping into dark battle mode. "So pointless."

"Not pointless," Jan, too, morphed into dark mode. "I enjoyed it very much," she sneered back at him. "Now, Charlie!"

Charlie threw an axe directly at Victor's back. He dissipated into cloud form again and the axe flew end over end through it, harmlessly. Anticipating this, Jan caught it by the handle and held it up at the ready, watching his dark fog swirl and dance over to the far side of the room like an angry swarm of gnats. He reappeared an equidistance from both of them now.

"You still have two minutes before sundown," he bellowed, running his hand through his disheveled hair. "Is this the whole of your strategy then? Marching bands and cheap tricks?"

"Do you mind, darling?" Jan teased, pushing out her bottom lip. "We're new to war and vastly inexperienced." She batted her eyelashes at him.

"That much is abundantly clear," Victor growled. "But one way or another, we leave here tonight with a wedding."

Charlie suddenly perked up with an idea of her own. "A wedding," she said to herself. "I am such an idiot. That's it." She took one of Dan's small books from her pouch and eagerly flipped through it. Victor and Jan faced off like two high noon gunslingers waiting for the clock tower to chime.

CHAPTER 9

I ran towards the boiler room but stopped short when I saw another Hell hound lurking just inside the entrance. I called past it with a calm, soothing voice, so as not to rile the beast, "How we coming, guys?" I sing-songed. "Got about sixty seconds until things get messy."

"Almost there," Sister Marguerite called back to me.

"Hi, Mr. Dan," Liam said, happy to see me. "We cast a spell on the salt and water. Now we just have to mix it all up."

"It's a prayer, not a magic spell," the nun admonished, "Focus over here. Watch your work."

Liam slowly poured out the salt from the mixing bowl into the vat of water below him as Sister Marguerite read the final prayer from her book. "May this salt and water be mixed together; in the name of the Father, and of the Son, and of the Holy Spirit. Amen."

"Amen," Liam and I said at the same time.

While I watched the last of the consecration ritual, I zipped my duffel open and pulled the crossbow out. With practiced ease, I snapped the two outriggers into place and inserted a magazine of seven short arrows and cocked it back into place with a sharp *ka-clack*.

Locked and loaded.

"All set?" Sister Marguerite asked over her shoulder at me. "Where's the closest fire alarm station, again?"

"Next floor up, right next to the hive," I looked back uneasily at the beast that had followed me all the way down here. Then, off the one guarding the boiler room, I asked, "Are you sure you two will be able to manage here?"

"You just worry about your portion of the battle, we'll take care of ours," she said confidently. Who was this lady? She pulled on some black leather gloves like she was freakin' Chili Palmer. Then, from their gear bag, she handed a small Roman Centurion-style sword to Liam.

"Cooooooool," he said, drawing the blade from the scabbard. *Shhhhhlikt.*

"Steady on," she cautioned him. Next, she lifted out a metal ring the size of a door knocker. It was attached to a ten foot chain and had a viciously hooked knife-spike at the other end. She coiled the chain into a loop. "This is not our first rodeo," the nun smiled at me, reassuringly; her dainty, British accent made it sound like roh-DAY-oh.

"Yeah," I shook my head respectfully, "that's what Charlie said. I just didn't want to—"

I stopped short at the spine tingling chorus of shofar war horns that blasted throughout the entire building. If you didn't know, Vampires can be so extra. I didn't even have to check my watch. It was 5:19pm.

"Sundown," I announced, raising the tip of my crossbow defensively into place. The once passive Hell hounds now shook their rankles, growling and hissing and slowly encircled me.

"Hey!" *Ting, ting, ting.* Sister Marguerite walked down the metal stairs tapping the flat of her blade loudly against the railing. It worked and the second Hell hound peeled off panther-like in her direction. I turned my full attention to the fire moose behind me.

My walkie crackled. "Come in, Dan, this is Charlie, over," she said, excitedly. He could hear some battle commotion on her end of the radio, too.

I kept the crossbow aimed true on my hideous stalker and with my other hand, triggered the mic. "Not really a good time, Chuckles. Kinda busy."

"You've got to marry Jan. Right now. That will nullify Victor's covenant and release the ring power. Do you copy? Over." Charlie said.

I wasn't sure that I had copied that correctly. "You want me and Jan to get hitched? Right now?" I repeated. "I mean, does Jan even want to—"

"Right now," she repeated. "Over!"

Rawr, the Hell hound swiped at me with its claws or talons or whatever devilish spikes it had on its ugly toes. It caught my shin as I jumped back just out of range again. "Ow," I said checking my ripped pants leg.

"Sister Marguerite, can you perform a wedding," Charlie crackled, again, over the radio.

The nun crouched low encircling her own beast and told Liam, "Tell her I can only perform Catholic weddings. Dan, are you willing to convert?"

"It's asking a lot, sister," I yelled back at her. "You can't un-dunk a Baptist."

"Charlie, Shishter shays she can only do Catholic-sh. Sho, negatory on that wedding sheremony," Liam spoke into his handset.

"Fine," Charlie replied, annoyed. "Gimme a minute to get ordained online. Then we do the wedding."

"Again, now?!" I vented aloud. "This is—."

The Hell hound leapt at me, high attack this time, and as Charlie and I had practiced, I rolled down to a knee, falling to the right where I had a clean shot to its ribcage and fired. *Ka-thunk.* It yelped in pain. I landed two more before I pierced the heart and it burst into a splash of neon.

"How we doin', sister?" I turned to check on Marguerite right as she slung the knife at the beast's head clipping the side of its cheek as it slipped aside. Neon blood splashed the floor. And then she jerked the chain and the knife snapped back again, whistling as she twirled it in a large arcing motion. "Okay, then," I said. "Ninja grambo bringing the heat."

"Go," she said, winding up for her next strike. "We've got this."

"Yesh," Liam added with a flourish. "As the Supreme Commander of Catan I will—"

"Not now, Liam. Just remember the pointy end goes in the bad guys," I said.

"You never let me finish my shpeech," he whined.

"Monologues are for cartoon villains," I explained. "Or Russell Crowe."

Just then the Hell hound pounced at Liam, landing halfway up the metal stairs; Liam backed against the wall screaming a high pitched scream. Whether it was an intentional thrust or an accidental flail, he managed a half-decent parry and knicked its front paw. Sister Marguerite took the diversion opportunity to attack the beast in the haunches with her knife. More blood splattered. It dropped back to the floor and spun back around towards her, now limping.

"Good luck," I ran from the room pulling up the walkie and said, "Jada, how's our live stream?"

"Interesting," Jada reported back. "Streamers loved Charlie and Jan fighting the shadow ghost. Lots of comments on the wedding dress. HairyBoi98 and Erect-Dictator are arguing in the comments whether it's real or staged. Anyway, we're over $160,000 now. Over ten thousand viewers."

"Wild," I said, a little surprised. "Obi-Juan, how's our marching band?"

"Headed there now with the drone cam," Obi-Juan replied back over the comms. "It's gonna be tight."

Obi-Juan was right, the tail section of the marching band was about a hundred yards away from the house and getting closer towards the safety of their Greyhound busses. As magic hour receded and the sky darkened, Obi-Juan's drone flew high overhead watching them egress. Launching through a broken hospital window, three Hell hounds locked onto the marching band like cheetahs running down a herd of springboks.

"We got two, no, three shadow bogies coming in hot," Obi-Juan's voice squeaked with excitement.

"Phase three," I yelled into the walkie, gasping as I ran, "Let's kick the tires and light the choirs."

Hidden within the shadows of the tree line, thirty six members of the Holy Cross Vocal Choir appeared in their red robes and white sashes. Friends of Sister Marguerite and freelancers for the Hunter's Union, they were clumped in groups of three spread out in an arc of 250 yards across. Each trio had one of Dan's ornate, fire stone staffs and they lit the wick on top, lighting up the whole area. There was a good twenty yards between torches. The firelight glinted off of a special gemstone at the base of each flame. But this did not deter the Hell hounds. If anything, their bloodlust propelled them faster.

The marching band finished their last song with a flourish and that was the cue for the choir who began a stirring a cappella rendition of "The Hallelujah Chorus." The choir advanced toward the haunted hospital as the drum line finally cleared past. They high-fived each other as they passed to the inside.

The Hell hounds raced forward. The grotesque beasts weren't slowing or stopping. The marching band —civilians that they were—couldn't actually see their demonic pursuers but could feel the evil presence drawing close. The hairs on the back of their necks and arms began to raise. They began to break ranks and move towards the busses, but the Holy Cross choir held its ceremonial fire line. Meanwhile, drooling with eager anticipation, the front two Hell hounds leapt powerfully at the last straggling drummer who tripped and fell to the ground. But as the Hell hounds passed through the fire line barrier, the gemstones activated a protective shield barrier and the beasts disintegrated from head to toe in fiery splash of embers, spraying all over the drum line, harmlessly. The last Hell hound skidded to a halt and began to back away, confused. Angry.

"It worked!" Obi Juan shouted into comms. "The fire stones worked!"

"Hallelujah. Hallelujah," the choir continued to sing.

The whole marching band cheered at the cool fireworks display, never knowing how close they came to actual death and dismemberment. The stragglers happily climbed onto the last bus, celebrating with their friends. Meanwhile, the singer's fire line curled around the ends until they had created a large protective perimeter around the remaining Hell hound. It hissed and growled and backed away from the multiple fires and the singing.

I rounded a corner and stopped so quickly my shoes squeaked. This was not the way I had come downstairs. It was one of those proverbial shortcuts that ends up never being a shortcut. Up the hallway on the right was the hive. But none of the longtooths were in their den. Of course not. No, all nine of them were scattered about the hallway in front of me like drones awaiting a kill order.

Fortunately, on the wall to my right was the fire alarm switch. And lining the ceiling every fifteen feet were the water spigots. And standing directly beneath those nozzles were nine clueless fang-bangers. I smiled and mumbled to myself, "Like shooting vampire fish in a barrel."

"Okay, finished the online sign-up," Charlie returned over radio. "You're up, Dan."

"That was extremely fast and, also, ready Phase 4," I said moving my hand to the red and white lever. "Skyfall."

Charlie began the ceremony, speaking so fast she sounded like an auctioneer. "Do you Dan Helsing take Jan Switcher to be your lawfully wedded wife—?"

"I do? Is this the part I say I do?" I paused to clarify.

"Let me finish," Charlie snarled. "To have and to hold, in sickness and in health, in good times and not so good times, for richer or poorer…"

I took the moment to enfold the lever in my fingertips and, with a deep breath and the flourish of a magician enacting his big trick, I ripped the emergency handle down and the whole empty shell fell off the wall and crashed to the ground. A single washer bounced loudly and rolled away into the stairwell, pinging each and every stair.

"…keeping yourself unto her for as long as you both shall live?" Charlie clicked off the radio and waited.

"Sh*t, I'm dead," I said kneeling down to inspect the useless box. "I mean, I do," I fumbled into the walkie. "I do! Over," I looked up and now I had the vampires' full attention. They were making their way towards me, hissing and baring their fangs. I stood back up and I could see down the hallway another emergency box. From my belt I grabbed a grenade looking device, pulled the pin and tossed it down the hall, skipping atop the tile and coming to a rest between them. It emitted a smoke that the Vampires could care less about, but then a garlic odor that they did care about. In fact, it pissed them off and I suddenly went from an annoying bystander to a person of interest.   I looked closer as they approached and recognized the sourpuss in the lead that was still dressed as Santa. "Holberman?" I asked. It *was* him. I couldn't tell if he recognized me or not since they all had the same expression on their faces like they had just been invited to a Hootie concert.

They couldn't do the cloud vapor thing like Victor since they were essentially baby vampires, emotionally speaking, but they could use advanced speeds to run by really fast and punch or slash at me with their claws and then move out of range before I could block or retaliate. They took turns coming at me from every direction. I took out two short spears and just started swinging them tornado style and ran right into the middle of them. They were hardly taking any damage, but I was getting absolutely wrecked. It was like fighting a wood chipper.

>— >——< — >——< —<

Jan and Victor battled feverishly against each other but with Victor's ghost mode or whatever he called it, she could land no hits with her axe. And she had no target for her orbital pistol. But, Victor could swoop in, spiral around her, taunting her and then slash at her with his own wicked nails. She was fast, but he was still quicker.

Charlie had assembled her double-bladed staff and wheeled it around herself with one hand to keep the nipping, snarling Hell hound from sinking its teeth into her flesh. With the other hand she continued reading the ceremony from her iPhone.

"Do you Jan Switcher take Dan Helsing to be your lawfully wedded husband? To have and to hold, in sickness and in health, in good times and not so good times, for richer or poorer, keeping yourself unto him for as long as you both shall live?"

"If I have to. Augh," Jan yelled swiping mightily at the nebulous form before her and again finding no purchase with her blade. "I do."

"Great, okay, Jan, repeat after me," Charlie instructed. "Dan, I give you the Piscatory Warrior ring as a symbol of my love with the pledge: to love you today, tomorrow, always, and forever."

"Yeah okay," Jan poked and jabbed into the air with her axe. Charlie held the radio out toward her. "Dan, I give you the piscatory ring, uh, what else?"

"As a symbol of my love with the pledge," Charlie chimed in.

"As a symbol of my love with this pledge to you," Jan waited for another prompt.

"To love you today, tomorrow, always and forever," Charlie read from memory.

"To love you today, tomorrow, always and for a thousand years," she emphasized the last part shouting it directly into the swirly black cloud. The cloud retreated back to a distant corner of the room and then materialized into Victor's human form.

He scowled disappointedly at her, "A thousand years? Really? That was so very hurtful, my love."

"Not as hurtful as this," she aimed the slingshot gun over his head and shot three orbs at the janky ceiling above him. It exploded to pieces as sections fell to the floor. And then the weight of all that debris collapsed that floor section down to the next level below. "Keep going, Charlie. I'll check this out," Jan jumped down through the hole to follow. It was darker under the ballroom, where she landed in a very controlled crouch.

"Dan," Charlie said over radio, "have you got a ring for Jan?"

"A ring?" I gasped for breath under the barrage of fists and claws. I'd sustained lacerations all over my face and arms. Fortunately, these narcissistic vamps were just toying with me. They weren't going for the kill shot, but rather the mere torture of it all. Death by a thousand cuts. Fun. I had worked my way down the hallway and now stood with my back to the wall. Trapped, to their dumb, red eyes. They paused their assault and stood before me like some meth'd out glee club.

"Yeah," I said with a smile playing at my lips. "I've got a ring."

"Okay, repeat after me," Charlie said, "Jan, I give you this ring as a symbol of my love with the pledge: to love you today, tomorrow, always, and forever."

"Janeane Abigail Switcher," I breathed heavily into the walkie. "I give you this ring as a symbol of my love with the pledge: to love you yesterday, today, and forever. Always and in all ways."

And with that, I pulled the fire alarm handle. Nothing happened. At first, that is. Then there was a faint ticking in the pipes just behind the wall, followed by an increasingly loud groaning throughout the archaic deluge system. Holberman and his vamp tramps looked around suspiciously. The main pipe began to shake and rattle starting down at the other end of the hall. As the sound approached each sprinkler head, a ring of water spewed forth.

The restless vampires looked at me, curiously, then back to the halo sprays of water spouting off closer and closer to us. "Oh, you guys aren't afraid of a little water are you?" Holberman hissed at me for even hinting such a thing. "Yeah, nor should you be." I paused to let a couple more water heads erupt. "Unless, what if, say, a Catholic nun had blessed the water tanks and turned all of it… into Holy Water?"

I pursed my lips into a thoughtful expression at this outrageous idea as it sunk into the group. They didn't even have time to panic as the sprinklers overhead activated and rained down holy destruction upon their heads. Their faces and skin were melting from the sacred solution, their skin smoked and they grabbed themselves and one by one, exploded. "Helsing!" Holberman yelled and then in a spastic flash of dust, he was gone.

"There can be only one, Holberman," I saluted the dust.

On the radio, Charlie wrapped up our wedding ceremony, "By the authority vested in me by GetOrdained.com I now pronounce you husband and wife."

Two of the vampires were huddled back in a safe zone just out of reach between two sprinklers. They watched, furiously, as their comrades all got dusted. Yet, fearfully as the water pooled closer to their disgusting, scraggly hobbit toes. I stepped under the water spigot, and raised my Piscatory ring high in the air and said, "By the power of Greyskull!"

But, once again, nothing happened.

"Anything?" Charlie checked in.

"Nothing, piece of garbage, son of a…biscotti," I ranted, not able to hide my disappointment. "Not even a how do you do or Bob's your uncle."

Liam chimed in on the radio, "Isn't there shupposed to be a kissh?"

"Okay, Mr. Hormones, that's enough of that," I said.

"No," he answered back, "that'sh what Shister Marguerite shaid to tell you."

"Dan, you gotta get up here, now," Charlie called, "Jan's going up against Victor alone."

"On my way," I said. The water was still pouring down from the nozzles and I was drenched. The two lady vamps scowled and hissed as I ran past so I flicked my blade at them and droplets splashed them and sizzled on their delicate skins, "BRB, guys. I'd stop the world and melt with you," I taunted them with my horrible singing all the way down the hallway.

Jan stalked along, eyes glowing red, brow darkened like a Valkyrie. Fangs bared. She had her pistol extended in front of her and the axe beside it as she negotiated carefully over the floor debris. This room looked like it was an emergency room at one point, except it was almost completely gutted. Graffiti all over the walls. And lots of dark shadows which made tracking Victor's amorphous cloud more difficult.

"Darling, are you hurt?" she asked in mock sympathy. "Mommy's here."

Suddenly the pipes began clanging and moaning like the whole room was possessed.

"Uh, oh, hashtag time's up—," she said as the sprinkler heads opened like a floodgate spouting rings of glorious holy water saturating the whole room. It didn't bother Jan's face and skin; some advantage to being a halfling after all. But she heard a frustrated groan and turned to see a dark cloud fallen to the floor, taking the shape of a man.

"Darling! Are you allergic to holy water?" she needled him. "Have you got your epipen?"

He writhed in agony, but with tremendous con-centration he just flipped the pain off like a light switch. He recovered to his feet, though his skin continued to smoke and flake and peel off when the water hit it. New skin regenerated almost as fast as the old skin was shed. Like a snake.

"It seems," his speech was very constricted, and even though he held his head high and proud, it belied the intensity of his struggle. "I…may have underestimat-ed…the math teacher."

Jan fired the gun and two orbitals cut through the indoor rain straight towards Victor's chest. One he batted away, exploding it to his left and blackening his whole forearm. The other detonated into his abdomen knocking him back against the wall. With tremendous effort he climbed back on his feet, ignoring the softball-sized hole in his midsection but fingering the burnt edges of his shirt, perturbed.

"This shirt was a gift…from the viceroy of Malta. Two hundred years ago," he blustered.

Just then a Hell hound carcass fell through the ceiling hole beside him with a spear shish kebab'ing its ribcage. It hit the floor and exploded, splashing Victor's shirt with neon fibers. Charlie dropped through the hole, herself and landed lithely like a cat. She plucked her spear out of the floor and with one smooth motion, shook off the excess viscera. It hit Victor's shoes and he growled at her.

That's when I ran into the room shouting, "What'd I miss, what'd I miss," panting as I pulled up short beside Jan. I bent over, hands on my knees gasping for breath.

"Not much," Jan shrugged. "Hello, husband."

I stood up grinning ear to ear, "Hello, wife."

"Ugh," she said.

"Same," I grimaced, too. "Weird, right?"

"Too soon," she agreed.

Victor took that moment to muster his last ounce of super speed and raced over behind Charlie, craning her head to the side, his sharp fingernails at her throat. "I think… we shall negotiate… the terms of your surrender… and then—"

While he droned on, I caught eyes with Charlie, who was unphased. She subtly tapped the protective cross on the chain around her neck. I nodded at her.

"Hold up, Vic," I said with a finger in the air. I squared up to Jan and looked deep into her red eyes. "Do you suppose we should at least try the kiss? You know, tactically speaking."

"Oh," Jan rested her weapons at her side mulling it over, "I guess from a tactical standpoint it would be the expedient thing."

"Okay, then," I leaned in closer to her, rain water still pouring down on all of us. "Here I go."

"You don't have to narrate it," she chided, stepping closer. "Just do it."

"I'm getting there," I said, now inches from her. "Don't rush it."

"Don't rush it?" she morphed from dark mode back to regular, angelic Jan-face. "I have been waiting for this kiss since the 7th grade."

"No," I corrected her, "I have been waiting for this kiss since the 7th grade."

"Guys, please…," Charlie prompted.

I cupped her face in my hand and leaned into the kiss. Our lips met once, twice, and then it got really good. And boy did she kiss back. She even dropped her axe in order to wrap an arm around me and pull me closer. City water dripped down our faces. And then I felt a stirring. No, not that, you perv, the warrior ring. It moved on my finger. It tightened and bit into my flesh, latching onto me. And a shockwave, way bigger than the last ones shot out from us and blew everything backwards.

Victor raised a hand to block his face as the shockwave had an irradiating effect on him like a nuclear blast. He screamed and released Charlie just enough so that she could reach the wooden spike she carried in her pants holster. Before the winds even subsided she lunged at Victor driving it deep into his heart and out the back.

He growled at her, "Ow, you little b—," and then exploded into a thousand dust particles.

"Cuss bucket," Charlie said, spitting some blood from her lip.

Jan and I pulled apart still staring into each others eyes. "Wow," I said softly.

"Same," Jan nodded in agreement, wiping away the lipstick with her thumb. "Your face—"

I touched my face and looked at my arms where a thousand little cuts were all healing super fast. I gasped in awe, "Whoa, am I wolverine now?"

"Let's not get ahead of ourselves, Dan Helsing," she smiled.

"Whatever you say, Jan Helsing," I countered playfully.

"Nope!" she deadpanned. "Too soon."

"Guys, don't worry about Charlie," Charlie picked up the stake off the ground and replaced it in her pocket. "Charlie's gonna be just fine."

"What's going on up there," Obi-Juan shouted into the walkies.

Charlie raised her own radio and said into it flatly, "Victor's dead. The magic kiss worked. I'm headed down to help Liam and Sister Marguerite with cleanup."

"No need," Liam said proudly, as he and Marguerite entered the room. They were battle weary but none the worse for wear. "We shorta kinda finished 'em all off."

"Well," Charlie sounded almost disappointed. "Sh*t—"

"Cuss bucket," Jan and I said together, staring into each others' eyes.

"—ake mushrooms," Charlie finished.

"Nice fake out, Chuckles," I smiled still looking at Jan, though.

Jan cocked her head to one side. "What...?" she asked coyly.

"I knew it," I confessed. "I knew you tasted like a summer vacation."

"Ew!" Charlie objected. "Minor in the room. And a nun! Let's dial it back to 'E' for 'Everyone.'"

"Yeah," Jan pulled away and threw a thumb over her shoulder. "And we should probably wrap the special choir. It being Christmas Eve and all."

"Oh yeah," I lifted up my walkie talkie. "Well done team! Choir you are wrapped. Please leave the fire sticks with Jada on the way out and have a Merry Christmas Day Parade!"

"Almost done," Choir lead reported back over radio.

Outside, the Holy Cross Choir had closed the circle tighter and tighter on the last Hell hound. As they powered into the big finish of "The Hallelujah Chorus" they slowly moved their stick flames toward the ground. As the height of the gemstones lowered, an invisible ceiling began to disintegrate the last hellhound into a fiery tornado fury. It crouched down, but that only bought it a few seconds of reprieve. The stones touched the ground about the time the choir finished singing the last drawn out, "Hallelujah." And only a whirly-dervish of embers was all that was left of the killer brute.

Back inside, everyone was hobbling off the battlefield like a bone-weary Hockey team after three periods and an overtime.

"May I just say," Marguerite smiled delicately at me, "Not bad, Daniel."

"For a math teacher?" I pressed.

"For anyone," she added with a twinkle in her eye. "Seriously, Charlie and I figured you'd be dead a long time ago."

"Day one," Charlie added morosely.

"Oh that's—how comforting," I said, but then conceded the point. "Statistically, you were correct of course."

Just then a giant crow flew into the hallway, startling us all into attack position. We relaxed when we saw it land on some rubble beside Charlie. "Oh, boy," she said unenthusiastically, "Fitz." She grabbed the small scroll from his leg. We all gathered around while she unravelled the message and turned it right side up.

"Banner Elk Slayer. Stop. Power spikes all over town. Stop. Suspected hive activity at abandoned hospital. Stop. Wait for reinforcements. Stop." We all groaned and boo'd as she balled up the parchment and tossed it over her shoulder. "We're done here," Charlie said shooing the bird away with both hands. "Go, I'm not paying for historical trivia, Fitz. Get outta here before we cook you for dinner. Go!" The crow flapped away, cursing all of us in its salty, bird language.

We all filed into the lobby, sloshing through the wet remains of the holy water.

"Whoever sends that message bird is the worst," I said and then added in my best transatlantic accent, "Banner Elk Slayer. Stop. You know the Titanic ship that sank in 1912? Don't get on it with Leonardo DiCaprio. Stop."

Obi-Juan and Jada met us with a bunch of thermal blankets like the marathon runners used. Our whole bedraggled crew exited the haunted hospital's lobby all wrapped in silvery warmth. Good thing, too. The temperature had dropped and now fat snow flakes had begun to dump down on us. We all squealed with delight at the festivus miracle. Next week we'd all be sick of it but for now, just for today, this was a nice Christmas Eve moment.

My phone buzzed in my pocket and I pulled it out, showed Jan the caller ID and answered, "Hello, Mayor Doug." Everyone around got real quiet. And real tense. "Oh, and a Merry Christmas to you, too. The final total was what, so far?" The corners of my mouth drew down and my eyebrows shot up, impressed. "I will pass that note along to the team. No, thank you, sir." I offered the phone to Jan but she shook her head no. "Okay, sir. Good night, sir," I hung up.

Jan whispered in my ear, "If you want me to draculize him, I'd do that for you. Like a wedding present."

"That is so tempting. I'm not saying no," I said. "But let me think about it. For like a thousand years." She nudged me, playfully. Then I turned to the others who were waiting expectantly. "Two point one million dollars," I exclaimed proudly.

Cheers rose up from the small, rag tag group. Everyone exchanged sloppy, wet hugs and high-fives. Not Charlie, of course. Charlie was Charlie. I cocked an eyebrow and held a fist out toward her, testing the waters. She rolled her eyes and bumped it reluctantly with her own.

"Ooooohhhh, Jan, did you see that? The Banner Elk Slayer likes me," I said teasingly.

"Oh, I know," Jan said with a wink to Charlie.

"Ugh, you people have no chill whatsoever," Charlie groaned. "I hope I'm transferred outta here tomorrow." She began to walk off.

I laughed, "Yeah right, fast forward ten years from now when the Hunter's Union is all, 'Banner Elk Slayer. Stop. Good job on the haunted hospital. Stop. Please report for new assignment. Stop."

Charlie almost cracked a smile. Almost. It was nice. We were all laughing and caught up in the after glow. Someone spontaneously began to sing Winter Wonderland beginning with "Slay bells ring, are you listening…" and we all chimed in, recklessly singing it in as many different keys as there were singers.

I'm not gonna lie, it was good to be alive.

>— >——< **THE END** >——< —<

CREDITS

(in alphabetical order)

David Acuff   Cover Layout & Design
MidjourneyAI.com

Nicole A. Bailey   Beta Readers
Betty Anne Davidson
Scott Davidson
Frank Marquez
Joe Wilson

AUTHOR'S JOURNAL:
BEHIND THE BOOK

Monday, August 1, 2022
7:44am // 3635 Words

Welcome to the behind the scenes. Under the hood, so to speak. Inside the sausage factory. Wait, what?! You heard me. This will be my raw and unfiltered thoughts that have not been sanitized, edited and cleaned up for prime time television. It's just a journal. Off the cuff. The A-cuff! Ha. It shows the date I wrote it, time of day, and how many words the story had in it. So, here goes…

I first got the idea for SLAY BELLS RING while I was home for Christmas last year, 2021. You know there's so many sappy Christmas movies out and I'm not talking about the greats like ELF or WHITE CHRISTMAS or DIE HARD. I'm talking about the schlocky formula Christmas paint by numbers films that a Hallmark Channel, for example, churns out hand over fist.

Mom and I watched a couple of them because she was hooked. And maybe there were some on Netflix, too. But, besides DIE HARD, there's not a lot of counter-Christmas or dark Christmas stories. Sure you've got your BAD SANTAS and your KRAMPUS and NIGHTMARE BE-FORE CHRISTMAS but those are either TOO dark or TOO bloody or TOO mind-numbingly idiotic.

Also, I had just seen a Ryan Reynolds movie or Tik Tok or Aviation Gin commercial—it doesn't matter—but that's when the idea first sprang into existence. The fact that we desperately need a Ryan Reynolds Christmas vehicle that skews a little darker but adheres to EVERY LAST Hallmark plot convention from the small town under fire (parade cancelled for lack of funds) to the big city hot shot that reluctantly comes home and dreads it all but falls in love with the home town guy who doesn't just work at the tree lot (surprise, surprise) he actually is a hidden and secret prince. And then it snows.

Anyway, I've looked up some Hallmark must-have tropes and will research more because yes, please!

The thematic wrap around this story is discovering your hidden potential Aladdin diamond in the rough and yes secret prince through line. We've all heard of Van Helsing, Vampire Slayer extraordinaire. Well, this is his great great great grandson, Dan Helsing. And this can grow into an adventure series with his soon-to-be soul mate Jan Switcher.

Spoiler!

Also, as I'm convinced RyanR does amazing with kid foils as in THE ADAM PROJECT and DEADPOOL so this, too, needs a precocious 12- to 14-year-old orphan named Charlotte "Charlie" Summers. It was so great looking up these names and researching iconic vampire stories to weave them in as Easter eggs. Did you know that Buffy the Vampire slayer had a little sister named Charlotte Summers? Iconic. And Jan Switcher is a play on the Witcher series. Don't know if I love that connection yet or not, but leaving it in for the time being.

This one has started the way many other projects have begun; with a vision for very specific humorous scenes or comedy bits or dialogue. Just writing those in my phone or a pages doc free flow as they come down. Like a transcriptionist. More ideas turn up through researching the historical story elements. Like, I know there will need to be a portal in this novel and as I ground it in reality I found a tree very specific to the Transylvania/Romania area that could end up being a wardrobe or dresser or door frame. Not a wardrobe. Don't want to infringe on ye ole Narnia transport devices.

So then you have all the main ingredients. A Math Teacher (modeled after my brother-in-law, Scott) who is an extreme introvert and loves his alone time but teaches math and wants to be an actuary because a cubicle job doing spreadsheets all day would be his Valhalla. Just a regular shmoe non-superhero, minding his own business as a background player in his own life that will be forced to step into his calling and family legacy of monster slaying.

Janeane (just figured that name out the other day, probably because of seeing my brother Erik and his wife, Janeane, at SDCC 2022 Anaheim) will be the big city girl just in town for Christmas, albeit reluctantly. Her name shortens easily to Jan. As in, Dan and Jan Helsing. Power couple. Along with little scrappy doo, Charlie Summers.

What is not to love?

Here's another style inspiration. I haven't worked on this particular story from January until May bc I was hardcore pressing in on SEMI-CENTURION my semi memoir comedy book. Those stories were so fun and stream of conscious and very VERY first person delusional unreliable narrator at its finest. But loosely based on true fictional events.

So, after I finished that book and launched it, I was kind of stuck on this fun and quirky writing style I'd been honing for six months and so I leaned into it as I began Chapter one. Got a few paragraphs in and felt that it was funny, engaging stuff. Starts in the middle of the big boss battle where Dan's getting his ass kicked and he's in a dungeon trying to hold a huge door closed and something is growling and ferociously tearing into the other side of it. Then we flash back to two weeks prior to let the narrative unfold. Sort of a "Yuuuuup, that's me…" moment.

Yesterday was a lazy Sunday afternoon. I picked up the laptop to go back over what I'd written. Sharpened it up a bit and then started seeing what could be the next steps. Not the whole thing, but I needed our protag to get down to orphan game night in the basement.

I went back to re-read and tweak and sharpen and then in the middle of that refining process I hit upon a flashback to him at the bar. I didn't intend to do that initially. Dan just mentioned his therapist Chrissinde and so at some point it just seemed natural to jump right into one of their prior conversations. And as the scene widens out, we discover he's in a bar and she's a bartender. Obviously that's modeled somewhat after my sister Nik who bartends at Foggy Rock Eatery and Pub in Blowing Rock, NC. So, armed with plenty of character insights to her as well as my brother-in-law, Scott, I continued to dig in.

Mind you, that helps me a lot to craft details and flesh out these characters in very unique ways. For example, to draw on Scott's love for table games (Catan, etc) as well as his deeply competitive streak even with his wife (my other non-bartending sister) and there's just some delicious conundrums and opposites to yank him along through the story as he slowly becomes reluctant hero. Our favorite kind.

I am all about stealing from real life people around you and their traits and foibles, but you can't just take their most convenient traits. You can't just mine them for one fear and leave the rest. Because that fear is linked to a certain childhood event that was interpreted in their mind a certain way that completely drives how they now interact with people or make certain life governing decisions.

At first, I didn't know Chrissinde was a bartender. I thought she was actually a Therapist as I began writing the scene. But it just made sense and its a fun intra-scene twist to discover the extent of our unreliable narrator's unreliable narration. Haha.

I didn't know either that Chrissinde was Janeane's sister (edit: changed this later by necessity but this was originally the plan), but as I wrote, I knew that needed to happen. At the end of the conversation Dan reluctantly brings up an old flame, much to the bartender's amusement. And then Dan just falls to pieces. He is not suave. He has no game. Now we can't wait to see the first time with Dan and Jan together because the sparks will fly.

I was unsure how to put Charlie in the gaming scene. She didn't naturally fit. If she did ever go to Orphan Fight Club I saw her sitting off in a corner. A loner, Dottie. A Rebel. She doesn't talk. Doesn't play well with others. So, I just added her at the end of the scene where they hear a noise in the hall and she pops up there and Dan screams like a girl and then they all run upstairs. Fine.

But, this morning I'm running on the treadmill and I came to realize that she's been down there fighting a monster. We don't know that. There was just the hint of a trowel in the hall and paint splotches. But that's enough of a thread for me to begin pulling on. I had the foresight to write the trowel in and have her pop up even before I knew what she was doing down there. Now I know. She's been down there kicking ass and *saving their lives*. Every game night. Every Thursday. That's why she sits by the door, too. Reading. Waiting. Guarding.

That's amazing. So, in this small town, creatures are already leaking through the portal somehow. Sure, Dan and Jan will have to defeat the main baddie but this cool, spunky adolescent has been saving lives all along.

I love that. Sets up another collision later on with Dan being the big adult and Charlie really having to explain monster-hunting to him. Also I'm pretty sure monster blood is neon colors so the Jackson Pollack-looking paintings in her bedroom are really her death trophies. Whoa.

Having Charlie as an OG slayer allows her to become the kind of Obi-Wan to train the others in all the horror rules they need to know. That's always been the intent but now instead of her just being a book worm, she will be a ferocious little warrior from the such-and-such clan or whatever the lore turns out to be.

I've got to go back on a second Chapter 1 pass and rework some of Charlie's pieces. I can't decide if I need to add the part of Dan reading from one of his family heirloom books to the orphans because of some funny little ritual they perform with them and these ancient words just sound cool. But little does he know (ha!) little does he's spell casting and bringing things through the portal.

I don't know if that incantation element organically works into the scene. We'll see.

I think Dan's gonna have to touch one of Charlie's paintings and get flashes of something. That's when he knows there's more to her and maybe when she realizes he's the anointed one or whatever.

So far I haven't left Chapter One on a cliffhanger. Yes there's a lot going on and of course his life's in jeopardy on page one so there's that, but building up more of Charlie's underworld might help propel us—rather than just her looking creepily out the second floor window as he drives away. Something more with that neon blood trail idea. "What are you… Banksy?"

Then what?

Hard to say what chapter two holds at this moment. We're still in the Meet the Town phase so we have to establish some more scenes and places that we'll revisit and wreck later on. But also remember this is a Hallmark movie at its core so by page so-and-so this thing or that thing needs to happen. Gotta keep that in mind as I weave this tangled tale.

Anyway, I'm having fun. Hope you're having fun!!

Saturday, August 6, 2022
11:32am // 3635 Words

Just got back from Aroma Cafe. What a delightful little breakfast nook. I hit Chapter One again to revise, rethink and rework the words. Obviously the narrator babbles a lot but it's got to be a funny stream of consciousness that moves the story along and intrigues the audience and not bores them with random soufflé asides and such. It'll be a delicate balance but we'll get there.

Still staring into the void that is chapter two. I mean, could one of you read it and then go back in time to right now and tell me what happens. Because I don't know what happens. I know where the story sorta needs to go. And I know I need to bring Janeane into town in a big reveal sorta way. But… uh… beyond that?

I'm looking at chapter one, again, to make sure it successfully sets up a lot of the gags and character stuff that comes out later. Like setting up all this fine china all over that we end up smashing by act III.

Also I need to study the Hallmark plot points so I can write specifically to that formula. That's why chapter two feels like it should be Jan's return. Big city girl not happy to have to come home to this quaint little small town life. But also this story narrator is Dan so I've got to watch out for scenes that he's not in, I think, because… how would he know what happened? Hmm.

This story is difficult because in some respects it is so high concept and the big story beats are as obvious as the ending I have in mind so in some respects it feels like it's written itself. But then to actually sit down pen to paper or fingers to pixels it's not obvious at all. Every new sentence is a struggle.

And am I right to dream-cast Blake Lively in my head as Janeane? I don't really have a personality lock on her other than prettier, female-er Ryan Reynolds. She doesn't play a "type" in all her films like her hubs. So maybe I need to re-cast to someone new that I can lock onto personality-wise and then Blake can morph into the role if she wants it. Obviously a Sandra Bullock would be an easier target to write for. An Anna Kendrick but I'm already using her for Devon Ayre. Ooohhh, what about an Emily Blunt?

Actually this dynamic is a lot more like Wall-E and Eve. Wall-E the lo-tech disheveled grunt haplessly going through life's motions. Eve, the buttoned up high tech efficient order following and deadly commander in control at all times with no time for things like love and romance and whatever the robot equivalent of the penis is.

Anyway, I'm off to stare at Chapter Two again.

11:32am // 4506 Words

Okay I didn't dive into Chapter Two, I went back and added the Charlie moment at the end of Chapter One where the other orphans are all getting ready for bed and she goes back to the basement to finish off the wookalaar. I think it plays a lot better for the audience here at the end of the chapter to be reminded of some of the stakes that we opened the chapter with. Which is that bad creatures are out there. And to learn that Charlie is a bad ass.

That was it. Just a simple scene, but could be pretty powerful and visual. And most importantly propels the reader into the next chapter. If this was a 22-min series this would be almost the end credits scene that takes place.

There I go ruining another movie idea by projecting it into a TV series. Stop it, Acuff!

Sunday, August 7, 2022
11:30am // 4672 Words

Guys I did a thing last night in the story (still Chapter One, hey, DON'T YOU ROLL YOUR EYES AT ME, BETHANY, WE'LL GET TO TWO WHEN WE GET TO TWO!!!) I'm reworking the opening stuff and as I get to the "counsel session" at the bar suddenly I change one of Dan's lines from like "How's your sister?" to "How's your clone?" And I made Chrissinde and Janeane twins!! I can't even imagine the hijinks and possibilities this opens up but at the very least its a super delicious fun selling point for the actress to play them both.

Again, I just changed one little word and suddenly a world of possibilities opened up. Now I'll let it play out in a few chapters to see if it sets well with the rest of the story or not (Narrator: It did not). For example, you can't just suddenly say "How's that martian sister of yours?" You add one little word, suddenly opens your story into some weird sci-fi direction that actually detracts from the rest of what essentially is a fantasy creature feature type story. Wookalaars are one thing, martians are a whole other entity and genre and just no thank you. This is why we walk out the new ideas and test their sea legs within the story. If suddenly the whole thing takes a sharp left turn and has nothing to do with EVERY OTHER SCENE BEFORE IT then as Gordon Ramsey says, "YOU'VE LOST THE PLOT!!"

So, if you've read the book and/or watched the film don't spoil it for me. Because I haven't. So maybe they stay twins, maybe I trash that idea in a future draft. Anyway, back to revise chapter one to get another great running start and then… launch into chapter two.

Maybe.

Still so damn foggy.

Also, if I do keep the twins thing I may change Chrissinde's name to simplify it a little. Make it more twins-y of a name to complement Janeane. Another "J" name, perhaps. We'll see.

3:05pm // 4920 Words

Added some interesting Grinch and Die Hard references to Charlie's reverie at the end of Chapter one. That can be the other fun part of this movie is that it can be hyper aware of every other Christmas movie that's come before it. That's more of a window dressing and not a plot point fixture so it can be lightly sprinkled on top after the rest of the story is written and it moves into the edit.

Like, how fun would it be to have a scene where Dan and Charlie have to lure out the monsters so they start singing "Baby, it's cold outside" duet from Elf. So good.

Tuesday, August 9, 2022
6:16pm // 7548 Words

Woohoo! Into Chapter Two. Finally.

How do you know when you're ready to start writing a new chapter?

Well, first of all, toots, remember that everyone outlines. Everyone. And some people even do it before they start writing.

(Rim shot)

So I really needed to know a few things about the direction of this chapter:

> Meet-Cute Jan & Dan (and - *shocker* - Brodie)
> Brodie touches the Ankh necklace and triggers the wookalaar attack
> Charlie feels the wookalaar emerging and goes to stop it only it's hella huge — bigger than any she'd

> ever fought before so she just opens the outside
> doors to prevent it from going upstairs
> And I think that can be the end of the chapter because
> it's a great cliff hanger and page turner. Where is
> this monster going? What is it going to do?

So, I knew those things but I couldn't decide on the very first sentence and first paragraph. I considered flashing back to Dan receiving the magic necklace at his Uncle's funeral but don't love the idea of using any flashbacks. Plus, there needs to be more mystery surrounding this jewelry and what it does.

Then, I suddenly imagined Dan dressed in a Santa outfit. Like he's doing it for the kids, but he hates it. And it reminds us we're at Christmas. And so I just had him rolling up to the diner as Santa. Then having a testosterone moment with another Santa doing Salvation Army bell ringing. Then he goes inside and we meet sweet Gladys. He gets distracted by the pastries. Then BOOM! There's Jan serendipitously appearing from the heavens above.

So, it just all kind of worked starting with the dueling Santas conflict right off the bat.

It's fun to write this one because Dan has jokes he says to other characters, but then he also has jokes with us the audience in the narration. Also, I didn't know before I started writing this chapter that Brodie was Swedish and muscular and blonde with an accent. That just came out in the story. It'll be interesting to find out how he and Jan met along the way.

Anyway, I've been going over and over Chapter One again and again polishing it because I didn't know how to launch into two. Now I'm launched! Feels good. And I'll have to go back and add some more tidbits here and there to finish setting up the world we're gonna break later. But it feels really great to have a draft of it. Phew!

Good job team! High fives.

Friday, September 2, 2022
11:41am // 7628 Words

I've got to get back to this book. I've not done any heavy writing for the past 3 weeks since that last entry. I have been working on the outline for "The Edge" script and having fun canoodling with a whole new spin on a 30 year old idea my brother-in-law Erik and I had in the 90s.

So, to stay on track, what I decided was to do my own NaNoWriMo in September. 1000 words per day goal. 30000 words total. On this one project. No hopping around. That should get us close to something like a first draft by month's end.

Sometimes its hard to maintain the mental space for writing. Like, I've been stressed over finances for a while now. Stressed over rent increase of $300/month. Stressed that even though I'm making more salary than I've ever made, I still seem to be underwater every single freaking week and month. And September even has 5 paychecks. That's like a whole extra bonus. Where's the money go?

Blerg.

I mean don't feel too sorry for me bc I'm living in a kick-ass, expensive apartment. And driving a kickass, expensive car. And I 100% eat out every meal. So it's all financially draining. What the eff am I doing to myself? Ridiculous.

And so that weighs on me. Big time. I need a breakthrough. A winning lottery ticket. A stock option or crypto that moons. Wen moon, Shiba Inu?

Anyway, so there's always life stuff that's gonna eat into your writing time; crippling you with emotional fatigue to the point where you don't even want to write when you have time because you're depressed and worrying about stuff. That's all part of the writing process. The compartmentalization. It's very important. To continue moving ahead even though you've, hypothetically speaking, written four books that all total have made you less than $300. And not even that because you've spent $5K on editors and cover designs, etc.

This book I decided would be fun for a Christmas release. This Christmas. That's a crazy deadline I'm giving myself. And then I can push BATTLE TIDES to May of next year for its big, BIG release (also to give it some space to pitch out to Lit Agents in case traditional publishing is in my future? Maybe?).

As I write this main character specifically for Ryan Reynolds I thought about how I could have some sort of fun drawn cover with a sticker that points to him and says "Not Ryan Reynolds". So, that's a fun non-attachment to promote with the book as long as I don't get sued.

To recap: sinking exorbitant amount of time and energy and money I don't have into another novel to self-pub and sell only 50 copies? Yes please! Sounds good.

What's the definition of insanity again?

Okay. So, writing. Christmas story. Murderous beasts on the rampage. Orphans and slayers. Ryan Reynolds. There's the windup annnnnnnnnnd…GO WRITE!!

Friday, September 2, 2022
8:35p // 9304 Words

Phew. Okay, I've broken through another blank section. Gotten a little further.

Here's what I was chewing on. I need to kill Brodie the fiancé. And to do that I need him to activate the Ankh family ring or whatever we're calling it. So at first I was toying with Jan having the ring that Dan had given her and maybe she was bringing it back to return it now that she was engaged to Swedish golden boy. But that wasn't working out in my mind. It was problematic. Convenient but problematic.

Also, I had thought about having a scene with Dan's dead Uncle who passes on the special ring to him. Thought about doing that in flashback but then decided early on I didn't want to mess with flashbacks. Just tell the story. Nothing fancy. So that ruled that out.

Then I landed upon this giant Sarcophagus just showing up on Dan's doorstep. It's so huge he can't move it. Later Jan and Brodie come over to pick him up for dinner and they decide to help him crack it open. So, the skeletons will fall out on Dan. He'll scream bloody murder fall back into the yard off the porch. Once in the sunlight the skeletons will immediately turn to dust. Except for the ring. Brodie comes to help Dan up. Grabs the ring. Puts it on. Foom! The call is activated and he can't get the ring off. Later, in next chapter he gets murdered and ring is freed up.

Eventually, Dan will put the ring on. Again, the power of the ring is that it calls to the dark creatures and brings them forth. Because he's the slayer, see, so they're drawn to him and he dispenses with them one by one. At least that's how VAN Helsing would have done it. Dan could die trying. Probably would, too, if Charlie didn't help out.

Oh and inside the casket are all manner of odd weapons and stuff that they'll have to figure out. Anyway, that takes us through the end of this Chapter when Charlie goes down to the basement to head off what she thinks is another baby wookalaar and it's a huge frikkin full grown beast. She lures it out into the open, so it won't go upstairs through the orphan house. End Chapter Two.

Saturday, September 3, 2022
1:50pm // 10663 Words

Okay, I accomplished today's goal of 1300 words. So that completes today 1K and Thursdays 1K. That's great. And I just left off where they're on the porch opening the huge box. They've just gotten to the inside box.

That leaves me exactly where I know what happens next so I might even come back in a few hours from now and keep working on it. Later this week I'll be at D23 with long hours so I want to get good and ahead of schedule before that craziness.

It's so interesting how these scenes play out. Like, going in I have my scene goal. For example, Jan and Brodie arrive to pick up Dan and offer to help him open the mystery box and hilarity ensues. So that's the mental outline. But getting into it I discover as I write that Jan and Brodie climb in to his home through the front window which is the new door and hang out inside for a moment. They have a discussion about his adult furniture and even bedbugs. None of which I knew anything about these characters before this but totally makes sense.

Jan gets to pet Smeagol but then the cat runs from Brodie which makes Dan super proud. Didn't know that was gonna happen, either. Just started giving them business in the room and knew Jan had to acknowledge the cat bc she would have known him. Also the fact she knew about the refugee furniture he used to own hints at some time spent together there in the past. So, little hints like that getting dropped and weaving a richer tapestry together.

And Brodie is just being Brodie. A swell guy helping out and being Mr. Perfect. Little did he know in the very next chapter he'd be eaten by a demagorgon. Or whatever we're calling those things. Sigh. Ah well. Is it a commentary on perfect boyfriends who have it all together? Lord, I hope not. Just need to feed the beast its first victim and the one with the MOST impact will be Brodie. Bye bye, Brodie.

Also I'll have to figure out along the way on the second pass if I've peppered in too much Christmas stuff or not along the way. I definitely don't want to lose that sense of season as we go. Hence the Santa suits and light decorations and music playing. Lots of touch points. Will this story be considered "heartwarming" in the end? Mmm. I dunno. Not as easy to do as "Elf" or "The Santa Clause" or whatever. But still a possibility and an actual goal. I think hence the orphans and Charlie especially being so antagonistic to Dan and vice versa up front. Paves the way for some sweeter moments later.

We. Shall. See.

Sunday, September 4, 2022
5:21pm // 12963 Words

And that's 2300 more words for today. Good job, Acuff. I started about Noon-Thirty. Took the morning to run to the grocery store, then cook myself a burger and home-made fries and corn on the cob yumminess. Then settled down on the couch about 12:30p to write. And, fortunately, I had left off yesterday with plenty of idea runway of where today was headed. At least through the end of Chapter Two. Which I've done.

Brodie, Jan and Dan have cracked open the box. Brodie has put on the ring that's triggered the call and then cut to Charlie who is going in the basement to fight what she thinks is the usual cutesy little beast and OMG it's huge and she has to lure it out of the basement through the cellar doors and then it disappears into the twilight. Zoinks.

        Chapter 1   5566
        Chapter 2   7387

That's approximately where we're at Chapter wise.

But as far as plot wise, we're still not really out of Act 1. No choice has been made by our hero Dan Helsing.

Oooh I just thought of the start of the next chapter would be great to have Dan outdoors on his own and some-things crackling in the woods and he gets spooked and Smeagol gets spooked and then Charlie pops out. Bam! It is time for Charlie to let him in on the big secret and let him know what the casket is and the weapons cache and all of that. Enough for him to REJECT the idea. Uh, hello, Hero's Journey outline.

Then meanwhile the thing EATS Brodie. Oh, spoiler alert people! And then Dan is forced to… something. Fight the beast I guess. Before his training, though. So, it's gonna be a bad one. And Jan will have to help.

Now before I was all about Dan and Jan partnering up like Daphne and Fred and solving this whole case. But she's also a grieving widow. So how is she gonna fall in love with Dan if she's just had her fiancé eaten. It's tricky. This is a tricky, tricky holiday film. Not as tricky as, say, sitting with your parents watching "Love Actually" and the porn stand-in scene comes on and scars your mom for life. But still tricky, I must say.

And we're not even into Sid Field's intimidating SEA OF ACT TWO yet! That large, daunting white expanse of nada and bupkiss. Many well intentioned writers have begun crossing the Sea of Act Two without enough fuel from Act One (Conflict + Characters + Goals/Intentions) and their story petered out half-way across and sank to the bottom of "I'll finish this some other day" ocean. RIP.

By the way, just for giggles I started watching the TV version of the Van Helsing (2016) show. I'm about 5 episodes in and it is, well, horrible. Just terrible, clunky writing and terrible action. Not good. Not helpful to the overall Van Helsing vibe I was hoping to glean from it. Ah well. I mean, technically, their character Vanessa (she's the One, Neo!) wakes up after a 3-year coma and the world's gone to shyte with Vampires but not in the cool way, more of the dystopian "Walking Dead" sorta way. Anyway, hero wakes up and has no idea she's the hero and no desire to be the hero. That's where our two story similarities end. A clueless/reluctant hero. And also the fact both stories are modern day vampire reboots or what I like to call re-vamps. Ha! Other than that, I'm not even doing vampires. Or am I?

Just hell hounds called *Wookalaars* or whatever. May add in other creatures, though.

I've got to balance back in some Christmas goals. Like, not dying from a hell beast is a very good goal but at the same time all these holiday movies have some big town takeover or the pageant is in jeopardy or the parade might be cancelled and then the town will go bankrupt. So, it needs that very Christmas-y entanglement for the plot to keep it more fun and less murdery.

But definitely gonna be a fun conundrum that Dan will have to don the ring of power in order to access some of his family dynasty but—LOL—he doesn't want to bc it means immediately he's a target as it CALLS out to all the beasts to come get him. So that's a nice and juicy future train collision we're building towards.

Anyway, did I mention I bought groceries today? Yup. Meant to spend $100 since things are tight but ended up at $150. So right now there's a rigatoni dinner with my name on it. Too bad I couldn't afford the wine to go with. Sigh. Is this how Coppola started?!?

This living paycheck to paycheck is for the birds. Y'all gonna have to start buying up my books by the truck-full! I need some vino to go with my pseudo-Italiano!

You know what else is weird? Sitting here with YouTube on TV playing Christmas and Christmas Jazz music in September in Burbank when it's 108 degrees outside. Yowza. Last week and this week, too. Hotcha! I don't know when we'll get a break. But a little Christmas spirit right now is fun. Even if there's hell hounds involved..

Tuesday, September 6, 2022
5:23pm // 15785 Words

So far I'm still on track for my September writing sprint goal. Yesterday I cranked out 1300 words or so and about the same today. I'm well into Chapter 3. It's going a-okay.

Brodie's just met with an untimely demise and Charlie and Dan have finally geared up to check on Brodie and Jan and the ring.

I was looking up Banner's Elk AirBNB places to discover where I wanted our lovey dove couple to be and there was a great one called: Glass Tree House. Very chic and modern and perfect layout. It's even an all white interior so how great will that juxtapose the Brodie bloodbath?

I didn't do that yet for Dan's house. I have in mind what it looks like and it'll have some yard space on either side as some of those homes do up there; he can have neighbors but still have privacy. But I haven't looked up on a map to decide where it'd be. Mostly bc their Banner's Elk Street photos in Google are, uh, lacking. I guess the google bots haven't mapped that far off road yet into the mountains. We be off the map here, Cap'n Barbossa!

May have to do some more exploring this Christmas while I'm down there.

A couple things that surprised me this chapter was the Jacuzzi scene. That's gonna be hot—literally and romantically. And then when Jan accidentally (and drunkenly) says "I love you, Dan" to the wrong person. Wowza. Did not see that coming but it's interesting. And spicy.

Anyway, technically I'm still in Act One. And could conceivably be there for another 4K words which means 20K Act One which leads me to believe a 40K Act Two and

20K Act Three but that's 80K words. Geez. That's a lot for a small book-to-movie like this.

I'm also considering changing up Jan's backstory a little. I don't really feel like she's got a full on cop vibe like I'd originally planned. And it's difficult if she's the tough one trying to buck Dan up into taking the mantle of his family since that seems to be Charlie's whole thing now. Which I love. But once Charlie became a slayer—and that was not even discovered until writing the end of Chapter One—then it forces Jan to be in a different role. Also I toyed with if there was some way to bring in one of the legends from the past, a Hugh Jackman or Kate Beckinsale, through the portal but I don't love that either. This is messier but serves the same purpose with Charlie as mentor and Obi-wan.

I'll have to canoodle on these things.

Act Two is a mystery right now. Obviously there has to be some training involved. Some Dagobah stuff. He's dead set against wearing the ring bc that means accepting the mantle and challenging death to a duel. It's the ultimate walkabout.

I do know that Act Three needs to take place down town amidst all the Christmas decorations. Possibly several hell hounds at once. Don't know what to do with the towns people yet. Maybe they're all at midnight mass like good little Christians while Jan, Dan and Charlie rock the town like Rambo. I dunno. Still canoodling on that too.

See, there's two types of horror films. The one where the things escape and go everywhere and kill everyone and it's a huge disaster pic and the second ones where some team is trying to keep the carnage undercover; the fact that all these things exist out there. Like Stranger Things. I'm leaning towards the town being oblivious to the extraordinary battle going on. That means we can't tear through the center of town. It'll have to be somewhere else more destructible. We'll see how the story evolves.

Wednesday, September 7, 2022
9:06pm // 16904 Words

Phew. By God's grace I've kept up with the 1K words per day minimum. I'm down for the weekend in Anaheim at the Marriot by the Convention Center for Disney's biannual D23. But I got in some writing time this morning before I left to drive down in the Z. A real Hank Moody moment.

It was a bloody 1K today as the Wookalaar devoured Brodie in the glass treehouse. I had a lot of choices and I'm not convinced I made the right ones but it felt instinctually correct. I could have had Jan enter the home and see the bloody aftermath but there's no creature or anything. Then we have to spend another 1/2 chapter or whole chapter of them trying to get the creature before it could get back to the Sylvania Home portal.

That was the original idea. But then I went with this second, newer idea where Jan grabbed her gun and found the beast still chewing on poor Brodie. She unloads a clip and that gets its attention and then as its about to pounce at her, in from the front door is (*cue Highway to Hell soundtrack*) Dan and Charlie with their crossbow and spears. And between the three of them they take care of the thing in fairly short order. And then of course it explodes and is gone forever.

But am I showing too much? Have we learned nothing from Jaws? Less is more? Only show shadows and glimpses and insinuations (like the bobbing barrels in the water) to hint at the horror and not show it outright. And did our three amigos take care of this thing too easily? I did have Charlie get whacked across the room. That's fun. But is it a Pyrrhic enough victory? Brodie's gone. So there's that. Yeah maybe Dan needs to get sliced across his belly by the beast. That's good. That would also be reminiscent of Charlie's last fight where she had the belly wound. Ties them together ironically.

Now that we've had a sick and monster-y horror chapter we need to go back and have a slower Christmas-y chapter. Get back to the b-plot of saving the city's _______ (Christmas tree farm, parade, live nativity, or whatever). And some training. And I have to figure out how Jan actually gets over Brodie. This is more of a comedy so it can't be treated completely dramatically and realistic. Need to lace more with humor and get her "eye of the tiger" back. Again, Jan is kind of blasé to me right now. She needs a whole other layer to her to click into place.

So the surprise in this last writing section was not only the beast dying then and there instead of being hunted down across Banner Elk, but also Jan's line at the last part "Leave a note so if Brodie returns he won't be worried." This is her mentally checking out from the situation because it's easier than believing that Brodie is gone. And that's a deeply interesting twist to me. For her to continue like he could be coming back any second. Like he just stepped out for an errand. When really she watched him die. Deliciously interesting.

Tomorrow, Friday and Saturday I have a ton of filming to do here at D23 so I'm not sure I'll have the time to put in pages. We shall see. But that's why we overwrote the past 4 days. Anyway, poor, poor Janeane. Oh and Brodie.

Monday, September 12, 2022
3:53pm // 16904 Words

Eagle eyes will recognize the word count hasn't changed since the last entry. Just finished up yesterday at D23 Expo after some long, arduous days. I was mentally spent. Even today I'm just sort of flopping around like a sunstroke'd walrus.

So, I'm about 2800 words short right now of my 1K/day. But I've got some time now to crack into it, so I'll do that. I'll make another pass from page one to edit and build momentum on previously-laid groundwork and then hopefully launch out where we left off after the melee of poor Brodie the human lunchable.

On my three or four day hiatus I started each day on the hotel treadmill and cracked into a new audiobook "Dialogue" by Robert McKee. I've read his "Story" which is superb. This one specifically deals with dialogue and not just scripts but plays and books, too. So it's a great study in all three at the same time. With a lot of great samples from books, novels and plays where he excerpts to prove a point and brings in actors to voice the scenes.

I know I have to go back to Charlie's dialogue throughout and rewrite it in character for her. Right now she sounds vanilla bean. And I especially think that after two chapters of her not talking at all, that when she does, it needs to be unique. Especially as a slayer. What does a 12 year old wise beyond her years trained assassin sound like? Welp, we'll find out.

Also my instinct is that Jan needs to be back in town for more than just Christmas. And more than just to announce her fiancé. Almost like she needs to be receiving some town award for some act of bravery she's done in the big city. Or is there some family legacy thing like playing Mary in the parade? With a solo? Really need to flesh her backstory out more because, like Charlie, it will then dictate every word of dialogue and action along the way.

And like I said last entry, make Dan a little less on point with his crossbow shots. He needs to be hitting walls and shattering lamps at first. Perhaps he can't use the power of the family legacy until he puts the ring on. Because it inherently holds a level of skillset that will be helpful to him, a christening as it were, but of course it leaves him completely exposed and on the radar to whatever dark forces lurk around.

Ye ol' catch-22.

Monday, September 12, 2022
8:24pm // 18038 Words

Well, that was interesting. I wrote and wrote and wrote and only got them from the AirBNB back to Dan's place. One measly car ride home. Haha. But some crazy interesting stuff going on in there. Jan's displasia or whatever you want to call it is gonna be fun to play with. Because now not only does she think Brodie is still alive but she will pop in and out of thinking Dan is Brodie? While they're still searching for Brodie?

Yes, she is broken and delusional in brave new ways.

Got out a little more exposition from Charlie about the ring and its power. Jan is almost bipolar in a way. Or split personality. And she's a twin so how does that work? Writing this last scene reminded me of Crazy Cora in "Quigley Down Under" only that was infinitely better written. The sad backstory. The comedy and the tragedy interwoven. Calling him Roy. Haha. So good. Anyway, mental health is definitely front and center in a way I had not ever expected it to be. But this is so much more interesting to me than Jan mourning for 300 pages about a fiancé that got eaten. This has so much more intrigue and tantalizing possibilities. She can be spooning and getting frisky with Dan one second bc she thinks he's Brodie and then the next second yelling at him to get out of her room pervert!

Just wild. Maybe too wild.

Anyway, just wanted to pop in and let y'all know I got my 1100 words today. Plus a little more. So that's cool. Making good headway. Also, I didn't go all the way back to Chapter 1. I started with Chapter 3 and just progressed from there. That's where I gained a little time. But I was excited to get to the new stuff because I knew it started with the car ride home. I'd left that dangling from last time so it gave myself somewhere easier to pick up. Like tomorrow I'm pretty sure it'll pick up in Chapter 4 with Dan and Jan waking up in the bedroom. And kicking Dan out of her space.

Thursday, September 15, 2022
10:29am // 19,549 Words

Here's something I learned in my last 1K word writing sprint that I didn't know about Janeane Switcher. She's not a real cop from Atlanta or Charlotte. She a Museum Cop in Raleigh at the North Carolina Museum of Art. Which I've been to a few times and know very well. All this time I thought she was a regular cop or a detective and was trying to build her up as this bigger badder tougher chick. But this, to me, is far more interesting.

Everyone in her hometown *thinks* she's this big time cop because that's the rumor her sister is floating around town as her hype woman. But in reality, she couldn't hack that life so she works in a nice, quiet museum of art. Still conceal-carries on her person and knows how to shoot. But it makes her less John Wick-y.

And part of that evolved naturally as the story unfolded because I saw how Charlie became MORE John Wick-y. And it doesn't work to have two of the exact same character. Then one would be unnecessary. And then Jan had the mental break down after Brodie got eaten where she's still pretending in her fantasy world that not only is he still alive (missing) but that she's projecting him onto Dan which causes its own awkwardness. That's a far more interesting person to me to write — dealing with a mental breakdown, dealing with a career that's not as glam as she let people believe her life is... way more interesting. Because she's more fragile. She and Dan are both more fragile so that as they ascend into their own arc to "Dan & Jan Helsing: Monster Hunters" it will be much more satisfying.

I'm pretty sure Jan and Chrissinde's dad is the mayor of the town, so I need to go back and build that b-story up more. Could be the reason he's so particular about the big parade or tree lighting ceremony going well for tourism so the town doesn't go bankrupt. As you might have guessed, horror does not blend seamlessly with Christmas nostalgia. They are in fact competing emotions of love and contentment versus fear and unease. And they both have to be built in parallel in the story as we rail hop from one side to the other. It's tricky!

I've been leaning heavily on the horror side getting the monster out of the house and on the prowl with an actual victim, so I need to go back at some point and build up the Christmas-y side. Build up those warm family moments that are just slightly off-kilter because of some underlying threat. Ooohhh, the perfect place to do that would be the orphans actual home. Great to have a town-wide who's who Christmas party there with creatures lurking in the basement trying to eat people.

Other than that, I have an idea for the big ending where Dan finally dons the ring of power and has to go help Jan before this huge creature runs rampant over the whole town and it starts snowing and stuff. But from here (death of Brodie) to there (Act 3) is that huge sea of Act 2 that's supposed to be 2x bigger than Act 1 or Act 3. At least in script form. Remember Act 2 doesn't begin until the main character makes a BIG DECISION that sets the story off on a certain path.

I'm 19K words in and Dan and Jan finally have realized there's an existential threat out there. Dan has chosen NOT to take the ring at this time. So perhaps here we are in Chapter 4 which is Act 2. So I need (in general terms) 3 chapters up to the big turnaround mid-point and then 3 more chapters til the low of lows and then the final 3 for Act 3. That's a 60K word book my friends. That's a lot for something that's supposed to be a screenplay…which usually clocks out as a 35K word novel or so.

Yikes. Not sure if I'm gonna get this thing out by Christmas 2022.

Wait, now that Jan works in a museum, does she need to steal an ancient weapon that they need to kill the boss monster or to close the portal? Hmmmmm. Is Jan Switcher more "The Witcher" based or is she someone else? She might need to get bit by a creature and become the hybrid like Selene from "Underworld". She could even die but come back as a vamp. Or half vamp. But whatever it is, she's not the same and has some new fun powers.

That would be great for Act 2. Could even be on the heels of this last attack where Brodie died or could be a new monster that breaks through and they train and they fight and she dies. And we're sad. And then she comes back. And Charlie wants to kill her but they need her to fight the big baddie at the end. "We can kill her later."

Friday, September 16, 2022
1:45pm // 20,481 Words

So I'm stalling getting into the next part. We're in Chapter 4. Everyone has just woken up, Jan screamed at Dan for being in the bed, they see the painting in the living room and realize the stuff in the painting is the stuff being sent to Dan and family heritage he's been avoiding and blah blah blah. I left off with Dan revealing this wasn't even the first Weapons box he'd received. He had other stuff in storage that was just sitting there collecting dust. And Charlie socks him bc she's been working her ass off to fight these things (earlier I imagined her fighting four over the past year, but I'll up that to 14) and then next scene will be them rummaging through stuff.

Wasn't sure how to make that next stuff pop. Or what came after. I have ideas of what COULD come after but nothing was presenting itself as THE STORY GODS DEMAND YOU GO THIS WAY which is really what I love to work from. Until now.

I'm going back over my screenwriting guru Scott Myers' Narrative through line. Ignore the page numbers because those are for screenplays, not books. But it looks like this so far:

ACT I – vibe: is this thing for real?

THE OPENING HOOK (P. 1-5)
Either a soft (character focused) or hard (action focused) opening which gets the story rolling
Fighting for their lives in the basement against the creature coming at them… also great trailer moment

INCITING INCIDENT (P. 10-15)
Something big happens which jumbles the Protagonist's world. The Reader gets an indication what the story will be
Charlie battles/kills little Wookalaar. Ancient weapons case sent to Dan. Full of weapons and THE RING OF POWER. Monster Wookalaar RELEASED.

THE LOCK (P. 25-30)
Can Jan's fiancé/Sheriff get eaten? Everything was under control until then. Or is that end of Act 1?
DECISION: Dan decides to help Charlie go save Jan and Brodie.

ACT II – vibe: yes it's real. real deadly

THE FIRST BIG TEST (P. 40-45)
Where the Protagonist confronts significant opposition/ odds. Survives mostly through luck, not skill
First huge wookalaar battle where Brodie is killed.

THE TRANSITION (P. 55-60) aka MIDPOINT RE-VERSAL

And Jan goes a little crazy saying he's still alive and at times thinking Dan is Brodie. And info about another weapons chest and goods in storage collecting dust.

THE SECOND BIG TEST (P. 70-75)

Where the Protagonist tests out their emerging confidence. More skill and courage in use, although still lucky

???

ALL IS LOST (P. 85-90)

Despite Protagonist's best efforts, it appears they have lost the Bad Guys have it all on their side

???

ACT III – kill it dead. For real this time.

ON THE DEFENSIVE (P. 90-100)

The first part of Act III, the Protagonist is on their heels Reacting based on their 'old' self, and haunted by self-doubt

ON THE OFFENSIVE (P. 100-110)

The Protagonist digs down to reserves of inner strength they did not know they had, and in tandem with lessons learned along the way in Act II, mounts a counter-attack

FINAL STRUGGLE/DENOUMENT (P. 110-120)
The Protagonist prevails against the Antagonist forces in this final test of their transformation. Followed by wrapping up lose ends, and positioning the 'new' Protagonist in his 'new' world

Obviously I haven't written very much from mid-Act 2 and beyond. It was great for me to clarify to myself that we're further along than I thought. I mean I may have to beef up the DECISION moment of Dan's, but the first big test is already there. And the big reversal of Brodie's death and Jan's little psychoses or delusion. Phew. This thing is half written at 20K words which is much better than I thought yesterday where we were at end of Act 1 and needed 60K more words to finish.

Again, all of this adhering to the SM Narrative Spine is only bc I want to do a novel and script from same. And have it more of a 1:1 correlation unlike BATTLE TIDES which is 90K words which is already like three scripts long. And not in the good way. BT has the length of a Season One of Premiere TV. That's where that's headed. Otherwise if I weren't trying to prep a script as I write a novel then I wouldn't be so adamant about keeping them tightly matched.

Okay so the SECOND BIG TEST needs to happen like this: See, Charlie has already told Jan they're not ready for Dan to take on the ring (not that he wants it anyway) because they all need to train more. So now, when they go to the storage unit whatever else happens, that scene needs to end with Jan putting on the ring. She wants to force another confrontation in order to get Brodie back.

Obviously the moment the ring goes on, the portal opens and they have to get back over there to fight whatever is coming out of there AND OH NO it's the big Orphan Christmas Party where half the town shows up every year to do whatever it is they're doing there. Meanwhile a monster is on the loose in the basement. And they think its gonna be another huge Wookalaar like Brodie faced but maybe it's a Vampire this time. Something different. And that whole thing ends with Jan getting bitten and dragged into the portal and Dan and Charlie left behind and BOOM that is the low of lows. Or maybe she's not dragged into the portal, maybe she dies from the bite and THAT'S the low of lows. Jan's dead. Sorry Jan.

Only next scene she comes back to life as a Vamp hybrid with special powers now. Because of her own family history (which is what again, Acuff?! Do tell!).

So, yeah. Gonna get exciting over the next few pages again. Which means the rummaging through the storage can be a little slower and more explainer-y (which honestly we need some exposition here) because sh*t's about to get real at the scene's end. Kaboom.

That's the causality we need. If Jan puts the ring on that demands the very next scene be them racing to protect the orphans from the monster. And complicated by a HUGE CHRISTMAS PARTY and also IT'S A BRAND

NEW MONSTER THEY'VE NEVER FOUGHT. And then Jan gets bit and dies and the ring falls off. That to me reads like a page turner. And up until about 20 minutes ago I had NO FREAKIN CLUE that Jan was gonna steal the ring and put it on but it absolutely makes so much sense because it's exactly what her character needs to do to achieve her goal of finding Brodie.

Phew.

So glad it's Friday and I'm coming up on a weekend because I now wanna write my little brains out all weekend. Get me a 10K-15K word weekend.

What felt a little like writer's block and not knowing what came after the storage unit scene, only opened up to me once I got the characters further into the last scene. And then I hit my spine outline again to get my plot bearings and realized where we were on this sea of act 2 which helped dictate what needed to happen next.

Yowza.

Pantsing sure is like being a trapeze artist and letting go of one scene sometimes not knowing if the next scene is even gonna show up, but then it does at the right moment and the act continues. Send in the clowns!!

Oh and speaking of clowns which sounds like clones I'm not sure if I'm loving the Chrissinde/Jan clone/twin thing. It hasn't presented any story benefit yet of why they'd need to be anything other than sisters. Obviously in a movie, it's great for a single actress to play both roles but so far in the novel, Chris isn't a vastly necessary role. I'm specifically NOT bringing her into scenes because I don't want two of the same people there. So it's limiting. That may be something I crack in Draft #2.

Anyway, onward and upward.

Saturday, September 17, 2022
4:35pm // 21,702 Words

Dang it feels so good to finish that 1K word sprint by day's end. Actually 1200 y'day which isn't bad. That brought us to the 21,702 total. Then you roll over to the new day and new time limit and new sprint and that is exhausting. Like 13 days left of this? Which will put us around 34K words? Ugh.

I mean that's really the goal of sticking to it. Just to be further along on September 30 than I was on Sept 1. That's it. Anything else like finishing an entire first draft or whatever is just gravy.

As you see it's 4:35pm on a Saturday. My big writing day. What have I accomplished so far? Procrastinating. Big time. I do wonder what some of that ADHD medicine would be like that the kids are taking to increase longer periods of concentration. Or Joe Rogan's ONNIT haha.

But the only drug I'll allow myself is some caffeine. A coffee now and then to punch up.

While I was running this morning (mostly walking) listening to McKee's "Dialogue" I was thinking again about how you create a good writer. How do you coach someone to be a good, effective writer and how do you train yourself for the same? Yeah, there's books and YouTube and English classes and creative writing and stuff. For sure. And I'm a school fan. I think it shortcuts the learning process at least 10-fold with the right class and teacher. Versus just blindly thrashing about in life to figure stuff out the hard way.

But, again, I am so thankful for my military brat upbringing. Knowing and observing up close all kinds of people from all over the US. Living in the north. Living in the south. Big city school versus small town school. It was an 18 year graduate level course on human psychology and anthropology really. How do you teach that?! You can't teach lived experience. You can boil it down to bullet points but they won't have near the impact as it did on you living it out and arriving at an epiphany on your own. That just takes time. And much patience.

Also, on my writing days I do tend to start with this journal to prime the pump so to speak but I never add this word count into my day's target word count. That's cheating! Like currently this journal sits at around 10,139 words. That means that as I write a book called "Slay Bells Ring" and I journal about it, I am actually working on a companion book called "Slay Bells Ring: The Making Of" or whatever the series will be referred to as.

So I'm definitely putting a lot of words down on paper. And I don't count any other books I'm working on concurrently to add to my day's target word count. I could easily do 1000 words on one book one day and then 1000 on another book, but that's a much slower process. The goal is to drill down and power through and all those other industrial metaphors in order to get across that finish line faster. Wait, that's a sports metaphor! Too many metaphors!

It was fun to write that last sentence last night:

"We both looked sadly at Jan. She was exuberant. In her own world. We had just had our teeth kicked in and the clock was ticking til imminent death. We had to move and move fast."

It'll change of course but for now talk about a hook to get you to the next part! Actually that'd be a great chapter break but I don't know if I have the length in this chapter yet. I was going for 4K to 6K words per chapter. Roughly. But this does feel like a fantastic dramatic turbo boost.

Yeah, I just checked, Chapter Four is at 2848 words. That's a little anemic by this book's standards. Even if in revisions and editing it will easily push into 3K. Hmmm. To start a new chapter or not. My gut is "yes". Do it.

Here's where it stands so far.

CHAPTER INDEX

Chapter 1   5590
Chapter 2   7946
Chapter 3   5295
Chapter 4   2848

Daaaaaaaang Chapter 2! Runaway train much? Sheesh. I definitely have to refigure these Chapter breaks at some point. That's not a big deal and there's no rule of thumb about it to my knowledge. Just as the author sees fit. I've seen an author do a one page chapter. And then their next chapter was normal length. So it's just a personal guide for me in this book to shoot for 4k to 6K. Another novel I was doing like 2K to 3K per chapter.

Personally, for those of us that like to read in the bathroom it's nice when a single chapter lasts about 15 to 20 minutes long. That's a good length to, uh, you know do my business while I knock out a chapter. That's all I'm saying. Not like some of those books where my legs are falling asleep and 40 minutes have passed with no chapter ending in sight. You're killing me, JK Rowling!

All right! Enough procrastinating. It is now 5:10pm. It's almost time for dinner!! What have I done? I know exactly what I've done. I've now created an inner amount of self-pressure to finish a large chunk in a shorter amount of time. Pressure I didn't have nearly so strong at the start of the day at 9am. And this is how I hack my own productivity and psych myself up. Haha.

Saturday, September 17, 2022
10:10pm // 25,070 Words

Dang dudes. That was an intense chapter, Chapter 5. I was just gonna go straight to bed after and cry for Jan but decided to stop by here again for a wrap up. From 4:35p to 10:10p I got about 3300 words. And this chapter really was rolling off the tongue so to speak. It was coming pretty fast and furiously with some more surprises along the way.

Victor for one. I needed someone to bite Jan and it didn't make sense for the Wookalaar. So here we are in the middle of the book introducing a new evil villain. We think he's come from the portal. Whether he does or not is TBD.

And now he's on the loose and Jan's dead and Dan and Charlie are beat to shyte. This here is what you might call the low of lows. The all is lost moment.

So are we moving in to Act Three? That might be a little too fast, but we are where we are. 25K words here. We have about 10K to 15k to wind the story down in a blaze of glory.

Oh wait, I thought I was gonna write that last scene as the trailer scene and the scene that opens the book with Dan leaning against the basement door and something banging to get through it. There's still a chance that could be at the end of the movie. But it is nice to put it here now so that everything from the trailer has been seen and everything from here forward is a complete surprise. That's something to consider.

Thought it was interesting when Charlie makes the "head on a swivel" comment and Dan's making fun of her bc he's never heard that and thinks its dumb and she mentions working with the Navy SEALs. That's new and fun info if it sticks. She mentions a special ops unit within the SEALs that they work with for unorthodox missions. Unorthodox meaning "monsters" and "Not human" and stuff.

I need to sit and consider Act Three and how it should unfold and to what exciting conclusion. And where. But... we are getting closer. So close. Light at the end of the tunnel close. Stay tuned.

Sunday, September 18, 2022
1:07pm // 25,070 Words

Before I get to writing today, let me just say it has been a little fun sitting here on the couch and I have the big TV in front of me playing "Cozy Christmas Shop Jazz" and other coffee shops + Christmas music vibes. Not that it's helping me write these traumatic horror scenes, but it's helping keep me grounded with a constant "HEY DUMMY DON'T FORGET IT'S CHRISTMAS" reminder to myself.

The push-pull or yin-yang of that in an actual film is much easier to pull off. Walking through a dark scary basement with weapons drawn, breathing heavily while Christmas singing from a huge party upstairs bleeds through and permeates the air. That's just a fun dichotomy to play with. In writing it's a little harder to keep the pressure of the music reminders sustained through a fight scene for example.

Anyway, each medium has its benefits to spiral up the drama.

Now what I HATE about YouTube or any Music App is the constant commercial breaks. But like I'm going to pay for free music. Pssssht. What am I, a Rockefeller? Sorry, outdated reference. Let me try again. What am I, Jeff Bezos? There, much better.

Well…sigh…I guess it's time to start writing. Again, even with the major success of the deeply inspired word vomit yesterday, today is a new day and a brand new blank page to stare at. It's like my friend Shun Lee says when we go running: "every day is a new run". Yesterday may have been a strong and fast four mile scorcher and then two days later you're walking every 50 yards gulping for air.

Merry Christmas in September, people!!

1:20p. I'm back. Ugh. Re-reading where I left last night with the death of poor Jan. The gut wrenching aftermath is where I'm headed on today's blank page. And meanwhile on the TV is a peppy jazz version of "Jingle Bells, Jingle Bells, Jingle all the wayyyyyyyy…" haha. Again, you don't necessarily need sad music to write sad scenes. Sometimes you need the disconnect of music and words to put you in an all together new head space.

So, here goes nothing. Okay buh-bye again. 1:23p.

Oh, back again… don't forget you want to rename the cat CK Dexter Haven instead of Smeagol. Maybe. We'll see. Bye. 1:24p.

Sunday, September 18, 2022
5:08pm // 26,970 Words

Well, okeedoke. Just knocked out about 1900 words. It's a tricky scene because it's mostly dialogue. The whole purpose at this low of lows is for Charlie to get Dan off his pity party and put the ring on and acknowledge that Jan might still be alive. And it's all going down in his living room late at night after he gets home. I was going to have him drinking but then that seemed like an overdone cliche. Sad guy with dead girlfriend at his all time low drinks himself silly. May go back and add him TRYING to get a drink to give more action during the scene. More movement. We'll see.

Haha so currently Chapter 6 is 1,666 words. Coincidence? I think not. Won't stay like that but it was just funny where it landed.

I'll have to let it sit before I revisit. There was some Vampire lore I dropped in there that I'll have to weigh and see if it made sense and some other stuff about monsterology laws that may need to get finessed as well along the way. He finally puts on the ring and after this huge buildup nothing happens. I don't know why yet. That's a later problem. All I know is there was no big power quasar when he put the ring on. Not even when he held his arm up and said "By the power of Greyskull!" Which I would LOVE to see in the theater because that line would SLAY!!!

Haha.

I also thought of the line "To the Victor goes the spoils" which would have double meaning for our new villain Victor. But if that line was dropped in sometime way way earlier thn here at the low point when it resurfaces on the piece of paper or notecard or whatever then it has some gravitas to it. What he thought was an old family saying was really an old family warning.

My plot flashlight or plot light only shows me a little way into the next section where they run to get Jan and are all reunited but now she's a bloodsucking half-vampire or something. But after that, besides figuring out how to turn the ring back on, hey maybe with a kiss between Jan and Dan. That would be cool visually to have the power quasar at that big kiss moment. Hmmm.

Anyway, good job team. Good writing session today. I think when I finish this first draft I am gonna do a steak dinner at LaLa's. I deserve it. Can't afford it, but I deserve it. Ha.

7:34pm

Just ate dinner and watched "Leaving Las Vegas" and forced myself to endure it. Hollywood ex-screenwriter drinking himself to death falls in love with Karate Kid's first girlfriend (Elisabeth Shue) who is now a hooker in Vegas and they spiral down together and he dies. Hooray for happy endings.

Anyway, one thing about these books of mine I'm wondering, especially the sci fi and the film noir detective and the horror Christmas… do I actually have anything to say? That's the difference with so much other great literature or even great films is that they can be about the fun genre thing but there's a deep level and layer to them that entices the intellect while the whiz-bang wow genre fluff stuff eye candy keeps your attention moving forward.

So even though I made my word count for the day, I'm gonna dive back in and start at the beginning and just see what my themes could be. See what I'm trying to say with this thing. I know the obvious part about accepting your call in life to do big things. Beta professor to Monster slayer warrior come up. Glow up. Whatever. But what else? What am I saying about society? About the genre? About comedy? About satire? About who the real monsters and vampires are?

Or, alternate thought, maybe I'm just doomed to be the Ed Wood of meaningless genre fiction for Bravo Bay Books. And maybe I'll be completely cool with that, too, just as long as I make money off of it to live and write the next mindless genre fiction. So let it be written, so let it be done.

Tuesday, September 20, 2022
10:23pm // 28,666 Words

Didn't make my day yesterday, with only 300 words. But today I got on a roll with Dan and Charlie going down into the Morgue to get Jan and just word vomited everywhere. And I would keep going bc Jan's only just woken up but it's 10:30p and I gotta be up at 5:18 am to go run with Shun Lee.

But that's actually really good because I'm pretty clear on what happens next. Mostly. So it'll be easier to jump back into it.

I can't believe I'm almost at 30K words. That is very cool. Amazing progress. 1400 words today. Also a thing I didn't know until I was writing tonight was that other people were in the morgue where Jan is. Other dead people. They were just kind of set decoration mostly. But then one of their feet started twitching and it was Bubba and he was also a Victor victim. So that's fun. They get to have a little mentor/training/life lesson session right then and there. I can beef it up or increase the tension more but it's fun as it plays out. And with the Arnold call back. All good stuff. Dan professing his undying love and devotion to Jan as Bubba slowly rises in the background?

I mean!

Wednesday, September 21, 2022
7:39pm // 28,666 Words

So tired of writing. G'aw. Every day an endless expectation of 1000 words. Get home from work all tired and today's deadline is looming large. Even after I left myself in a good spot yesterday really in the middle of high action so I had very obvious threads to follow. Still, it's an incessant drum beat.

I did just find some fun YouTube music to play on the TV while I write since I'm tired of Christmas music for now. It's called "Lord of the Rings Gandalf's Fireworks in the shire" and it's video playing of the shire fireworks with LOTR hobbit-y music underneath. Fun.

Making great progress, mind you, but it's just… a lot. 1K daily is a lot. I've ended up taking some veg out days and making them up later, but I really do need structured days to not write. And it can't be Sunday because that's one of the few large chunks of "me time" I have is on Saturday and Sunday to catch up and write large sections like last weekend.

I know, I'm just complaining just to complain. Don't mind me. I'll get back to it very shortly. Just needed a breather. Everything is coming together magically well and I'm staying on task for 21 days straight now. And I'm much further along now than when I began this month. And I still don't know how it ends fully. I know Dan can't get his power back until Jan kills Victor. Then the legal vampire loophole is fulfilled. Then Dan can fight and kill his boss beast.

I had the idea today that Jan is mistaking Dan for Brodie and that causes problems in the story obviously how to resolve such a thing. Well, I had the idea today that Dan, during the battle climax, convinces Jan that Victor is Brodie. Because she's in the very angry Brodie left her phase. She's super mad at Brodie. So now that Victor represents Brodie she unleashes full fury on him to kill him. And then she can finally have a body in her hands and cry over the fact he's gone. Or something like that. Anyway, it's a transference that Dan helps facilitate which frees him up to be himself again. Crazy.

Sure would be great for Rawson Thurber to direct the feature with Ryan Reynolds in the lead. I know Rawson does his own writing/directing but maybe he'd be into a special Christmas movie like this one. Would be so freakin good. Sigh. Make it so number one!

Make it so.

9:10pm // 29,216 Words

Okay not a complete 1000 words, but brought us to a small time jump. Jan has just sunk her teeth into Dan and sucked out his "top shelf van Helsing blood like a caprisun" and then she got woozy and Dan faints to the floor. That's a good little chunk right there.

I might take it back about the LOTR fireworks music. Seems like there's only two or three hobbit songs that keep repeating and repeating for 2 hours. It's nice background noise and I def tuned it out as I wrote, but still, very repetitive.

Alright, beddy bye time. Chat you kids up later.

Thursday, September 22, 2022
7:04am // 29,216 Words

Brief morning writer's sprint after workout and before breakfast. Go.

7:43am // 29,719 Words

Okay, boys and girls. That's our time. Headed off to a big Paty's Diner breakfast and then to work. Just wrote their exit from the hospital where they run into Grubbs (changed later to Gerald) and Jan hits on him. She wants to eat him or suck his blood or whatever and he thinks she's flirting. Will massage it more later. I like Grubbs as the pentultimate redneck friend. May need to drop him in the story sooner. Play with his thick accent some.

Anyway, off to Freeform TV. Byeeeeeeee.

8:12pm // 30,780 Words

That's a pretty good chunk I got through today. Almost 2K words. Really helped to start off early morning in the middle of big action sequence. In this last part a dead body of Grubbs (poor Grubbs) falls onto the truck and that's the last straw for Dan and he's like "Charlie, how do we end this tonight?"

And here I am as the AUTHOR of the story also begging Charlie to tell me how I'm supposed to end this thing. Here's what I know: There's gotta be a big show down.

But where? The Orphan Home? Giant Church/Cathedral? Downtown area with lots of Christmas decorations? Ski mountain? What makes sense? What loose thread has been planted all along? Maybe back at the storage unit? Maybe.

But also gotta be a big showdown between Jan and Victor. Then that opens the door to power for Dan to defeat his nemesis. And what does Charlie get out of it? What did she need, not want, but secretly desire this whole time? Significance, right? Family? Union hours to keep her Slayer guild insurance? Haha. That'd be funny.

I do love the new idea of the Hunters Union. Or HuntU. Could be could t-shirts. Local 666. HuntU. Or something.

I haven't done a whole lot so far with the big Hallmark subplot so on 2nd draft I have to go back through and paint those in. The worried mayor afraid someone will bankrupt the whole town or whatever. Also, the other orphan siblings get lost and we never really see them again. Chrissinde is worthless as a character. Started out super strong and then disappeared because she was not a plot necessity. Need to beef her role up throughout the story or ditch her.

I also need to know what Victor *need* needs. If I play my cards right, I could be done with this whole draft by Sunday night. That'd be awesome. A week early. To 35K total. Ish. But I may need to take a day off to puzzle over this ending. Really lock it down before I wade into the blank space unknown that is the final chapter.

Friday, September 23, 2022
4:32pm // 30,780 Words

Haven't written anything more, yet. Still chewing on this ending. Where should the big battle take place? What are the stakes? Is it at the abandoned hospital? Is it at the equivalent of main street? Or at a ski lodge? Might be nice if there's bodies or damage all over the ground that it starts snowing magically at the end. So they know their tracks are gonna be covered AND they get a nice white Christmas.

The Orphanage battle previously was perfection. There's great dramatic stakes. The orphans and all the party go-ers upstairs. There's Christmas music pouring down as they fight. Festivities. And a boss battle downstairs and intro to Victor. All deliciously woven.

Also, if there's a Hallmark-y element of the town needing tourists and money so they don't go bankrupt then this battle has to somewhat solve that issue too. Maybe someone is trying to buy the abandoned hospital and turn it into something dumb like a Crypto mining ware-house like I saw on the news. So this is good that their battle kills that operation and squashes their plans to take over the space. But that's not holiday related.

Currently I've got the Cannon hospital as an active hospital where Jan is taken. So maybe there's more to it. Like the bodies are taken to the abandoned hospital instead of the regular morgue and that's what tips Charlie off. And so it's more of a top secret mission to break in and get the body of Jan. And then Grubbs would have to be rewritten some. Would definitely amp that scene up if they're trying to avoid creatures and monsters and Vamps on their way to find Jan. And get out again. Would make more sense too if Jan were dressed as Bride. And she'd have to do the whole last battle as the bride. Especially with the Brodie resolution.

That's the other conundrum I'm trying to resolve today. Once Jan comes back as a vamp with all these new powers, doesn't seem like she'd be in the same weakened mental state where she'd be pretending Dan is Brodie. But that stuff is so juicy it can't just go away. So have to layer that more organically so it resolves correctly.

I may not write anything today. Just keep noodling on all these things until the moon and the stars align and that glowing path illuminates before me. I don't need a lot to go on in this creative fog, but I do need a light house to aim at. One major plot point needs to come into focus before I launch out headlong.

Saturday, September 24, 2022
3:45pm // 30,958 Words

I did the tiniest bit of cleanup y'day just to get about 200 words more. Didn't break new ground on the blank page yet. Chapter 7. Kicking my ass, still. Still a fog. I've got so much time to write today—been procrastinating all day til now—that I'm gonna start at the top and read through it all and sand down more rough spots and see what I'm missing. There's a thread that's in there that I'm not seeing. A missing piece of the puzzle that I need to hone in on to nail the big finish. Just not seeing it yet beyond the obvious: "There needs to be a big fight."

Okay, got that.

Am I panicked. Oh, heck no. This is process, baby. Young David would have been panicked. Moved right on to another story to write on that and then come back to this one. But David's a pro now, people. A real pro. And a real pro can stare down the blank page like a hunter in a blind and wait out the mystery plot point he or she KNOWS is lurking out there. It's there and it's close.

The rest of the story I'm willing to go in half-baked on an idea just to get words down on paper to give myself something to respond to on pass two. It's easier to rewrite than to write. And easier to see where the story should have turned or twisted after you picked the wrong turn. So you write it sloppy, just to get words out and get out some sort of direction. Then go back and refine and fix and add the missing character you forgot or add a dialogue layer where the character is suddenly making this about something else all together.

But not the end. I may have one or two chapters left in the story. Perfect for a screenplay adaptation later. And I want to stick the landing. The first six chapters is about throwing all the characters up in the air and shaking up their lives. The final chapter they've got to land it. Same with the open, actually. It's a runway in a very specific direction your plane has to take off and then later land on another small, specific runway. Up in the air, you've got a whole lot of latitude up and down side to side, etc. Loop de loos and barrel rolls. Whatever. Beginnings and endings are different. More important. And here we are at the end. The instrument panel and data says we're near the airport. We've reduced speed and let down the gear.

Just haven't seen the damn runway yet.

So I'm switching over to the story now. Wish me godspeed. Remember any landing you walk away from is a good landing. That's what the pilots say, anyway.

7:15pm // 30,976 Words

Okay to catch you up I reread Chapter One. Spent a lot of time revising and finessing the open because that's the most important piece to grab attention. It was too ramble-y before so I streamlined it. Then went off to dinner across the street for a wagyu cheeseburger and sweet potato fries and a couple of ciders. Acuff burgers on Saturday night! Tradition!

Anyway the more I thought about the ending and how to mix Christmas in to the battle I kept coming back to the list of Banner Elk Christmas activities my sister, Nik, sent me. They do a Banner Elk Christmas Variety Show. That's the nugget I need to explore.

A challenge to the vampire. Bring in the orphans and chorale groups and all that as the town watches this battle take place on an outdoor stage. Somehow Dan was responsible for the show. So he's now trying to host a battle and tell a Christmas musical story all interwoven together. Somehow.

That seems like the way to land this thing. I've got some EMO YouTube songlist with Skylar Grey and Christina Perri and Renee Dominique. Usually use that list for my Devon Ayre PI script writing sessions but I was a little tired of Christmas music haha. Need more somberness. Seriousness.

Here we go, off into Chapter 7.

9:00pm // 31,366Words

Sike! Okay, really just finished up Chapter 6. Didn't break ground into the new chapter. Had to finish up their conversation in the car and let them all speak their intent to Entente (see what I did there?) before moving into Chapter 7. Tomorrow we'll Chapter 7! So eat, drink and be merry, because tomorrow we go to war!

Sunday, September 25, 2022
12:27pm // 31,366 Words

Sunday Funday. Gorgeous day outside today. Crystal clear blue skies. So of course here I am, settling in to take a whack at Chapter Seven. Fresh as a daisy. Had my French toast and coffee at BeaBea's with my buddy Bill.

Ready to go.

I saw a TikTok from a dude named @danwillisauthor giving one piece of writing advice he wished he'd gotten sooner. His authorly advice was to dig in for the long haul because it takes at least 10 years to make an overnight success. He's like "some of you are in year 4 or 5 with multiple books under your belt and no traction. Keep at it." And that was a great reminder. Because I am keeping at it and I'll *keep* keeping at it because my goal is to have this writing thing profitable as a viable income stream by the time I'm 60 (in 10 years). So I've got the long game in mind, but that doesn't mean the thousand little kicks in the nards along the way don't get to you. It's rough.

It's rough not being able to sell one dumb Sci-Fi short story to the magazines. It's rough not hearing back from agents and publishers. It's also rough hearing back and getting a "No" from agents and publishers. It's rough spending $2000 on a self-pub'd book to earn $75 back on it. It's rough when you don't rank in any writing contests that would improve your marketability. It's rough being the new kid. It smarts. I get it. I'm there right now.

But I am a firm FIRM firm believer that if you pay your dues and if you grind out enough blood sweat and tears that eventually it must pay off. It's only a matter of time. It's the barrier to entry that everyone worth their salt has had to pay. Everyone that's left any mark on the writing industry whatsoever has paid their entry dues. Nepo babies can kiss our ass, right? We're out here trail blazing like our lives depend on it.

The onus is not on the industry to discover me and craft me into an author. The onus is on me to be a better writer every day. To have a library of work finished and ready to go. Each one better than the last. Not "ideas" on napkins, not folders crammed full of articles and pictures inside a filing cabinet. No, it has to be actual finished novels. "Be so good they can't ignore you anymore," is ye ole adage.

I've got four finished novels on Amazon and this story will make number five. Meanwhile I've got five future novels currently in the works that are at least two or three chapters into the writing. And at least five more on top of that in the idea gathering phase. And twenty more beyond that which are just vague ideas on napkins like "what would a post-apocalyptic BREAKFAST CLUB movie look like?" Or "what if CONDORMAN had a sequel?"

Because I'm a writer. This is my life goal. I want to get one idea out the door and move on to the next. Also, because I'm behind! Not really, there's no time table, it's just that I felt like I should be further along in my professional writer career. Magically manifesting a career because up until now I've not planted, watered, or tended that garden in any comprehensible way. I've dabbled. But not pursued it as a real viable career. Not before five years ago on the novel side of things.

And straining ever forward into the discovery of what lies beyond the next blank page, heigh ho, heigh ho, it's off to write I go.

8:19pm // 32,404 Words

Okay good news and bad news.

Good news is I totally made my 1000 words for the day. Bad news is I still haven't started chapter seven. I was still working on smoothing out the end of chapter six with some fun powerful stuff in there. Just really love what's there now.

And I've outlined chapter 7. A beat outline with step-by-step guide to how it should unfold. I'll hit that again tomorrow but I finally FINALLY should be able to launch into chapter 7.

As I go through the dialogue again and again in these scenes I've got Robert McKee's book in my head, leaning over my shoulder judging whether my conversations are too on the nose, too basic, too expositional, too ordinary and plain, or too ineffective. Maybe. Hard to say at this point.

"It's probably good enough," says my favorite Greek philosopher Mediocrites.

A little disappointing coming out of my last weekend of September with all that free time and I essentially only got about 1500 words cranked out. But again, we knew this was not going to be easy. And I did spend a ton of time sitting and staring and thinking about the ending and how it should land. So it wasn't wasted time. It was work. Brain work.

Just wanted to have another 5K word weekend and, sadly, that wasn't possible. Friday is the 30th, by the way. So there's that. The end of the 30-day/1K word per day challenge approacheth.

Thank the lord!!!

Yesterday I also saw on twitter that there's a pitch contest on October 20th. I believe it's called #PitDark and is specifically a pitch festival online for horror/thriller log-lines. Hey! My story is a horror/thriller logline! So if I can finish the draft this week and then polish polish polish by Oct 20th then I can submit to these lit agents and see if anyone's interested.

But, back to the story, this novel so far has not lived up to the stated goals of being a good Hallmark movie spoof. That hasn't happened and may not happen in the overt way I had originally planned. It just is what it is. It's evolved into this comedy-horror story. And I'm very okay with that.

Another question I have about this novel will be writing it in first person past tense. That works fine for most of the story but parts of it where Dan is not actually present for but the story is being told—for instance at the end of Chapter one with Charlie finishing off her kill—sometimes I need to break into more of a third person past tense. Just tricky sometimes. I need to know if I'm supposed to be able to do that.

Also I write "He smiled" a lot and "She smiled" after a lot of dialogue instead of "He said/She Said." I've got people smiling like all the time. Need to finesse that more. Cut back on the "smiles" and even the "grins." We just get hung up on certain phrases a lot on first draft. Funny to root them out and deal with them for draft two polish.

Also ALSO this behind the scenes diary is now 16,269 words. That's almost a full book on its own. That's about the length of HISTORIANS PROPER my first (short) story that I novelized through Amazon KDP. I'll have to decide if I put the behind the scenes at the end or if I make it its own separate book for sale. Or release it as a blog.

So much more to do.

Also also also happy birthday today to my buddy Melissa Nunnally. Another lap around the sun, girl. Congrats.

Anyway, here for posterity is the outline for Chapter 7. We'll see how closely we adhere to it or veer dramatically away as the characters necessitate.

Or the humor…

CHAPTER 7 OUTLINE NOTES

App State Marching Mountaineers — Christmas Marching band awakens Victor in his orgy bed. He tells all his "pets" to stay because he can't do anything until sundown at 5:19p

He goes up to watch the marching band parade through the abandoned hospital and then out the other side. (Are they tracking something through like Garlic? Holy water in the sprinklers?) Band gone.

When does the hallelujah chorus begin?

Sees Jan in bridal dress. Words exchanged. She tries to explode his head. Doesn't work. Charlie tries to shoot out from under the dress. He catches it in his hand before it strikes his heart. Sun drops below horizon. His turn to strike. Whistles for "pets"

Dan pulls the "stop I have the ring" line which halts all the pets after him briefly he picks up the blanket and does the disappearing corner/doorframe trick. It works until they hear him running and crashing down the hallway.

Fight between Charlie and Jan and Victor. He's got the upper hand.

Dan gets to the emergency fire alarm and pulls it proudly. Nothing happens. He panics with all the pets on his tail there's a slo mo around the corner shot as he runs away in a panic. Finally he reaches another emergency fire and pulls it and the alarm goes off and the sprinkler system douses everything.

In the Victor fight, his smokiness/apparition power can't work in the holy water. He can't cloud up and it's burning him like acid.

In the hallway the vampires all burn up and explode in neon colors. But not the wookalaars. Dan runs through a large wooden door and pulls it closed behind him. The wookalaars pound against the door, rattling it on its hinges. This is the scene from the open of the book. All is lost for him.

The girls, now, with an edge are doing better against Victor. Something happens, Charlie loses the cross pendant. Makes her vulnerable. Victor hypnotizes Charlie. Makes her fight Jan while he tries to escape. Jan tries to fight without hurting her but can't win that way. Charlie's too good. Finally Jan clouds up in a desperate attempt. And Charlie goes flying. Jan grabs Victor in a hug and kisses him. Charlie goes to shoot a stake into Jan but Jan clouds up at the last second and the stake goes into Victor. And then Victor explodes. Dusted. Charlie's red eyes return to normal. Jan's tattoo on her wrist disappears (the one from the Victor claim).

Downstairs, Dan suddenly gets the full power of the ring. Uses the Greyskull line again. Pulls the swords from his back or wherever and has a singularly bad ass fight with the remaining wookalaars.

What happens to the Choir singers? Does a wookalaar come after them and that's when Charlie slides and does her thing to kill it in mid leap?

Epilogue; they're all in the mayors office watching the video of the scary ghost hospital fundraiser video. They're all beat to sh*t and have arms bandaged etc. The go fund me has already raised $2M. All is right with the world. And it's beginning to snow.

And the portal is dead. Charlie finds. Maybe its smashed when Helsing steps to power.

— what about the orphans we haven't seen them in ages

— what about Chrissinde? Need to rewrite if she doesn't have a role

—what about Jan's museum job and past police failure? Where does that come into play?

—need more "save the town" hype or talk about some company (a crypto company?) coming in to use the abandoned building for mining but its so loud. And that's what is destroyed?

That, in general, is where we're headed.

Monday, September 26, 2022
11:42am // 32,404 Words

I was out for my morning run about 6am. 3x a week I run a dusty old park in NoHo with Shun Lee. I was thinking about this story and especially the big finish and got goosebumps TWICE. While I was running! *Goosebumps.*

What?!

The first time I was thinking about Dan getting a call from the Blue Cross Blue Shield interview lady in the middle of the marching band turn up. So he's gotta shush everyone and so he can take his important phone call. But meanwhile it's getting closer to 5:19pm which is sundown so he's putting lives at stake if the band stays there not moving. Plus, I think the goosebumps part was when I figured out Victor is there HELPING HIM OUT with the interview answers. Why? I dunno, because he has sworn to make Dan's life a living hell so he knows if he gets him this corporate cubicle job he'll be stuck in a fresh hell the rest of his days. Plus, then he won't be out on the street trying to stop Victor's shenanigans. Win-win for Victor.

Second goosebump flare-up was half way through the battle royale, Charlie remembers an obscure reference that says if Jan and he marry then the ring power returns. So over walkie talkies Charlie is doing a wedding between the two and signing up online to be an officiant. And at the end with the "I do's" nothing happens. Because there's no *kiss*. Dan has to get upstairs to kiss Jan. That's when he pulls the sprinklers sending down the holy water and confusing the enemy giving him time to get up there for the big smooch in the rain like some frikkin' scene out of "The Notebook."

Then they can kick Victor's butt with their new combined powers of Greyskull, haha.

Also a funny after credits scene would be the crow coming back with a new (way too late) message: "Banner Elk Slayer. Stop. Victor Von Lichtenstein is alive and very powerful. Stop. Stop what you're doing and leave town. Stop. He will kill you. Stop."

So this will leave Dan and Jan married by the end of the book. Somewhat implausibly but it kinda works. And Charlie can have a line about Vampire time. So that even though Jan lost Brodie, in her new vampire time she processes things very, very fast. So it's been 4 days or whatever but like 3 years in her mind. Or something crazy like that. We'll see. At least this fulfills the "Rise of Dan and Jan Helsing" promise from the cover. (Editor: which I changed to "Rise of the Banner Elk Slayer" because the other was way too spoiler-y)

Also I think Sister Margarite has been Charlie's mentor and trainer this whole time. Like she's known about the basement stuff. All part of her long long history. Maybe she really is 127 years old. Has she been training any of the other kids? Would they show up in the end to help fight? That seems a wee bit over the top. Haha right, Acuff, like everything else has been a study in understatement. Ha.

So that's the gist. Take the notes from yesterday and add in the moments from this morning's brainstorm/jogging sesh. And badda boom badda bing. Bob's your uncle.

Tuesday, September 27, 2022
3:25pm // 33,362 Words

Finally I've cracked into the vast nothingness that is Chapter 7. It's slow going but I mostly got my 1000 words yesterday. Unfortunately for my writing progress I was hanging out with Shun Lee y'day for dinner for a Cowboys game down at the Thirsty Merchant. And tonight he's got passes for the new David O. Russell movie "Amsterdam" at El Capitan Theater downtown.

Haha, tsk tsk tsk.

There's a lot about the end of Chapter 6 that I really love. Kind of a breaking point for the first time with Charlie. Where she comes clean about not wanting to be in Banner Elk or babysit Dan. And some great fireworks between Jan and Charlie while Dan is out parlaying with Victor for the Entente.

I'm having to learn as I write about Jan's vampire condition. It's new to all of us so we're learning together. But she obviously has vampire battle mode or "dark mode" and then her other flirty-spice glow-y phase to lure people in. And then somewhere in there is still just regular Jan. The girl with the broken heart trying to move on. Vampire mode helps me solve some problems story-wise though so I think all of this is coming together as it needs to.

Wednesday, September 28, 2022
9:04am // 33,932 Words

Chipping away at Chapter 7. Actually, not that you asked, Shun Lee and I went to a SAG screening of "Amsterdam" at the El Capitan theater so left work at 5pm and dragged home after 10p. Three days left to land this thing!

Doable.

And obviously as a fly-by-the-seat-of-my-pantser I already have 10 different things to go back and fix in the earlier chapters to set this last chapter up better. Smooth out the train tracks as it were so the plot unfolds more intentionally instead of suddenly in the last chapter, even though they said nobody can know about the monsters, the whole town is in on this big climactic battle event. It'll make much more sense in future passes. Like a scene with the mayor where he's bemoaning the Cannon Memorial Hospital and how it's sucking the town dry. Ha. I see what I did there.

And obviously playing up the Hallmark moments if that's going to continue to be a thing I'm aiming for. Or make it even broader and sprinkle in a lot more of all the Christmas movie tropes. That would be fun, too.

But first to get through the big bang finish.

Also I think I want to see if I can overlay Dante's nine circles of hell atop this story which would require breaking it down better into 9 total chapters instead of the 7 it's at currently. Which means that all my previous behind the scenes notes about particular chapters will either have to be tweaked or they won't reference the correct thing from your point of view. That might be okay since I mention chapters and then also what's going on in the scene so there's two ways to track the reference.

Back to 7. Or 9. Or 7 of 9. Rawr! Jeri Ryan! Insert Fire Emoji.

Wednesday, September 28, 2022
3:20pm // 35,860 Words

Another good chunk knocked out. Another pause to figure out logistics. How does Victor get upstairs to battle Jan? How does Dan get downstairs trapped by beasts? How does Charlie get away from Wookalaars to get upstairs and help Jan and facilitate the wedding/walkie talkie bit? Once the marching band leaves is there a gospel choir singing Hallelujah Chorus? How does that work? It looks cool but why endanger them like that?

So some issues at hand.

Dan's just got off the phone with the BCBS interview. Wookalaars are spreading out getting ready to go on attack. Tension is building building building.

Now fight!

Somehow.

Obviously reached my word count for the day, so any thing extra now is gravy. I'll have to calculate tonight and see if I'm still on track for the 30K for the month goal. Maybe so. I think I'm at a total of 28,232 words since starting this on Sept 2nd. So haha I am right on the money penny.

I need to query my brother-in-law—who this Dan character is LOOSELY based on—so that he can tell me about his BCBS interview so I can be a little more faithful to the original material. Got a little bit of back and forth with Victor that will be humorous to see played out. And cutting away to check on all the other members is good so that time passes before we get back so the bit doesn't carry on too long.

It's a mess is what I'm saying. It's kinda working but its a mess in this first draft. Here's where we stand with chapters:

Chapter 1	5651
Chapter 2	8182
Chapter 3	5312
Chapter 4	2966
Chapter 5	3674
Chapter 6	6991

Chapter 7   3061

So there's that. Chapter 2 and 6 seem to be the huge hogs that I'll have to look at when I'm revising the big second draft. And what's up Chapter 4? Pull your weight, dude!! C'mon! You look anemic.

Thursday, September 29, 2022
4:20pm // 38,176 Words

I may write some more once I get home tonight since I'm on a roll with this last chapter and things are steamrollering into a crazy cacophony of controlled chaos.

Also I needed another Helsing weapon so I googled Christian gemstones and found this:

> "There are also twelve gemstones listed in Revelation, Chapter 21. Despite the confusion surrounding the various names and translations of them, many believe that the gems listed in Revelation, Chapter 21 are the same twelve sacred gemstones from the Mountain of God, "The Stones of Fire", that were in Aaron's BreastPlate of Judgement.
>
> The twelve sacred gemstones of Revelations are Jasper, Sapphire, Chalcedony, Emerald, Sardonyx, Sardius, Chrysolite, Beryl, Topaz, Chrysoprasus, Jacinth, and Amethyst."

So twelve gemstones on twelve staffs becomes exactly what I need for a circle of protection around the marching band. Who should that line be? Oh, well remember that choir I was trying to figure out how to work them back inside? Now I've got it. There's 36 of them all together. All singing in robes. Every group of three has the staff and torch and a stone on it. So they'll walk towards the haunted hospital, kill off a couple rogue wookalaars who tried to pass the barrier and slowly draw in a circle in the hospital, a fire circle for the big final showdown. Now you've got flames and fire and a circle of magic protection where Jan and Victor have to finally duke it out with Dan's help once he gets his ring working again after the marriage.

Phew. I'm telling you. A lot going on in this grande finale. Throwing everything in there plus the kitchen sink.

I do have to take a moment to pat myself on the back because I have just crossed over the 30K words in a month goal line. Even though I need about 3K-5K more to finish the novel, I have at least accomplished this goal. So well done, me!

And thank you Jesus for helping me keep on track along the way. Because there have been other times I've started the NaNoWriMo 50K word challenge and not even made it two days and quit. So this is good. The Christmas Horror Comedy anointing is upon me! Ha.

Anyway, I'm way further down the road on this whole story. It all makes sense and by EOD tomorrow I'll have the end of first draft. Then I can go back and fix all the rough stuff along the way and smooth out the arcs. Who knows. Maybe late November this thing will get out there. Rush rush rush!

Ohhhhh you know what I deserve for finishing? I deserve a Cadillac margarita! Oohhhh yeah! Haven't done Don Cuco's in a month now. May be how I celebrate tonight's achievement. Via con Dios, amigos!

Friday, September 30, 2022
9:06am // 38,176 Words

Almost didn't get my Cadillac Margarita last night to celebrate. I did the dumbest thing you can do which is check your bank balance to see if there's money. D'oh. And the fact that rent is due tomorrow and that I'm not as liquid as I'd like to be right now—*BUY MY BOOKS PEOPLE*—and so I was gonna nix it and throw a pity party instead. Like a last meal on a Pirate ship: "Here's a crust of bread and some mustard. Eat and drink up me hearties, for tomorrow we perish in a cruel and unusual death." But then I decided to step out on faith, throw caution to the wind and do it anyway.

Anyway, this isn't a financial blog! I'm not GaryV! This is a *writing* journal. So I used my credit card. Sorry, Dave Ramsey!

Meanwhile, today I need to wrap out this first draft and put 'er to bed. So I'm on my way to begin that now. Again, anyone who has ever chopped down a huge tree or seen it done knows you don't do it in one fell swoop unless you're Superman. Otherwise, you have to chip away at it a little bit at a time. That's what I've done this whole month. Chipped away consistently .

Today the tree falls. The story is mine. And tomorrow we begin shaping the tree, the raw material into the final work of art it intends to be. Like a beautiful story canoe!

Saturday, October 1, 2022
6:39pm // 40,929 Words

"The End."

Those are the words I just typed. That last chapter is a mess. And there's a plethora of story points I had wanted to hit but didn't so I have to go decide on draft 2 if I'm going to add them in or if they don't matter anymore. As much as it felt good to type, I know there's still so much work involved to rewrite. And maybe I'm feeling it wasn't quite as satisfying as I'd hoped originally when I thought up specific scenes.

So lots to rework.

I mean there have been multiple times when I've finished writing along the way and thought about how much I loved what I'd just written. And that's common. Even if the next day in a new light it all looks like garbage. Ha. At least while the ink is still wet it seems like genius verbiage written in the language of the gods.

But this last few pages feels like it's lacking. And it is. In my notes and outline plans the Victor battle was gonna be so huge. And Jan was gonna have to kill Victor so that Dan could get his power of the ring back. Then Dan would have to kill all the wookalaars and lesser vampires. Once I decided the wedding/kiss angle to bring back the ring power then that changed things up.

And plus we're waiting all this time for him to get his ring and it doesn't really do anything. I'll have to think through that. I mean he's not suddenly gonna turn into Green Lantern but it does seem to need something.

See? This is why you let things simmer on the back burner for a while after you write a draft. Let it settle a bit. Then get back to it with fresh eyes to make all the changes and approach it with new vim and vigor.

Also on my morning treadmill walk I listened to Dean Koontz's "Frankenstein: Prodigal Son." And guys his description is so good. Paints the perfect succinct picture and the most unique characterizations. It's perfect. So then I go back to MY STUFF and I'm like, "Meh." So that's part of my current problem too. That I'm apparently not a world class writer.

Yet.

But for now: Victory. Goal is met. September sprint was a success. Whew. Rent paid. Haha. By the hair of my chinny chin chin. May not eat for a week til next paycheck but for now, bills are paid. Phew.

Sunday, October 2, 2022
2:35pm // 40,929 Words

Haha, guys, Chapter 7 is 8130 words. And Chapter 2 is 8182. That's outrageously long for me! Where's the Chapter police? This is unacceptable. And meanwhile this Dean Koontz "Frankenstein" audiobook I'm listening to has a new chapter every two minutes. Are his chapters like a paragraph long? Now I'm interested to hold his book in my hands. That's the downside of audio books when you're a visual learner.

Meanwhile, my sister in Boone, NC was texting me this morning pictures of the Banner Elk Cafe where she and hubby, John, are brunching today for "research" purposes only, haha!

The cat's name there is "Gandolfini the Grey" so that's pretty perfect (and serendipitous) considering my Tony Soprano reference in Chapter One. So, if there's a cat here, will I have to change Dan's fuzzy little plus one at his house to, I dunno, a three legged raccoon? That'd be fun and mountain-ous. Pet raccoon named CK Dexter Haven.

Also instead of having a Bar with Chrissinde and then a separate breakfast place I made up called "Toot n Tell", in the book as it currently is, I will combine it all into one location. Makes great sense because the real Banner Elk Café does breakfast, lunch and dinner *and* has a bar *and* has a pastry case with all the latest yummies in it. It's name is simple: Banner Elk Cafe so that's less folksy than I'd like but not horrible. And very on brand.

And apparently locals just call their town B.E. for short. All good knowledge! Good location scouting, Nik! Haha.

I will poll my sister a la Mad Libs for 1) A name of a server she loves and 2) A name of someone she loathes to the core that we can fictionally eviscerate and 3) A town doofus etc. Because literature should be about showering affection on those we love… even indirectly… and skewering the real life villains. Obviously not recommending you use people's real first and last names in your fiction. However, if the guy in my story who I called a "Duck Dynasty looking fella" can have a real first name? That's just good poignant writing.

And when readers go to B.E. and eat at this fine establishment and get to meet Gandolfini the Grey it makes it all that more rich of a reading experience. And that's how

I write. I start with maybe a cliché sketch of a person like the town mayor. Then on future drafts I try to overlay them with a real person with real habits and choices and expressions. Maybe even real life events that fit into the scene. Like the cat who stands on the ground with front paws on the window sill watching outside is a very real event I've witnessed. So Dan's cat gets that quirk. Along with the chirrup sound it makes instead of a real cat's meow.

It'll be fun to visit B.E. this winter while I'm home for Christmas break. Obviously I'm trying to get the book out before then, but we'll see. And the reason for that is I want SLAY BELLS RING to get out there into Ryan Reynolds' grubby little Canadian paws so he can green light it and make it for NEXT Christmas. Because obviously movies are written, green lit and put into the pipeline in less than a 12 month turnaround all the time. Right? RIGHT?!

Narrator Ron Howard: In fact, they did not. David was smoking HOPE-ium.

Shut up, Ron! Respectfully. Haha. You dream squasher.

Also I looked up some fun Romanian sayings/expressions so I could try to sprinkle some in for Victor and even Jan after her draculization.

Like:

> "Threw his boogers in the beans" meaning "screwed up"
> "Throw vapors at you" meaning "try to fool you"
> "Rub on a wooden leg" meaning "useless"

Stuff like that. Those are some solid metaphors. Other than some expressions like that and making his speech a little more formal, I haven't done any kind of accents in the dialogue for Victor other than to mention it is a Euro-chic accent. Only Gerald the good ol' boy's extreme southern dialect and Dominic's lisp are worked into conversations. I may even scale those back a little for readability.

So what do I have to fix. Well a lot of things. Thank you for asking. But for starters, Chrissinde the twin sister is maybe seen a couple times in Chapter one and two I think and then gone forever. Has no bearing on the story whatsoever. Especially the twin thing was a loose end that never gets utilized so its more of a waste. So that's a thing I need to decide on and change.

And in the last chapter this whole idea of saving the haunted hospital as a goal the town needed to Go-FundMe as a big Christmas charity thing needs to be back-filled into the story. We never dealt with the police following up with Brodie's disappearance. Or the Air-BNB fire at the Glass Treehouse. Other deaths are better explained away because the people are dusted so there's less to go on. MIA. Police wouldn't think there's a huge serial killer incident happening if people are just missing versus if dead bodies were stacking up all over the place.

The choir with the fire sticks have no job or point whatsoever beyond dusting a few wookalaars when I conveniently needed those things to disappear. I had wanted them singing inside the hospital holding their flames, but that's difficult to pull off with sprinklers dousing everything in there.

The drones at the top of the chapter disappear never to be heard from again. Need to keep the pressure on to have them in more scenes. The nun and Dominic go away for a good while and kill some creatures off screen but that's not too terrible.

And of course the Brody-ness of it all. Jan never grieves or works through all the stages of grief and just seems to flip over to loving Dan all of a sudden. Need to plot that out better. Currently Jan and Brody are hopelessly in love when we see them. May need to dial that back so there's more contentiousness to their relationship so it's on the rocks and not full honeymoon phase. Something as small as that could help the reader imprint on to them differently than they do currently. Now it's as if she's found her soulmate and then he's gone. That's gonna wreck some people and require a lot more emotional triage along the way. But if it's more obvious that he's not the one and the relationship is a ticking time bomb and she only just met him or something then the audience is actually happier when he gets his face eaten off and she moves on to Dan.

There was a lot of good Dan v Charlie stuff in the beginning that I loved. I want to make sure I maintain that animosity even though it intentionally arcs towards a quirky partnership. Like, he has new respect for her when he finds out she's been defending them all and keeping him alive. And he hugs her. That's new for them. And I loved when Jan says Charlie likes him and Charlie goes off on her. Just need to make sure I land that relationship right at the end.

See? Lots to fix.

And of course reconcile all the notes I'd made before writing. Like I really loved the scene of Jan getting pulled into the portal and them having to go after her. But part of that felt too "Stranger Things Season 4" and upside down-ish so I shied away. Then, I didn't know Jan was going to be bitten and "die" for a hot minute. So that threw her trajectory off.

Maybe if they just dipped into it briefly during the Sylvanian Christmas party battle. Just enough to see that it's not an upside down but actual 15th century underworld. Or whatever it is. Just a glimpse to stoke the fires and imagination.

Monday, October 3, 2022

1:01pm // 41,244 Words

Chipping away at Chapter One again today. Changed Chrissinde's nickname to Sinde from Chris. Changed Jan into her former roommate instead of twin sister. Basically Sinde just got downgraded because there was no plot reason that motivated the twins thing or even the sisters thing. That just complicated things more, in fact.

Also since the Hunter's moon is generally in October then I may have that be the start of these wookalaars coming through the portal. In the last draft they've been coming through and Charlie's been fighting them for a year. So now if it's almost Christmas and the portal has been open since October then it makes sense that Charlie could have fought 14 of those things. And killed them. Trophies. Also I made it so that when they're playing games in the basement and Dan wants to get them upstairs that he uses a trick he heard Sister Marguerite use. The wookalaars come out at 10pm trick. He doesn't know they actually exist at this point. He thinks they're just scaring the kids straight. But we'll know that the orphans know more about life in that house and potential death in that house because the nun is training them. Anyway, that fixes things I didn't even know needed fixing.

I changed the bar to the B.E. Cafe. And I still have to add the cat in. Maybe to the top of the scene.

On Saturday, as you read, I seemed a little down on the last novel chapter, currently Chapter 7. But re-reading it yesterday it wasn't the disaster I first thought it was and in fact reads very well. And works. When I was seeing a disaster I'm coming from a design point of view and factoring in early EARLY intentions I had for that scene that didn't pan out for one reason or another. But don't conflate "different" with "bad" which I was doing initially. I had to let go of some alternate ending expectations. So I thought I'd explain that a little better.

Plus, I think it was a mistake for me to celebrate on Thursday night because I'd officially completed the 30K word count. Friday I wrote almost nothing and I was so close to the end. So Saturday I finished 2700 words or so and then there wasn't as much to celebrate since I'd prematurely done so two days before.

So, lots of things swirling about on Saturday. I had just paid a huge amount of rent and was not looking forward to the next 5 days of eating ramen only until I got paid again. Haha. Play that sad violin music for me please. All these things are ancillary writerly things we all have to deal with. Life. We don't just wrestle with the words and our characters and their motivations. We wrestle with our own lives and creating space for our writing and the characters in our lives and our *own* freakin motivations. It's tricky. Or it can be.

Now as I move into Chapter Two with its 8K+ words I need to stay on the lookout for how to break that into two different chapters.

2:20pm // 41,263 Words

Okay I've split Chapter 2 after the Santa handing out gift bags after school section and before Dan gets picked up for the date with Jan and Brodie. That's now Chapter 3.

Too, what I'm refining is dialogue and jokes. I want this thing snappy. There's gotta be a laugh in every paragraph, or at least a punchline. A guffaw or a teehee. I'm not picky. The other part of what I feel like I lost in the later chapters is the comedy riffing in the narration. But some of that is warranted because it's the big scary climax of the book. Lives are at stake and there's some serious moments happening.

What did Chaplin say? To end with a tear, start with a laugh?

Maybe that's what I'm doing. Anyway Chapter 7 is now Chapter 8. And I have a feeling I'll split it, too, to get my final Dante's Inferno nine rings of hell corollary. Not that they line up in any way to what his chapters were about, but at least I'll get my nine chapters and an epilogue.

3:45pm // 41,263 Words

And I just chopped chapter 8 into 8 and 9. Right after Charlie gets the idea they need to do a wedding. Also it's like 2 minutes before sundown so the battle is about to shift in a big way. It's not really a whole new chapter thematically or requiring a time shift of any sort. I just didn't like an 8K word behemoth mountain for the reader to climb. This will be a page turner, I suspect. And that is the first goal at the end of every chapter is to propel the audience forward with curiosity as to what comes next.

Like, end of Chapter one is perfect. We find out about Charlie and her basement killing adventure and it's suddenly a whole new book. Game on! Turn that freakin page and get to Chapter 2. That's something I'll have to make sure of at each chapter's end. Must propel. Just like we say the end of Act I or the first 20 to 30 pp of a screenplay something huge has to propel the main character into Act II. A choice. Eliot says he's keeping ET. Matt Damon wakes up alone on Mars and decides he wants to live. Luke says he wants to go with ObiWan to Alderaan and learn the ways of the Force.

The point is a big moment that launches the plot into act two. Same at the end of Act two into three. But here with chapters we have to spice up the chapter ending enough so that they want to flip to next section. So at the end of Act 2 I need to put a line like "What I wanted to do was go to the Cafe and have a margarita. But I had to get ready for the worst double date ever." I mean, not that but something along those lines and more clever.

And now in Chapter 9 I need to come back in with "It was a minute and a half until Sunset. We all braced ourselves for what was about to come our way." That sorta thing. Recap and then pick right back up with where I left off.

Friday, October 7, 2022
12:36pm // 41,410 Words

Haven't done too much with the story this week but I HAVE been tweaking on the cover design. I got inspired so I had to put some ideas down on paper. This will be a much more simple cover than BATTLE TIDES and HISTORIANS PROPER and all the others, actually. I mean, my memoir was pretty simple, too. Just a glam shot of me on the Oscars red carpet. This one started with the idea of like a Christmas gift-wrapped book sitting on your bedside table like a present. And evolved from there.

Messed with some different wrapping paper designs but stuff was just so busy it competed with all the verbiage in the title. Then I thought of that gold foil lettering that looks so Christmas-y and that was perfection and adding in a torn red swipe was more perfection. Looks like a real cover now and hints at all the things I want hinted at. Helsing + Christmas + killer creature.

I was going to do the torn white swipe behind the title. And was working in that direction but when I flashed through the overlay settings in Photoshop it reverted back to its original red color and I was like, "Intriguing" because it matched the blood at the bottom of the page which was, pardon my French, pretty bloody perfect.

I also reached out to my good pal Joe Wilson back in NC. Editor and graphics genius and horror enthusiast. So I told him I wanted him to read the story next week when I had it in better shape (still filling plot holes and tying up narrative loose ends). And would like for him to take a crack at the PSD file that is the cover once he reads it.

Guys, Joe is amazing. I sent him my trailer cut for "Historians Proper" and he grunged the hell out of it and added some out of focus racks and some audio nastiness and skips which was all perfect! Juuuuuust perfect. I worked with Joe for years at Trailblazer Studios watching him do great and wonderful things with all manner of video project and short films. And then he went on to Epic games where he cuts trailers and such there in RTP. He's by far the best thing Sanford, NC ever pooped out onto this planet, haha.

The goal by next weekend is to have a draft #2 that I can send to my sister and her husband in Boone, NC so I can get the in-person, birds-eye mountain life Banner Elk insider scoop. I'll sent it to Betty Anne's husband Scott since he's like a good piece of the main character in real life. Minus the vampires and wookalaars. Well, I take that back, they've got three kids under 10 years old so that can be like living with wookalaars when they're all hungry and tired and cranky.

Then, based on their feedback I'd like to have this thing ready for Twitter's #PitDark on October 20th. Zoinks, like whoa, Scoob that's only 13 days away! Ruh-roh.

Exactly.

I won't have all the feedback in from my "Beta Readers" but I'll have enough to hook a Lit Agent's interest. That I feel fairly certain of. I'll have to spend time polishing the logline, too.

That's my plan. Today at Disney is a "refresh day" which is a rando day off they've given us just because life is hard? I dunno, I'll take it! So I'll be spending the next three days writing. Unlike before I don't expect to come away with huge advances in the word count. I do feel like there's one or two scenes I need to add in, but for the most part it's paring the story and verbiage down to a concise and crisp narrative patter. Clean dialogue and descriptions that just bite into your soul through your eyeballs. Good stuff like that.

I made it through the last week on ramen noodles and scrambled eggs. Not together, mind you. Eggs and bagels for Bfast and noodles for dinner. Yesterday I was pretty much out of soups and breakfast things but I had a free Chik-fil-a chicken biscuit offer on my app and as I looked through my accrued points I was able to get the biscuit, hash rounds and Sunjoy tea for breakfast and then I stopped back for dinner and used up my remaining 800 points on a deluxe chicken sandwich.

Oh, man, so good. Very yum! Such a Godsend. And free refills on that Arnold Palmer… I was in heaven. Why am I telling you this whole sob story? I dunno. But I've got to work really hard to balance out my personal finances and eating out and giving so that I'm not in the same position next 1st of the month.

Again, you play stupid games, you win stupid prizes. You spend all yo cash eating out and high rent apartment and fancy car? Welp, it ain't good. It means you get to skip some meals when it's time to Pay the Piper. So be a smart saver and not an egg-nah-ray-moose money pit like me! And cut to "The more you know" NBC logo and theme.

Saturday, October 8, 2022
5:34pm // 43,305 Words

Just finished another pass on the whole story. A lot of cleanup. I think I still need to add into the final scene instead of a GoFundMe video that they have to go make, that this thing is live on the site and money is coming in hand over fist. And maybe just Obi-Juan is flying the drone and Juan is tracking the site stats.

Also probably needs a final moment with the Mayor. The revamp project (ah ah ah) is funded at $2M or whatever. But he's got to agree to use the money for ________ . A math wing? A museum? What would the best use of the new building be? Or save that for the sequel surprise?

But the story is so close I want to just send it off to Joe Wilson now. I'll wait til EOD tomorrow because I definitely want to go through that last chapter again. It's been revised the least throughout this whole process as always happens. So it needs to be gone over a bunch more to make sure everything is wrapped up as awesomely as possible.

Also, the only non-satisfactory thing is that once Dan puts on the ring and kisses Jan and is imbued with power, he doesn't have to accomplish anything. Charlie stabs Vic and the movie is done. Roll credits. Earlier outlines had it so that Jan needed to kill Vic so Dan could get the power to kill the monster boss Wookalaar.

Ohhhh, what if the ring of power is used on the last wookalaar and he actually transforms it into a human. Like it turns out wookalaars are actually more like werewolves. By the power of Greyskull, haha, it transforms back to its human form and it's dum dum tadahhhhhh... Brodie!

That's kind of interesting. Jan's happy to see him but she's married now. I'll have to chew on that possibility. Here she is, then, with her fiancé *and* her husband. Haha.

We're running about 183 pages. That's about 200pp with all the front matter and other stuff in there. Again, unless

I want to tack this BTS journal on the back. But why do that when it can be it's own thing? (Edit: Insert side-eye emoji. Ha.)

Sunday, October 9, 2022
8:25am // 43,305 Words

Just chilling out in Aroma Coffee & Tea on Tujunga, guys. Already Tiktok'd an IG reel in the lobby with the pastries and did a mini-photo shoot with my Chilaquiles for the 'gram. So now I'm diving back in to the final Chapter for another brush over. See what we can see. Maybe a new and active location will cause ideas to pop off in new and wonderful ways. Remember, the thing about routine is that you can't keep putting in the same input variables and expect different results each time.

Routine is vital. Supremely necessary. It's how we get anything done. But once in a while take your story for a walk. Go sit in a park or on a boat or in the corner of a cafe in London. And let new sights and sounds and smells invigorate you and inform your story. Gotta get outta that she-shed from time to time. Out of the man cave. The writing corner.

Also, total non-sequitur here, I've got a goofy IG Reel of me dancing to classical music that's blowing up over the past week. Especially in the last three days. Up to 500K views and 50K likes. Great. Whatever. I'm adding visibility and about 150 new followers. All good especially if it keeps going. But... even now as I type, my phone is over there on the chair buzzing and lighting up every 90 seconds with a new IG notification. That constant interruption DESTROYS focus.

To me there's a very distinct difference between the analog stimuli of sitting in a cafe with people walking by and conversations happening and dishes clinking... all of that works on one level. An acceptable level engaging the lower function brain with base auditory and visual stimulus. That's good. As opposed to digital stimuli which would be my phone freakin buzzing off the rails. Or sometimes if there's another diner in the room having a conversation on speakerphone. That digital high-pitched scratchy loud conversation is very different from even two people speaking loudly in regular tones IRL.

Analog vs Digital. Somebody do a study and get back with me on results. It's real. Now, high pitched screaming toddlers? That can be real or digital and drive you nuts. I can put on my "dad ears" which all parents learn to do over time to ignore levels of whining and screeching. It's a life saving evolutionary tool. Saves the lives of our own children haha from getting yeeted into a volcano. We simply tune them out.

Anyway, back to the story... I'm still struck with Dean Koontz's level of chapter breaking. Auditorially it's daunting when the narrator is like, "Chapter 72..." and I'm like WTF! Why the face! But this last chapter didn't use the chapter break to change time or location or character POVs. Carson and what's his bucket ran into the apartment and started shooting up the perp and it paused in the middle with a chapter break and then continued right where it left off in the next chapter. That's sorta how I decided to break Chapter 7 into 7 + 8... which is now 8 + 9. But I am tempted for some of those early paragraph breaks—the double space time/location jumps in earlier chapters —to break them into individual Chapters, too.

Lastly, before I get back to actual writing, I am real tempted to not use an editor for this first round release. Now I say this as a 50 year old who's been writing a long time with a Master's Degree which speaks to some level of class instruction and massive amounts of paper writing along the way where spelling and grammar and citations counted. And also this being the fourth novel when I worked closely with a paid editor to comb through the first three and give massive feedback. That's my disclaimer.

I'm hoping for a "The Martian" situation. People just love it so much and help it go viral that it grabs the attention of a publisher and a movie mogul like a Rawson Thurber or a James Gunn who wants to bring it to life on the big stage with a Ryan Reynolds attached.

That is the goal.

Does it actually happen? Well go check IMDB and get back to me. Since you're reading this from the future, I'd like to know. Tell me!

5:03pm // 44,538 Words

Worked at Aroma til about 11am then packed up and moshed on home. Been working since then on a third pass on the last two chapters. I wanted to add the live stream of the GoFundMe so there could be some semblance of a story counter or measurement of progress for the town. That helps tie that loose end up. I don't think I totally pulled it off. One difficult part is the one drone has to be so many places at once that it's missing some of the action. I may need to go back to two drones.

But, also the idea that I threw in that Vampires can't be seen on camera. And wookalaars are seen as shadows on camera. That helps explain why they're doing all this because they know nobody will see the monsters. Just the good guys and the sparks and the wind effects. So it really does look like they're battling ghosts.

In a feature film it's easy to write "INTERCUT BE-TWEEN SCENES" and then you can keep cutting back to the boys in the truck responding to various events that the streamers love. It results in giving increases. Or things they hate resulting in streaming gifts slowing down. But in book form that's not as easy to convey so we lose some of the truck business.

I toyed with bringing Brodie back. And if you're reading this and he's back then I guess I figured it out. But currently it's too messy because they have a lot of business indoors after Victor is gone and the crow shows up and they walk to the lobby and get the blankets and go outside and then it's starting to snow and they celebrate.

Well that flow gets messed up if they have to go from Victor, to outside to raise Brodie scene, then to the crow and celebration and snow, etc. It's not great.

At the end of all this re-working there's still a nagging problem, IMHO, with Jan getting over Brodie so quickly. Even being draculized she might still need a moment. Or at least the scene I might need to add earlier where Charlie is explaining to Dan that with Jan's advanced metabolism etc that it's been 24 hours in real time but in vampire time months and years have passed by. Meaning she's grieved and moved on.

Also Jan and her dad the Mayor—that whole arc is not as neat and tidy currently as it needs to be. Like we never see them together ever. So does that even need to be her dad? Or do we downgrade him like we did to Sinde when we made her a regular shmoe versus making her a twin sister? These are all good questions y'all are asking. Good notes, people. Good notes.

Alright, well having done a major writing accomplishment—as I may be sending this story out tomorrow to my inner circle—I think I deserve a victory Fajita and Cadillac margarita? Who's in?

Tuesday, October 11, 2022
2:46p // 44,885 Words

Okay I started reworking the ending where the ring suddenly bursts with power after "The Kiss" and then as the shockwaves roll out it interacts with the fire stones and transforms that wookalaar into a human. A human named, Brodie.

Dum dum dahhhhhhh.

I'm not even finished writing it yet and I don't love what it's doing to the end. It's actually having the opposite effect that I intended. I started writing it in because some might find it is a happy ending that Brodie is not dead after all. But it really brought the ending down. It already was happy and celebratory. And then he shows up outta the blue and suddenly right at the end the whole ending is thrown out of equilibrium.

Here's what I think I want to do. Keep the happy ending where they all walk off singing "Slay bell rings" and such. That's the Christmas Hallmark ending. With the snow and everything. Then in Book #2 (SPOILER ALERT) we come back and find the narrator, Dan, has lied about that ending. And Brodie was brought back to life as a were-creature of some sort. Were-wookalaar? I dunno. But he's back. But Dan's on trial for hiding that part from the Hunter's Union.

Oh, also at the end of the current book we find out this whole story is basically a report that Dan has made to the Hunter's Union. Maybe that's an epilogue. An actual letter that's signed and everything. That'd be interesting.

So I've got to go back and re-un-fix the new ending. Yeah.

Hey, also while I've got you here I just got back from a lunch welcoming a coworker back from maternity leave and I got to make the rounds and see everyone in the ABC Building. And Patty O'Leary told me about this thing called Kindle Vella. Where you publish through Amazon but chapters at a time. Made available to readers and paid out to writers.

From the site:

"We're introducing a new storytelling option: Kindle Vella. With Kindle Vella, U.S. based authors can publish serialized stories, one short episode at a time. Readers can explore Kindle Vella stories in the Kindle app by going to the Discover tab in app on iOS devices or the store tab in app on Android and Fire devices and tapping the Kindle Vella link, and they can also visit the Kindle Vella store at http://www.amazon.com/kindle-vella."

That's very interesting. Have to look into it. Sometimes these new programs are incentivized and weighted more so maybe it's pushed out to more eyeballs or maybe there's some marketing behind it or whatever. Until they get enough writers utilizing the service. Sometimes there's a short cut when you're one of the first guinea pigs. Like the early TikTok adopters who now have 1M followers. I'm almost there by the way. I've got 350. Sooooooo close.

Food for thought. Here's the latest chapter breakdown by the numbers:

```
CH01  5892
CH02  4843
CH03  4030
CH04  5430
CH05  2983
CH06  4165
CH07  7378
CH08  4984
Ch09  5108
```

Seven sure did go off the rails. Meanwhile, five seems fairly anemic. Again, this is not the important stuff, people. It literally doesn't even matter the size of these chapters. It's just for my own info. And I am still really tempted to make each in-chapter break into a new chapter.

Wednesday, October 12, 2022
10:37am // 44,829 Words

Ohhhh and the word count went down! Yes, exactly right. Plus 10 points for Gryffindor. A very keen eye you have. It may continue to flux around this word count. But I really was hitting the first five pages hard. That's the intro to the whole story so it's vital the right tone and humor and info is getting across. It's gotta sing, baby. SING!

Obviously the catch-22 is that the narrator is an unreliable and rambling chatty Cathy. But humor, the best humor, has a certain precision to it and succinctness. So I pared down some of the longer buildups to get through to the punchlines quicker. I should include the first whack I took at page one so you can see for reference. The jokes were in there but you had to dig around and DIY quite a bit. Not great for comedy. Not this type anyway.

On each successive pass I am also trying to up the ante with the jokes. Like in an early version Dan is surrounded by vampires he says "stood before me like some Billy Idol cosplayers." Now it reads "stood before me like some meth'd out glee club." And it may change again before the end. Tighter wording and higher concept word pictures really help close the gap between reading and understanding and laughing. You don't want them to read it and have to think about the meaning too long. They need to read it and just get it. Meth'd out glee club is as succinctly visual as I can get. The instant image of bedraggled nerds burned onto your emotional retinas.

You get the point.

Especially the first few pages of any book has to blow people's minds and hook them to their core. Same with the whole of Chapter One. Every stylistic promise and most of your main characters better be all in there for the most part.

In this current nine chapter version it unfolds very much like a nine episode TV series.

ACT 1	Ch 1, 2, 3
ACT 2	Ch 4, 5, 6, 7
ACT 3	Ch 8 & 9

So that helps me know my narrative through line and backbone of the story are on track.

I was talking to a friend yesterday who has moved away from LA. He asked what I was up to with personal projects (we always keep each other posted on fun stuff in the works) so I told him about this Christmas horror comedy I was trying to publish by Dec 1.

And by the way this aside gets filed under "listening to clueless people's feedback on your story." Because he immediately dug in like "oh his name can't be Dan that's too simple, it needs to be bigger." I'm like the whole joke is that his grandpappy was *Van* Helsing and so here we are with the dollar store version of that great hunter/ killer and so we have *Dan* Helsing. And my friend gets all left-brained about Van is like a surname and his real name was Lawrence Van Helsing or whatever and I'm all EARTH TO DOOFUS! Stop making it so complicated. Stop trying to dissect with your left brain. It's funnier for ALL OF THOSE REASONS for it to be Dan Helsing. And for Janeane to be Jan Helsing.

Then he said he loved the title "Slay Bells Ring" but I might want to have a backup title because people pushing Christmas movies lean toward softer titles and holiday warmth and again I'm like WHAT THE HELL ARE YOU TALKING ABOUT?!? This film is counter programming to all of that. Yes it's got elements of the Hallmark Christmas underpinnings but I'm not calling it "Miracle on Banner Elk Avenue" just to make it sound less murder-y. To wit, this season we've got an action packed "Violent Night" coming out with a bad ass Santa avenging all over the bad guys in the trailer. Stabbing them with candy canes and such. That's where I'm headed. Not "White Christmas: Grandfather's Mountain".

Geez. Some people will really try to put their grubby thumb prints all over your work without taking into account, uh, YOUR ACTUAL STORY. Drives me nuts. "You may want to release it in late October to make the Christmas rush." Dude! Stop talking! Traditional publishing has to do that because they have to ramp up their whole marketing plan and saturate the market for 6 weeks prior to a release and get the biggest launch possible. They're trying to make deadlines for Christmas catalogs that come out early which their stores and distributors buy from. They have a long tail they have to manage.

I do not.

I finish the thing November 30 and flip a switch and it's on the market December 1st.

So, take people's feedback with a grain of salt. Haha, I almost wrote a grain of *thought*. Also, oddly appropriate. Now, if I send this out to my five beta readers and they ALL hate the Dan Helsing name then I have a problem. But it'll be a real problem and not a Rainman glitching out on random over-generalizations problem.

Okay, rant over. Phew.

12:43p

Just made the big story call to change Dominic to Monica. There were just too many little boys in the Orphan Fight Club and I didn't want to have a huge rewrite to add in action for a female. Flipping Dominic to Monica just seemed like an expedient choice. So the find/replace worked great for that. But now I have to go through with a fine-tooth comb to change all the he/she and him/her etc. Blerg.

Also I'm trying to keep the cussing down. But the f-bomb is just so hilarious. I know, Jerry Seinfeld, it's low hanging fruit. But still. When someone says, "F*ck Soufflés and f*ck meringues too" that's good stuff and *very* on brand for Ryan Reynolds.

Which reminds me I'm trying to think in this Dean Koontz novel I'm listening to if I've ever heard a cuss word. It's amazing but I don't think I have. And characters have gotten mad at other characters and exploded at them viciously with out it. Masterfully done, Koontz!

Friday, October 14, 2022
10:02am // 44,970 Words

Hitting this draft hard this week. Getting it polished for the Beta Test Readers. Need to send that out this afternoon so they can have a weekend read.

Also, I discovered another thing on this pass. Mayor Doug (is that his name?) is *not* Jan's dad. That arc didn't go anywhere and felt like it needed a lot more work if it was her dad. Father-daughter relationships are very complicated. Just like changing Chrissinde from her twin sister to former roommate. So, I turned the Mayor into Jan's ex-boyfriend instead of her dad. Yeah, Freud would have a field day with that. But the story and relationship is even better this way. Sexual tension and animosity with an ex-partner can be very funny. Abandonment issues with a dad are sad and depressing. As an ex, the mayor still gives off the right amount of sordid history vibes. The old jilted lover she has to confront. And it gives he and Dan even more backstory of animosity instantly and rivalry between them which is more delicious.

What do you do in a small town when the current mayor is your dream girl's horrible ex and you still have to work with him on a regular basis? Happens all the time. The fact that the perfect boyfriend Brodie gets munched but the douchebag ex-boyfriend lives is just a sad social commentary. Who knows, maybe in a later pass he gets eaten, too. Perhaps the audience needs that relief like Jurassic Park when the T-rex chomps the sniveling lawyer.

Let's see what else am I fixing? Still working on better jokes and references. I had one about Jan and Brodie having to come in Dan's window "Like they were in a Shakespeare play." That was okay. Not bad, not good. A little ecclectic. I changed it to "like they were in a Soderberg film" which is better, but still not great. But THEN. Then, I stumbled on the answer. They had to come in the window "like they were a Duke boy."

Ahhhhhh perfection. Comedy. Works on many levels. First that's a uniquely southern reference which is important that Dan would have seen the show and loved it and it would be part of his lexicon. Soderberg film was a stretch for his character although he does mention Oceans 11 later. Also funny because Duke boys expectation is that they go in car windows and so this is funny because it assumes the Dukes never used doors anywhere and instead preferred to enter everything through windows. And plus Duke Boys has an instant and obvious connection with a lot of people. It's just a funny word.

Again, the importance is as a writer to get out the general idea on the first draft. However obtuse or jumbled up or ham fisted and awkward it has to be. Just get it down. Then refine it later with more better words! See? Brilliant. Don't try to get it letter perfect and crisp on the first pass. Don't be a George R. R. Martin perfectionist on the first draft. Be a Stephen King. Keep the momentum going and get all the words out and on paper. Fix it in post! Ha.

Still working on turning Dominic into Monica. Found some loose "he's" I had to turn into "she's." I've gotta be honest, I'm not loving the switch. I mean it keeps their core group a little more diversified. I'm almost tempted to change her back to a him and change Juan into Elisa or something and lose the Juan/Obi Juan joke which I'm not convinced works anyway.

The thing is, the abuse that Dan heaps on Dominic plays better if he's a he. Then it's more balanced because he heaps abuse on Charlie and Dominic the whole time. Girl and boy. Very balanced. But when the two he's railing hardest against is Monica and Charlie, then that doesn't feel as right. Still chewing on it. It's a thousand little tweaks to flip the gender. I changed up one joke when Dan is getting on Dominic about using deodorant. That joke doesn't play as well with little girls as with little boys.

So, still working out the dynamic of that core group. I think there are still a couple of kids in the Orphan fight Club that are mentioned as a number but never mentioned by name. So, they're currently background extras and placeholders. We'll see how that evolves.

I think I may give Charlie long white Khaleesi hair. Kinda like X-Men's storm. That would be a great visual. Especially as she creeps through the dark basement. Good contrast for an actress to pop off screen. But also how many kids you know with white hair? Like, none.

Okay, bumping back over to the story in progress. Stay tuned.

4:29pm // 45,285 Words

Okay, phew. Did it. Changed some names and swapped some genders. The hispanic twins are now a boy and a girl named Jada and Obi Juan. Dominic who was Monica is now Liam. He's also a he again. Feeling much better about that. Put the deodorant joke back in. It's brilliant! Now Dan has two main kids he heckles the most: Liam the boy and Charlie the girl. Equality! Ha.

And I made up a fun new word. I have to figure out how early I can place it in the story and then not wear it out.

It's such a strong word I can only use it like once per chapter. Here it is:

Fangbangers

See? Isn't that a fun word? Like gang bangers but… fangs. You get it. It's the perfect little description to their vamp tramp club. I like it.

Finished making Mayor Switcher the father into Mayor Doug the ex-boyfriend. So that works. Jan threatens to draculize him as a wedding present in the end. It's sweet. I like it. He can be an even bigger pain in the ass in book 2. Incidentally, I'm already writing the opening of that book in my head. Guantanemo style interrogation of Dan by the Guild about his last 'report' to them. And keeping Brodie a secret, etc. And how Dan never got the ring off of Victor so that means he's not dead. So that's a fun problem.

But one book at a time people.

Also decided that I don't really want this journal combined with the book. (Edit: the first-release paperback book, that is) I want to be able to add some last entries about the release, or fun marketing things that happen or book signings (ha) or getting signed by a literary agent. You know, I just wanna leave some room for distro stuff. So that'll be a great addendum. And maybe it's not paperback. Maybe it's hardback only.

So the only thing I'm not happy about in this current version is the f-bombs. Yes, they're used sparingly but f*ck! It's hard to drop them out and keep the intensity and the humor.

Haha.

I'll run it by my beta readers and see what they say.

Thursday, October 20, 2022
11:05a // 45,600 Words

Today on Twitter is the #PITDARK pitching session. You tweet out your story's logline and if an agent likes the tweet you followup with them with a query and whatever they ask for (20pp or a first chapter or whatever).

Here's what I pitched out so far…

> 6am
> SLAY BELLS RING
> Math teacher Dan Helsing—great, great, great grandson of Van Helsing—must take up the family business to save his small NC mountain town… or die trying. Worst. Christmas. Ever.
> A Christmas Comedy Horror
> #PITDARK #A #CH

> 7am
> SLAY BELLS RING

Taking up the family biz was the last thing he wanted but when a hellish portal opens beneath a local orphanage, math teacher Dan Helsing must pull on his big boy monster-slayer britches for the first and probably last time
Xmas Comedy Horror
#PITDARK #A #CH

11am
SLAY BELLS RING
It's 2022 and Dan Helsing's family curse is a real pain in the neck. It's eggnog and carolers and vampires and hell hounds. With help from his Orphan Fight Club and an old crush back in town Christmas just might not suck.
#PITDARK #A #CH

Which one do you think is the best representation. I tried to add different pieces to each logline so if they read them all together they get the full story and not just the same old same old. Anyway a refined version of those three will end up being my official one that I use for marketing and promotion and such.

So far I've gotten a couple retweets and a few likes… from friends. Not Lit Agents. Yet. Looks like—from the tweet metrics—a couple of people viewed my profile from the tweets. I've got the header as a graphic tease for the book (Christmas tree wrapping paper ripped with claw marks and blood splatters) and of course my pinned tweet is "Semi-Centurion" book and link so they can see comedy and humor.

Guys, it's a little frustrating. Okay I mean a lot frustrating. These things like #pitdark and writing contests and such have traditionally been very disappointing endeavors for me. Always. Now, the silver lining is that I'm pushing this book out there whether some lit agent likes it or not. Whether it gets read by "pros" or not I'm going to market with it. Make it the absolute best I possibly can and then push it out to the *real* readers that matter: you.

And, then, of course mail copies to Ryan Reynolds and Ryan Gosling and any other Ryan's or non-Ryan's that I can possibly get to that would be a great fit. Since Reynolds and Ferrell are coming out with their musical take on Scrooge this year, I don't foresee them wanting to do another Christmas movie so soon. That's not great since I basically wrote it for Mr. Deadpool.

Another random thought I had was how great would it be if you could take money from the book sales or movie distro or visibility from that and work it into some program to revitalize the real live Cannon Hospital there in Banner Elk and turn it into something usable for Lees-McRae college. That would be awesome. Make a novel/movie and do good for Banner Elk community. And of course create some tourist traffic based on those buildings and landmarks and such.

Turn one room into a virtual zombie/vampire slaying escape room. As it should be.

Anyway, so expectations are very VERY low for #Pit-Dark. Meanwhile, I still have about another week before I get manuscripts back from my beta readers. Otherwise just sitting on the story for now. I've looked at Chapter One again and again. Trying to smooth that out even more.

I just want something to spark. Career-wise. You can launch an entire wildfire inferno with just a spark, but you need that one random editor or agent to see it and fall in love immediately. You need a friend of a friend on LinkedIn to like a post that suddenly puts it in front of the right eyeballs. Or like that Screenwriter who wrote "Violent Night" where I DM him and he DMs back. Only unlike real life where he's not interested in paranormal horror, then maybe it's just the thing he's been looking for and *SPARK*

This boy is on fiy-aaaaaaaaaahhhhhhhhh!

What I thought about the other day is that in 2022, guys, I have written two books from start to finish! Yes, technically novellas at 35K to 45K range but the point is that I didn't start writing these 15 years ago like I did with BATTLE TIDES. Especially SLAY BELLS RING. It came to me in bits and pieces last Christmas at my parents' house and then after I finished writing my Semi-Centurion memoir then I hopped on it towards the end of summer.

I mean, look at the first date of this behind-the-book file. It is August 1st. That's when I dipped a toe into the waters. And began the big push through September so that two months later I've got a draft. That is not nothing. Two books conceived, launched, written, produced, slathered smattered, smothered and covered in 12 months. Could they use some more work? Absolutely. I didn't use Editors for these or paid cover designers to intentionally keep costs down. That's not great. But necessary for expediency.

Now I have to figure out a trailer for the book. It'll be much more teaser-y than the other books where I actually had footage to work from. Or animation elements in the case of HISTORIANS PROPER. But that is so November's problem!! Haha.

Oh, and I forgot, I will throw this story query out to a couple of Lit Agents I'm trying to connect with because I've sent them other stuff but not a Horror Comedy. Gonna keep hitting up the same Lit Agents, too, until they finally see the light like in that Woody Allen joke: "This food is terrible, yes and such small portions." Only it's "Acuff's writing is terrible, yeah and such large volume of books. We should rep him!"

Isn't that how it works?

Sunday, November 6, 2022

9:51a // 45,366 Words

Okay so it's been a few weeks since I sent this thing out to all my Beta testers. I've heard back from FrankM (whose medieval knights and kingdoms book I'm helping edit now), and my sister Betty Anne and brother-in-law Scott who is basically the main character in this book with a Ryan Reynolds coat of paint. And of course from Joe Wilson the gamer guru from NC and horror aficionado.

Guys, all thumbs up from everyone so far. I was most nervous about what Joe would have to say, but he had a bunch of great notes about the whole story and how it unfolded. Everyone loves the crazy action ending and the world building. I know it's a small sample but an important sample. Joe gave some great story ideas and I'll retool the open based on his feedback to move the first flashback bit into a Prologue. So Chapter One starts at the bar conversation.

Betty Anne felt over all this is not her cup of tea. Ye ol' horror thriller. Same. Me too, girl! She didn't know anything about Van Helsing from literature/film and missed the slay/sleigh reference but her Spidey sense began to tingle she said in the hot tub scene like every thing was going just a little toooooooo perfectly and she's all "Brodie gonna die!" Hahaha. Yep that's some solid Jurassic Park and Predator when you're 5 years old type trauma/ptsd kicking in!

But the female perspective is important, too, for me to hear. As well as her mom perspective. So she's pointing mom-things out like why is little Phoebe the 7-year-old on the top bunk and Charlie the 15-year old is on the bottom bunk? Stuff like that. But of course in boy world, I recall that the bottom bunk was pretty dang cool because it's like a cave and I voluntarily gave my younger brother the top bunk. Of course we were only a year apart. Anyway, I'm really hoping my other sister and brother in law in Boone (right next to the real Banner Elk) finish in time to get me feedback. I want to know their in-town perspective. I know she's talking it up bc someone up there wants to read it so I said sure even though they're not family, but I made them promise to send me an email with notes. Especially since they both went to Lees McRae college.

So four beta readers got back and now I'm going to dive in over the next week and make all the changes and corrections and make sure the questionable sections get explained out better.

Like every one of them to the person was a little confused—not when Jan gets traumatized after Brodie is eaten and says "lets leave a note for when he gets back"… that part makes sense that she's thinking he's still alive because she's in strong denial. But the part where she starts pretending that Dan is Brodie was confusing. Annnnnnnd it is.

Everyone loved the job interview during the climactic battle sequence. And Scott and Frank were great about going over a bunch of their LOL moments from the story. Everyone said they laughed at a bunch of spots. That it's really very funny.

Score!

Scott even mentioned by page three that he just knew that this was Ryan Reynolds narrating the story. And it's only words on paper at this point. So that's perfect because that means I nailed his quirky, witty narrative blathering word vomit perfectly. Noice.

Nobody necessarily foresaw Jan getting draculized as her end. As if she'd died for good. Everyone felt like she'd be around later and mostly because of the subheading on the book cover that LIT'rally says the rise of Dan and Jan Helsing. Which I'm torn on whether I want to keep that spoiler on the front cover or not.

As this becomes a series, then perhaps each cover needs to allude to the specific case they're working on. "The Case of the Banner Elk Slayer" or something similar. That sounds pretty good actually. Hmmm. Multiple meanings: wookalar is a slayer, Victor is a slayer and Charlie of course is a certified Slayer, MHG or whatever (monster hunter guild). Ha, I may have to throw that in. I hadn't considered that part of the unions where they add like ASC or ACE or PGA to their names. Hahaha.

Scott and Joe got ALL the pop references. Betty Anne missed a bunch because they were "Lord of the Rings" or "Game of Thrones" references. Again, she wasn't feeling like the book's target audience. I said, but the reason you ARE the target audience is your HUSBAND IS THE MAIN CHARACTER. Otherwise, I know it's not her cup of tea so ordinarily wouldn't have asked her to read it. Like I wouldn't expect my mom and dad to read it. Or MelissaN who has read EVERY one of my previous works in Beta.

Some notes are very specifically helpful like Scott pointed out I said Banner Elk Elementary and fifth graders but then later I mention middle schoolers. I think I do need these kids to all be around fourteen which means 7th grade-ish. Also, Elementary schools don't generally break kids up into different classes for different subjects except for like art and music. Otherwise one teacher teaches everything. So by bumping up to 7th grade then we got ourselves different periods and study halls and stuff. But still equally awkward teenagers.

Anyway, if you can, get yourself a Joe Wilson to read your genre stuff. He knows his stuff. He's like another David Acuff that can edit video and write and direct etc so he's got an eye for dramatic narrative and reordering for sentences or ideas for maximum compelling output and results! I think at least some of your beta readers should be fellow writers so they can speak to the technicals like a Joe. But then have other muggles (haha) that aren't writers, they're just genre fans that can speak instinctually to what is working or not. Very helpful.

Meanwhile I've been running three to four times a week and listening to audiobooks and just finished Stephen King's "On Writing." It's really two or three chapters of "On Writing" wrapped in another 20 chapters of biography. But the way he writes the biography part is just prime verbal expertise in action so, in fact, he is showing us how he writes fiction using real stories from his own life to expound upon. So it's good.

I can't remember if I mentioned this part but he's a pantser! Not a plotter. And that to me is deliciously satisfying. Both he and Aaron Sorkin are not fans of overly complicating the writing process with outlines and character biographies etc. Just dive in and see where the story takes you. I love that. My people!

Now my second Script BURGLAR EYES I tried that and it just meandered and didn't hit the right screenplay guidepost limits because it lacked a cohesive narrative throughline. So the story was just a bunch of bloated but funny scenes stitched together. But now, having gotten more rigid with the screenplay process and hitting those Act marks and specific turning points, I can apply that to the books and they clip along at a good pace as well as follow similar Act 1 (25%), Act 2 (50%) and Act 3 (25%) structures.

So you really do need to learn structure and plotting and that sort of thing before you become a pantser. That's my caveat.

And if anything, my writing is too lean. Scott and Joe still would have liked more information on the town and the layout and Charlie sprinkled in here and there. That was Joe's biggest help-note on BATTLE TIDES, too was he wanted to take time to look around and see the world more. So in future drafts I did and boosted the story from like 70K words to almost 90K at this point. Not fluff, mind you, but important, useful and entertaining details.

Never fluff.

Never padding just to pad the story. Readers hate that garbage. I remember the original "Left Behind" series was supposed to be 7 books long and then it become this cash cow so they decided to expand it out to 12 books so now suddenly the first few chapters of each book was so much fluff. I quit reading the series at some point. It had lost the edge.

Unlike "Harry Potter" where the books get longer and longer but it's not fluff. It's meat and bones, It's entertaining detail. That's the difference.

But my script writing background keeps my novel writing on the lean side so I have to watch that it's not too anemic. I mean, I don't want to pull a Tom Clancy and spend five pages describing a tank down to the oil pan bolts. No thank you. It's a delicate balance. My main barometer is never to bore myself. And I've got an everyman type sensibility so it works for me. I'm not too smart, not too dumb. Right there in the Goldilocks middle. Along with 80% of America. So I can use myself as a gauge. Other people are so eclectic that they can't use themselves as a guide for what the masses will like or dislike. They'll never hit the wider audience. Always a niche core group.

Not that I've tapped into any wide audience outside of my 1700 Facebook friends and family. Sheesh. And even that only adds up to about 50 book sales. Damn you marketing and distribution!! Foiled again!

Alright, so we've set our clocks back an hour. It feels like 11:33am body time but really it's 10:33a so I've got a chunk of time to work on the story. Yeehaw! Let's go, fangbangers!!

12:02pm

Okay I finally figured out where I think Dan lives...get this... SEVEN DEVILS, NC! It's about 8 miles from Banner Elk. Found an actual real estate listing on the place I want him to have. Very cabin in the woods-ish.

The exterior is perfection! Gravel driveway, just as written! Porch steps. Exactly as written. A black refrigerator sized package could easily block the door. Windows to climb in and out of into the living room! Guys! It's perfection. Go on Zillow and look up: 302 Hawks Lake Drive in Seven Devils, NC.

Amazing, right? The only downside is that it's in a proper neighborhood so there's houses close by on the left and right within 50 feet of the property. Not exactly the secluded bungalow, but who cares? Other than that it is drawn straight from the pages of my book! Haha.

And how about this stone castle looking space for the Sylvanian Orphan Home. Look up 5742 S. NC Highway 194 on Zillow. Booyah! That it! That's it exactly.

Well, close. None of these places really have the basement dungeon aspect I'm looking for as an all-in-one as is, but for filming purposes that could easily be another set piece somewhere else. (Like that's even my problem to worry about, pshht) And although it's an eight mile drive to Dan's place on the roads according to google maps, through the woods its only two miles away.

And the Glass Treehouse AirBNB is 10 minutes from Dan's place by road, about 3.3 miles, but through the woods it's like 3000 feet. Huh. Okay this geography is gonna be fun to play with.

Hahaha get this: the massive stone estate on Highway 53 overlooks THE VALLE CRUCIS !

Valle Crucis is latin for Vale of the Cross. Whaaaaaaat?! Yes. This is definitely the Orphan Sylvanian Home. Who is writing this story, anyway? Not me! Apparently I'm just discovering it, I'm not the author, but as Stephen King says, an archaeologist, carefully digging up the bones that have been preserved here for me.

Serendipity baby.

Monday, November 7, 2022
3:10p // 46,028 Words

One thing Stephen King wrote about in "On Writing" was the writing vs the editing process. How you write draft one with a closed door, he called it. No outside influences and readers and feedback allowed. Just you and the story wrestling it out. Then the second draft is with your trusted readers (for him it was his wife). King was told early on that the edited version should be about 20% leaner than the first draft.

The idea is to cut the fluff. Things it took you a paragraph to say, maybe now it takes a sentence. And instead of a sentence it now is a phrase.

I get that you have to go after your word choice like Edward Scissorhands on draft #2 slicing and dicing everything. But with my screenplay background my problem has always been my draft #1 is anemic. And so I have to add descriptions and character motions and location references and decorative notes and so my draft #2 is always more. Actually each draft generally is longer than the first, I've found.

He also is a big proponent (and I agree with this one for sure) of letting at least 6 weeks go between draft one and draft two so that you come back to it fresh. So fresh that it seems like someone else wrote it. And even though it is difficult to kill your darlings, as they say, its much EASIER to kill someone else's darlings. Haha. So he is a huge fan of sticking the draft in a drawer and getting some emotional distance before moving on.

I got three or four weeks between first and second draft so that's very helpful as I move back in on revisions. I've got Joe's notes open on one laptop and my story on the other and working my way through. Upgrading a lot of jokes, too, that I wasn't happy about on the first round. Making them tighter and cleaner and punching them up. That's exactly the process of "Semi-Centurion" which is what gave me the whole confidence to begin this story in this style with a first-person narrator as a Ryan Reynolds variety. It just made sense.

So I've gone through Chapter 1 and 2, added a Prologue and now diving into Chapter 3. Got everyone's notes in mind as I go so I can fix and move on.

Wednesday, November 9, 2022
10:03a // 45,808 Words

The astute observer will notice we're down some words as we revise along. Stephen King was right after all! There was a lot more back and forth business and dialogue with Jan/Dan when she thought he was Brodie. But that wasn't working and was confusing our Beta readers. They liked her having PTSD and pretending Brodie is still alive out there in need of rescue but they didn't understand why she was physically confusing Dan and Brodie.

So in paring that down it's done a couple things. Streamlined the narrative a little which is good. It's not as convoluted. But it also loses a bit of fun business during those scenes of her showing unbridled love to a guy she thinks is Brodie. A guy who is secretly in love with her and kind of likes this attention even though it's misplaced.

I'm not as thrilled with the revisions as I go through them taking that thread out because it feels like a fun part is being excised. But that's what kill your darlings is supposed to feel like right? So I'll continue through to the end and this weekend will give it another whole top to bottom, tit to tail read through and see if, in the new context and flow, if it is actually improving the story. Which in my gut I feel like it is. But in the gut of my mind it doesn't feel that way. Just seems less busy and more dull. But that's why we trust the stomach gut and not the mind gut, I suppose. One thing is for sure, it takes guts!!

Haha.

I believe I'm into Chapter 7 now. Yes, we just lost Janeane again at the end of Chapter 6. RIP Jan. And now we roll into seven.

Beta Reader JoeW had also mentioned—or wait no it was actually ScottD that mentioned—this could have fun chapter titles like JK Rowling did with Harry Potter. I've done that with SEMI-CENTURION and BATTLE TIDES. I really wanted someone reading through the table of contents on those to get inspired by the chapter titles. Like "OhhhhhHHHhhhhhh, a Bath House you say." And then dive into Chapter One because fun stuff is coming.

But I didn't do chapter titles for this book. I've just gone through and made fancier embellishments around the chapter numbers. I specifically experimented with letters and characters already on a regular keyboard instead of like a graphic file so it would translate better to Kindle eBook. More 1:1. Unlike the doodads in Historians Proper which looked cool but took some monkeying with for them to stay in the right place.

Also, per my read of Stephen King's "On Writing" I am trying to be mindful of all the -ly adverbs I've sprinkled in. Some we're just stuck with. They're fun and they add. But a lot can be removed and reworded better. Especially trying to take out "quickly" because I apparently LOVE to use that one. "He ran quickly" which could easily be "He scrambled for the door."

Anyway, feeling back on track for a Dec 1st release. Would I like a proper editor to take a gander? Yes I would. Would I like to pay someone to pimp out the cover? Yes I would. But I don't want to spend $2K out of pocket and get the same 50 book sales as I would have if I just did my own AAA full service by Acuff-o-rama Book Enterprises.

Now what may *not* be ready by Dec 1st is my kick ass trailer. It might just be a teaser. And what cuts into my time is an upcoming Thanksgiving holiday and a Texas road trip to visit friends.

Maybe instead of moving on to Ch7 I'll hit Ch6 again. Even on this latest pass I'm still picking up he/her mistakes left behind from the brief gender flip of Dominic to Monica and then back to Liam. So that's good. That's what this process is for.

Meanwhile in the back of my mind I'm considering what all of this content in the behind-the-scenes section should be. How it should be rolled out. In blog form first? In ebook only so it retains all the hyperlinks and you can do more show and tell? All good questions. What I do know is it will be offset/delayed from actual novel paperback release so that I can input some final chapters or entries on distribution and such.

Hopefully a fun, happy ending like "Hey guys guess who just called and wants to repackage and republish my book under their Harper Collins shingle?!?" You know, or brunch with Ryan and Blake or something.

Thursday, November 10, 2022
3:39pm // 46,555 Words

Okay thus endeth another complete read-through and revision. Pretty sure I got through all of Joe's notes. My older sister finished her read y'day so I still need to hear her specific feedback. Of course her notes will be on the previous draft so I may have already cleared it up. We'll see. She printed it out too as did the Davidsons bc it's easier to read and write comments. So she's mailing me her copy but I'll still hop on a call while its fresh in her mind to hear their thoughts.

What did you think about these vampire words I made up:

> Longtooths
> Fangbangers
> Vamp tramps
> Draculized

I like them. They're fun and, to my knowledge, completely original. I mean, I can't have been the first one to coin these phrases given the vast amount of Dracula lore and spin-offs and Twilight-y stuff but maybe.

Perhaps on Sunday I'll push all of this into the correct Amazon/Novel 5x8 format and get my cover up there too so I can get my first ARC test copy back.

I haven't really thought about any other material I need like front or back matter. Don't have a good foreword either. I do like the idea of having a Scott quote at the back. Like "Really really liked this story," Scott Davidson, Actuary and Former Middleschool Math Teacher

That would be funny.

And then a trailer. Yeeeesh. What to do about a trailer?

Sunday, November 13, 2022
12:27pm // 46,557 Words

Finally got to call my sister NikkiB yesterday and get her take on the story. This, from an *actual* Boone resident. So that's good. She was able to update some very specific things for me like distinctions between the southern accent and Gerald's mountain accent which she says would be more like "Gomer Pyle in the Mayberry show." Which makes sense bc of the actual location of where Mount Pleasant (the real life town that Mayberry is based on) is located. It's like right next door.

She's going to be sending me the print out bc she just wrote all her notes in real time on it. On the phone we just went over the broad strokes.

Overall very positive about everything and all the quirky characters. Loves Charlie. Of course as we all do. Loved Dan although she says he sounds more like he in his 30s and not 40s. Huh. And she felt Jan was a little under-written on her part but she likes her. Just wants more. And more Charlie and more Sister Marguerite. So that's good. Better than too much of the characters or too re-vealing. That's always the sweet spot to reach with the reader, giving them enough information and detail and backstory but leaving them wanting more. It's a delicious middle ground.

Her big concern was with the ending. She thought the BCBS phone call was hilarious but it let some of the ten-sion out of Victor's big baddie character. He was less threatening so that was an issue for her. And she men-tioned there's no marching bands around in December so there would be no App state band for this ending. And she didn't buy that Charlie went online to get ordained and suggested adding in a Pastor figure somewhere.

So, again, now I have to tune my reader ESP to high fre-quency in order to hear the notes behind the notes. Be-cause these are interesting gaps she's calling out. I also feel like the more we see Victor interact with our crew, the less deadly and intimidating he seems on one hand. So I want to balance that because we all know to make your good guy look awesome you need a badass bad guy. A Darth Vader. A Joker. A Borg hive mind, a Buzz Lightyear. Wait, who was the bad guy in Toy Story? It was Buzz, right? Stealing Woody's spotlight? And we all know how much our Woody's love the spotlight. Ahem.

Next pass I'll pay more attention to Victor. The marching band thing just may need to clarify more. The elements are there. Like originally I wanted a whole Christmas Parade kind of thing. But instead of, as she suggested, the parade being a the derelict hospital it's got to be more clear that Dan has cannibalized the parade by bringing a bunch of those people into his fundraiser. And that was another thing, what are they actually fundraising for? Because the hospital land currently is privately owned. So need to know more about what the $2M actually does. How it helps the town.

I think the Charlie ordination thing is what it is. It literally says you can fill out the thing and be ordained in 15 minutes online. So the only stretch there is that she does it in like 5 minutes. Plus I love the comedy/irony of Charlie now being an ordained minister. I think we've all had friends officiate weddings that have had no business officiating weddings because it's just too easy to get credentialed.

Nik had a couple more notes that were similar red flags as others had brought up so that's even more confirmation about those parts. Like she didn't realize Dan was dressed as Santa, too, when talking with Holberman the Salvation Army Santa. Easy fix.

She did mention one super cool thing that I really really really loved the idea of. And again, this is the most crucial part of how you take notes and feedback from people. It's why we don't argue with them about the story. Instead we make it seem like everything they say is a god-send that can be used and crucial information for the next draft. Because that opens them up to get all the feedback out. If you attack them back then they may close up and not share the one thing you really really needed to hear. So keep the communication open. Just receive and only ask questions to clarify and see if you can restate their note/concern. You're not trying to win People's Court here and trap them in their own logical fallacy. Put your ego aside and let them talk. And prod them with specific points about specific problematic sections that others have brought up. Lead them to those areas of your specific concern. Was the ending satisfying. Was there enough Christmas and Horror and Comedy in this Christmas Horror Comedy? That type of thing.

Her idea was that maybe Dan grew up in the Sylvanian Home himself. That's why he has such an affinity for it and a history with the town. And potentially that even Sister Marguerite had brought him over from wherever as a baby to raise him here in this area.

Brilliant!

That's gold right there. It makes total sense to the story and can add some cool new moments to the over arching back story. Plus it makes him a big brother to all the other orphans instead of just like he's doing volunteer charity case work that he's doing because he feels sorry for them.

Now how much of that comes out in this first novel? We'll see. That's another thing that I told Nik was that some of her feedback was great suggestions for the sequel. Like I don't know that we need to find out so much more about Marguerite in this book. The more mysterious the better. But in book two we need to delve into Marguerite's and Charlie's background and the Hunter's Union and all sorts of things. See more of the ring power. All of it.

Also a minor note Nik said in passing just about life in Boone is that their house is not in City of Boone, it's in County. So they don't have trash pickup. They have to load their trash into a pickup and haul it to the dump and sort it in the recycling. That's just a thing they have to put up with that I never knew. She said at the end of their street, the next street *is* on City property so they all get trash pickup. Weird. And they also don't have city water. They're on a well water system. No wonder their house reminds me so much of our Granny and Peepaw's Williamsburg country home.

That's wild!

But, again, that's just allowing the conversation to meander during the notes and feedback process and pulling at some threads that I saw along the way that lead to some interesting things being unearthed. By not being adversarial you get more good info from your Beta readers.

Also I used a line in our phone conversation where we were talking about the Crow and I'm like "what does the message bird say?!" And I then wrote that down (I was typing everything she said or ideas that it sparked) because that could be a funny thing to call it. The message bird.

So that concludes five really solid notes and feedback sessions. Three male and two female on the story. More could be coming in (looking at you, JerFilm!) but it won't be as helpful now since I really need to be going to press this week to get the first print sample in hand to check all the physical elements and make sure nothing is wonky.

But here we are.

Saturday, November 19, 2022
1:44pm // 46,566 Words

Finally got Nik's hard copy notes in the mail on Thursday. Very helpful. Especially because she marked the minutia edits including semicolons or changing "my" to "the" and stuff you might not think is that big of a deal but makes a much better book with all these little adjustments. Books aren't made or broken usually with one big thing. Movies either. It's a thousand little problems that drive audiences away. So she's given me a third eye on that stuff which is extremely helpful.

Also made me think for the first time about what if the orphans at Sylvanian home are from the past. Like they've been moved forward in time through the portal somehow (including Dan who was one of the first orphans) so they'd be safe. So what if Liam and the others were somehow from two hundred years ago. Interesting idea. Again, it'd just be a couple of small changes in this story but it sets up a bigger thing in Book #2 where we learn more of their origins.

Feeling some pressure. This weekend is supposed to be the last to get to press. I need to finish the story and formatting today and tomorrow so I can get it to Amazon and order my first copy of the book to hold in my hands. Always a fun moment.

But Dec 1st is coming, people! Gotta get this thing out there. I think 12/1 is a Thursday. If that matters at all. It's nice to release a book on a Thursday before a weekend.

So this next draft I've been going through Nik's hardcopy notes and addressing all of those issues. Some of which have already been addressed because I'm a full version ahead of her now. So things like Jan thinking Brodie is Dan and flipping back and forth is already gone. Fixed.

She mentioned another thing I'll consider. The term wookalaar is a pop culture reference to the Tim Conway and Don Knotts movie PRIVATE EYES. So while it makes sense for Dan to use this word even in narration from time to time since he's Pop culture reference king, eventually we need (probably from Charlie) the real name of the fire moose. Something as epic as a Demigorgon from Stranger Things.

Good call.

Off to write. Byeeeeeeeee.

Sunday, November 20, 2022
8:46a // 46,786 Words

And on Sundays we go to Aroma Café and order up some scrambled eggs and black beans and a Cran-Orange Muffin and a large Coffee. And we write.

Today's big goal is to get through the whole book in another pass since I really need to reformat for Amazon. Big goal. Yesterday, I finished with all of Nik's comments/notes. So this pass is making sure that all the changes that I made are consistent through the whole story stem to stern. Like on the last pass I was still finding Liam's pronouns as "she" from back when I gender-flipped him to a girl for a hot minute. Then flipped him right back because it wasn't working and being a girl felt more sympathetic and the name calling seemed more like bullying; a chubby little boy with a speech impediment and a hella high degree of confidence reads more comedically.

Everything you put in your story creates spiderweb tindrels to other parts of the story in an elaborate interconnectedness. So when someone comments on one thing you can't just remove or change it. You have to trace back all the links (both physical and emotional) and see how the change affects the whole web's infrastructure. Make sure you're not removing a load-bearing wall. It's a tight little choreographed dance. If written correctly.

Changing Liam to a girl weakened the story web overall and made parts less funny so I had to flip him back. Changing one of the twins to a girl strengthened the story web overall and made parts more funny so I kept that in and doubled down on Jada and Obi Juan.

So it's a trial and error and backtesting involved just like computer or structural engineers only the worlds we build are imaginary. But real. Lies that tell the truth.

Also a little thing I did y'day was I lightened the breaks from a black to a dark grey. Very subtle.

From:

>— >——< — >——< —<

To:

>— >——< — >——< —<

Again. Subtle. Don't even know if those stay through the whole process but I like them for now. To have the physical break that is more defined than the triple space. There's no confusion about these intentional breaks. With spaces only, from the bottom of one page to the top of a new page you might miss it and the new paragraph sounds like it's out of place and messes the reader up. The hard break leaves no question about the intended time/location change.

8:39pm // 47,343 words

Here's where the Chapters stand right now.

Prologue	778
Ch 1	5825
Ch 2	5227
Ch 3	4065
Ch 4	5449
Ch 5	3050
Ch 6	4200
Ch 7	8214
Ch 8	5298
Ch 9	5213

Did a lot more cleanup on the last pass. Including little things like instead of "fangbangers" I hyphenated the word as "fang-bangers" and I changed most of the "wookalaars" except some of the early few references to "Hell hounds." Because, at first, he's referring to a mythical creature so "Wookalaar" is fine. As per Nik's note. Later, though, we need the real name which is Hell hound. Fire moose is also acceptable in parts.

Added the marching band and their busses in Chapter 2 noting they're already in town for the big Christmas parade.

Made it more clear about what Dan's blood is doing for Jan. Also added a new part about it creating a bonded pair between Dan and Jan. I thought that was an interesting addition. Because now it makes Jan sound a little more like Dan with his pop culture references since they're connected more. That can build into anything later. Like in the sequel it can be almost ESP like communication between them. Where they finish each others... sandwiches. Ha.

Again, just leaving myself some loose threads to pull on later.

Otherwise, very deeply satisfied with the story and how it plays out. Cranked down a bunch of the jokes to make them smarter and funnier and snappier. I feel like I've addressed every beta reader's concern and note. And overall I think it's a fun ride.

I didn't delve into where all the orphans came from. I thought I might get into that a little but I didn't. Oh and I realized I had two Dougs. Mayor Doug and Doug Holberman. So I changed Holberman to Dennis. And since I mentioned Dan's ex-girlfriend Rachel Lynne then I made the waitress at the other restaurant (Mary Lynn or whatever it was) into Bernice. Doesn't really matter much except to me. Smoothed out the southern talk into more mountain talk. Not quite as twangy. More "Hons" and "Honeys" than "Sugars." That sorta thing.

I just sat through a First AD training session on Saturday through the Greenhouse Arts & Media (shameless plug) and this guy was advising some in the group to cut a rain scene from the end of their short film because they're so difficult (outdoors at night) and makes the actors miserable and just in general are not to be used. Only sparingly. Of course my whole final chapter is in a rain deluged indoor hospital with the sprinkler systems flowing.

Yeah. Easy to write for a book! Good luck filmmakers! Ha. Not my problem.

Also, this morning I posted the first look of the book cover on IG and FB and TT. Sadly it's been an underwhelming response. I mean for some reason it's not gotten the eyeballs on it first of all. And all my normal social media cheerleaders aren't cheering. Sadly, the Christmas Horror Comedy is not necessarily the home run I was hoping it would be among my usual friend circles.

Pshhhht. Christians, amiright?

Again, SEMI-CENTURION was an anomaly bc it was my face on the cover and it was a humorous semi-memoir. So there was a huge groundswell of friends and family that climbed out of the woodwork to read it and feedback. It was fun. But this one being a Rated-R dark comedy is a smaller slice of the pie. More niche. It's why Seinfeld never went blue. It's why Will Smith kept it PG-ish in the beginning. Bigger pie. Smart.

Anyway, I wouldn't do it any differently. I had to write it as is. I'm just saying, it was a disappointing roll-out. I thought Sunday morning was one of the IG reel hotspots around 10am but apparently not. Mondays at 10a, Thursdays at 10a and Fridays at 10a have all done very well for me.

I thought about the Hollywood power couples I'd like to send the book to. Because there's a few couples that would make a great Dan and Jan, including:

1 Ryan Reynolds and Blake Lively
2 John Krasinski and Emily Blunt
3 Jessica Biel and Justin Timberlake
4 Dax Shepherd and Kristen Bell

Can you imagine Krasinski and Blunt? Holy Mackerel. That would be amazing.

I mean I get that some couples like to schedule alternating his and her movies so they aren't both working at the same time for the kids sake. But wouldn't they also want to do a film together? Where's the love? Long odds to be sure. But dreamers gotta dream.

Monday, November 21, 2022
11:38am // 47,343 Words

Okay, I've formatted to my 5x8 document and laid everything in with placeholders for the Dedication page and some back matter. I exported my .jpg cover to this website (jpg2pdf.com) to turn it into a pdf for Amazon. I don't why I had such a hard problem with this task before.

Last time, I think I was trying to export straight out of Photoshop from PSD to PDF and kept getting white edges around the document because it was treating it as a print document with no bleed edges (this has now been fixed in Adobe and you can export from PSD into an Adobe PDF that works great for Amazon, FYI). For Amazon you need the colors all the way to the borders so that the colors "bleed" off the edges of the page. So frustrating. Not anymore. Now in Photoshop I use the Amazon template for the appropriate image size constraints and then spit out a .jpg and go to that site and flipped it to pdf.

Easy peasy.

Also by using my 5x8 template from *The Wrestling Girl* I was just able to swap out each chapter with the new material and voila. Always takes an hour or so to go through and fix page numbers and all of that but otherwise the layout is good.

I've selected these categories in Amazon for now:

> Fiction > Fantasy > Urban
> Fiction > Thrillers > Supernatural

I think Urban Fantasy might actually insinuate more magic use, you know, on a Harry Potter level. Not just vampires and werewolves but magic and sorcery. But for now those seemed to fit better than straight up Horror. The only down side is there's no Horror Comedy category. They had a Black Comedy category and I'm like, uhhhhh, does that mean Dark, Edgy Comedy or does that mean my lead characters gotta be Denzel Washington? Whatever, I stayed away all together from the controversy.

I proofed it online and everything looked good with zero errors. Zero. That's never happened before. And I've ordered a proof copy. Or I said I wanted a proof copy so they have to do some magic and small animal sacrifices down at headquarters, I dunno what they do. But four hours later they say okay now you can order your proof. I'll see if I can get it Wed or Friday. Always fun to hold that first copy in hand.

This one is ringing in all total (the whole pdf) at 240pp. The story meat is about 218pp so that is my goal weight for all of these novellas. 200+ pages. About 45K words.

That's my sweet spot I try to hit because they especially make easier novel-to-screenplay adaptations.

So, phew. One step closer to publishing. I couldn't decide if I wanted to do super cheap pricing and have the paperback be $9.99 where I get about $2.40 profit per book according to Amazon math. Or $14.99 where I get $5.28 profit per book. Generally, upon launch is when I have the most friends and family and the big push so that's the most sales so I should do $14.99 to maximize profits. But to me there's something psychologically tantalizing about a $9.99 book. But maybe there's another psychological negative about a book being too cheap. Maybe it should be $19.99 because who wouldn't buy a book for a measly $20?

I've got time to figure that out. And I still have to format an eBook. I don't have time to go in and create hyperlinks to each and every pop reference or location that I put in the book. That was an early idea I had and trashed. But maybe I still should. That would be a fun thing for people. Until someone changes their website and the links I added break. D'oh.

I keep thinking about this fact I discovered last night: I've only sold 190 books all total. Four novels on Amazon which is about 47 sales a piece. Haha, that's so terrible for the amount of blood and sweat and tears and MONEY that I have poured into each one of these things. That's what happens when you have no audience or social media following. You've gotta totally pay people to push it out there with PR and marketing and ads. Or you just sell 40 books and call it a day.

And I don't have a trailer for this one either. How are people supposed to glom on to it and make it the next Twilight hit? Huh?! Or Shadowhunters? Anyone?

Anyway, we're one step closer to finally finishing the journey from nebulous nothing idea into physical book. Still a remarkable process creating something from nada.

Thursday, December 23, 2022
4:00pm // 47,343 Words

"I'll be doing a book signing this weekend," I would tease people during my stand up comedy set at Flappers a few years back. "It will be down at the Barnes & Noble in Burbank…" Pause for effect and some appreciative nods from the crowd. "Now I haven't actually *written* any books but I'll just be signing everything I can like Banksy until the cops show up so come on down."

Ha. Well, five books later I had my first book signing and launch party:

> They braved the fog. They braved the rain. They braved the vampires. The Foggy Rock Eatery and Pub of Blowing Rock, NC hosted a festive book signing event last night for Author S. David Acuff's latest novel, "Slay Bells Ring".

"The location is perfect," Acuff explained, "since the story of this particular Christmas horror comedy takes place in the neighboring town of Banner Elk, NC. And it features local restaurants, the haunted hospital across from Lees-McRae College and even familiar felines that these Boone natives will all appreciate."

This event all began as a "what-if" phone call from Acuff (who lives in Burbank, California) to his sister, Nikki, who has lived in Boone for over ten years and is always up for masterminding a "fun shindig."

The enterprising bartenders of Foggy Rock went the extra mile and whipped up fun new cocktails in honor of the vampire-themed event. One was a cinnamon flavored hot toddy aptly named after the book's Ryan Reynolds-esque main character, "Dan Helsing". The other was a berry margarita-style beverage called the "Slay You Berry Much."

The signing was held from 4p until 7pm in order to beat the ice storm that was forecast to hit later that evening. A personalized, signed book + cocktail combo was offered to anyone who was interested. And people were interested. In fact, Acuff sold out his stash of 25 books with orders for more on top of that.

Acuff had a blast hanging out with friends and family and meeting new and enthusiastic readers who were all looking forward to diving into the local indie title.

And of course he heard that question that all authors simultaneously love and fear:

"Hey, when is the sequel gonna be available?"

Patrons were happy to hear that the follow-up story is already in the works.

So that was the press release that went out today. I was also able to leave some consignment copies at the Appalachian Apothecary and Tea Room. That's the power of having a sister that everyone adores in Boone, NC, so all of her friends pitch in to help launch this book. Haha.

I've heard a lot of negative stories about early book signings where zero people show up so I generally have avoided them because I barely have a crowd of fans across America, let alone all clustered in one spot enough to form a line. So we used my sister's local bartender celebrity status to woo them in the door.

Also it's great for marketing purposes to get a variety of happy people holding my book in real life. My first book "Historians Proper" I photoshopped the cover into the hands of all these famous people like Oprah in a satire sorta way. But it's nice to have pictures with actual real people.

So this was fun to have an inexpensive and themed event to kick off the release. Best Christmas ever!

Monday, March 27, 2023
1:50pm

And he's back! Ta-dahhhh. Three months later. I've decided to do another book release this year in 2023. See, wha' ha' happened was I started playing around with the Artificial Intelligence web site Midjourney.com that takes your written prompts and turns them into art work. Some is ridiculously bad. Other stuff is ridiculously good.

After tweaking on my verbiage/prompts I got some images that I thought would make for a great cover. The first cover I did for the Christmas 2022 book release was more of a tease. I had envisioned a book that looked like it was wrapped in Christmas paper just like a present and then had three claw marks across it. Very simple. Very effective.

Not having access to this cool new tech, I updated to this new cover you see on the front of *this* novel. So much more compelling to have faces and eyes and red portals opening up and black mist swirling around some questionable dude lurking at the bottom. Much more eye-grabbing than the last one. But you do what you have to do. Work with what you've got.

So all of those first 2022 covers will become like "collec-tors items." And I still have like twenty of them at the house. Moving forward, all the new hardcover books will have this awesome cover and this Author's Journal in-cluded as a bonus.

I thought the play-by-play "behind-the-book" would be fun and hopefully even helpful to other writers who could relate to the emotional seesaw of crafting a story and the evolution of a new fictional world and the headaches and triumphs therein.

I don't know if Amazon will let me do a 400+ hardback book if my paperback was like 240pp. Maybe the page counts don't have to match up. If it won't let me then I'll just release the 2.0 paperback and hardback with the new covers on them as their own title. But only the hardback will have these bonus materials. The author's journal. Gotta be some healthy perk for the peeps springing for the hardback.

Ordinarily I'd be concerned about not being able to use the first print paperback URL already setup on Amazon because I'd want all the reviews from it to apply to the hardback as well. But, guys, it is almost April and despite my begging and pleading with my beta readers and oth-ers, I've gotten one official review. One. Five stars, mind you (I love you, RachelZ!) but one review.

I'm seriously considering a review service where you pay a couple hundred dollars for 10-15 guaranteed reviews. I mean that's a non-debate really. That's the bare minimum just to begin getting your book some exposure. And I have to get a lot more press releases out there to drive more news articles and stories. And I need to fly a blimp over Ryan Reynolds' house. It's somewhere in Canada right? That's a small country, shouldn't be too hard to find.

Traditionally that's the part of this publishing process that I've done so poorly on the first 5 book releases. Zero paid sales and marketing. Who can afford it? Now, I've done videos and social media and book trailers for everything, it just doesn't seem to make a dent in book sales. I never paid Google or Facebook for ads. Just word of mouth. And to date, as I said, I maybe have sold about 47 copies of each title.

I'm slogging along out here on Writer-Wannabe Mountain but it's not easy to get traction. I want to build an empire but so far all I've got is a little mud hut. But believe me, I'm in it for the long haul. My goal is to continue writing and releasing and in ten years to be much MUCH further along than I am today. Hopefully to the point where it's paying all my bills and I can switch over to writing full time. But for now $70/month income from book sales is tough to live on. Thanks, Obama.

Haha.

Thursday, June 22, 2023
3:03pm // 47,216 Words

Just a couple more updates. We're about a month out before the official July 25th Christmas in July hardcover release. Since the last March 27 update I've been let go from Disney after seven years so I'm really going to be pushing hard into the BravoBay Books space. Added a website and an Instagram account.

I'm going to buy some follows initially just to prime the pump and then release the SEMI-CENTURION audiobook sometime in the next couple of weeks once its ready on audible. Then July 10th is international kitten day so I'll release Scruffy's brand new "Cat Scientists" book. Then 7/25 is this release. Then in early August will be FrankM's "A Kingdom Without a King" which he is super excited about. I'm trying, as his publisher, to manage expectations but some lessons are just learned the hard way.

I sent out a hard copy with cool new cover to Stephen King. I sent a query note to him on his website and his webmaster/intern got me his mailing address and said "no promises." So I said I'd read his "On Writing" and it was very instrumental. I told him this was my 5th book but first in the horror genre and would love his feedback. And hey, if he wanted to write a foreword then we'd burn that bridge when we came to it. That was in May sometime. Still haven't heard back. Not expecting to.

Next I sent a hard copy to Jessica Biel. Turns out I had her address so I wrote a cute and funny note. I reminded her of our interviews together over the past couple of years with "Cruel Summer" and then sent her the book.

Not expecting anything there either. But we gotta take these long-shot hail mary passes because once in a blue hunter's moon, they pan out. So we'll see.

Four weeks ago I paid the service for 13 reviews on Amazon and GoodReads. So far have heard nothing. Not even a single request for the book which is why I'm not mentioning their name. No use advertising for them if they're not reliable. Time will tell if they pull one out in time to be helpful for 7/25 release.

Tick tock tick tock.

Anyway, hope you've enjoyed the behind the scenes word vomit for Slay Bells Ringy Dinghy. It's been a fun little experiment to watch the story unfold and evolve in real time.

Onward and upward……………../d

BRAVOBAY BOOKS

BravoBay is a fictional top secret test facility for fighter jockeys and experimental aircraft in Acuff's yet-to-be-released sci-fi epic *Battle Tides*.

BravoBay Books, on the other hand, is a top-secret test facility for word jockeys and experimental ideas.

Those who have read our books, *Historians Proper* and *High School Masquerade, The Wrestling Girl* and *A Kingdom Without A King* know the high quality of our work and our commitment to first-rate story-telling.

Stay frosty and bleed the edge, my friends.

ABOUT THE AUTHOR

S. David Acuff grew up the son of an Air Force Colonel and lived all over the United States.

Being the new kid every year in school taught him a certain objectivity; to see through local prejudices, politics and predilections. It gave him the best vantage point to view all of these different lives and delicious stories and how they intersected and collided with often unexpected results.

Since 2014, Acuff has lived in Los Angeles, CA. He was a Producer-Editor for Walt Disney for seven years. And he enjoys doing voiceover work for Audible book projects as well as animated characters.

He has three *amazing* daughters—Caitlyn, Alexis and Raegan. And his life-motto is very simply, "What doesn't kill you makes you funnier!"

Keep tabs on his book, film, and TV shenanigans at: www.davidacuff.com.